TURNAROUND

TURNAROUND

Rick Ollerman

Copyright © 2000 by Rick Ollerman.

ISBN #:   Softcover   0-7388-2402-X

All rights reserved. No part of this book may be reproduced or transmitted in any form or by any means, electronic or mechanical, including photocopying, recording, or by any information storage and retrieval system, without permission in writing from the copyright owner.

This is a work of fiction. Names, characters, places and incidents either are the product of the author's imagination or are used fictitiously, and any resemblance to any actual persons, living or dead, events, or locales is entirely coincidental.

This book was printed in the United States of America.

To order additional copies of this book, contact:
Xlibris Corporation
1-888-7-XLIBRIS
www.Xlibris.com
Orders@Xlibris.com

CONTENTS

CHAPTER ONE	9
CHAPTER TWO	16
CHAPTER THREE	22
CHAPTER FOUR	28
CHAPTER FIVE	40
CHAPTER SIX	46
CHAPTER SEVEN	50
CHAPTER EIGHT	57
CHAPTER NINE	71
CHAPTER TEN	85
CHAPTER ELEVEN	90
CHAPTER TWELVE	107
CHAPTER THIRTEEN	119
CHAPTER FOURTEEN	127
CHAPTER FIFTEEN	138
CHAPTER SIXTEEN	145
CHAPTER SEVENTEEN	156
CHAPTER EIGHTEEN	165
CHAPTER NINETEEN	179
CHAPTER TWENTY	187
CHAPTER TWENTY ONE	198
CHAPTER TWENTY TWO	207
CHAPTER TWENTY THREE	213
CHAPTER TWENTY FOUR	220
CHAPTER TWENTY FIVE	232
CHAPTER TWENTY SIX	237
CHAPTER TWENTY SEVEN	247

CHAPTER TWENTY EIGHT 253
CHAPTER TWENTY NINE 271

TO MELISSA, WHO SAW THE WORDS, AND TO GI,
WHO SAW BEHIND THEM.

CHAPTER ONE

It was a clear spring Sunday and the park was full of people walking along the asphalt trails after church. Mothers were arriving at the wading pool with their children and some kids were playing baseball on one of the diamonds at the north end. Two basketball games were running side by side on adjacent courts, separated from the tennis players by a chain link fence.

It was pure street ball, very little passing, few jump shots, just do it off the dribble and take it to the hole, baby. More than a game, it was a way of life for some of them. The park was a low cost country club for Tampa's poor.

From the parking lot fifty yards away, two men in suits walked up and stood at the edge of one of the games. They watched patiently, waiting for a break in the game, not speaking to each other.

In the middle of a play, someone noticed them and called out, "Yo man, I've got to go." A number of the players looked around and moved to a picnic table where they snatched a tee shirt or a ball from the bench and filtered out of the park. The other game stopped and it too broke up.

The remaining players from both contests moved to one of the baskets away from the men in suits and began to shoot. One man stayed on the court where he had been playing. He was bent over with his hands on his knees, looking at the ground. "What are you doing here, Hill?"

"We need to talk to you, Nick," said the bigger of the two men. The other one grinned at him.

Nick Kingman straightened up and looked behind him. There were barely enough people left for one game. "Leave me the fuck alone, Hill."

He began to walk away from the policemen toward the remaining players, wondering if he'd still be welcome. Behind him Hill called, "Come on, Detective."

Kingman turned and marched back into the man's face. Hill was a few inches shorter than him but there was a hardness there, a discernible quality that had nothing to do with running miles in the park or lifting weights at the gym. He didn't flinch when Kingman jabbed an index finger into his chest.

"Where the hell do you come off coming down here calling me out in front of these guys? He kept his voice down but it was clear he was yelling. "And what's this 'Detective' shit? I stopped being one of you a long time ago."

"We just want to talk."

"Well fuck you, Hill. And you, too, Fetterman." Neither man moved. "There's probably fifteen guys here now that will associate me with you two and by next week that'll be everywhere. These guys don't like cops and they don't like assholes. I'm surprised they even let you park here."

"Now listen, Kingman–"

"No, you listen," Nick said jabbing his finger again. "You just fixed it so I can't play here anymore. Or anywhere else in the fucking city. These guys think I have anything to do with cops and even if I get on the court they'll have to roll me off on a stretcher. I'll be playing at the goddamned Y." He turned and walked across the court to the picnic table. He picked up his tee shirt and ball and started for the parking lot.

"We have to talk, Nick," said Hill.

Kingman didn't stop. "You want to talk to me, call me at the fucking office."

The two men turned and watched him leave. Fetterman spoke up. "I can stop him."

"No," said Hill. "Let him go. We'll get to him later. Or he'll get to us."

* * *

He threw the basketball at a chair as he walked into the house. Katy heard him come in and walked out of the kitchen wearing an old fashioned apron over a pair of shorts and a cut off tee shirt.

"What's wrong?" she asked as she stepped up to give him a kiss.

"Nothing," Nick told her, kissing her back. "I'm over it, anyway." He watched the basketball roll off the chair and stop under a table. "What are you doing in the kitchen? I was planning on making you lunch today."

Katy saw that he was fine and laughed at him. "Honey, you know you can't cook. I thought I'd whip something up both of us could eat."

Nick spread his arms wide and said, "At least let me help."

"Nicholas, if I asked you to separate an egg for me, what would you do?"

"Take it out of the box?"

"Uh huh." She turned to go back to the kitchen. "Go take a shower, Nick."

Nick peeled off his sweaty tee shirt and said, "You know if you give me a few more guesses I bet I can figure that one out." He turned and headed up the stairs leading to their bedroom.

Halfway up, Katy called from the kitchen. "Honey?"

Nick stopped climbing. "Yeah, sweets?"

"John called earlier and left a message on the machine. He wanted you to call him as soon as you got in."

"I'll do it up here." Nick made it to the bedroom and collapsed on one side of the bed. His body still allowed him to play ball every weekend but it demanded a harder and longer period of forgiveness after each episode. He scooped up the phone and speed dialed his partner. "John, hi, it's Nick."

"Nick."

Kingman pushed himself to a sitting position when he heard the way his friend said his name. "What's wrong, buddy?"

Nick heard the sound of a deep breath being drawn on the other end. "Where've you been?"

"Playing ball all morning at a park. Are you okay?"

John didn't answer right away. Nick waited, giving him some time. "I don't want to be the one telling you this."

A cloud of rising anxiety was making Nick nervous. "Don't want to be telling me what, John?"

"Marie Clayton called me. She said she tried to reach you but you weren't there."

The cloud turned cold. "What happened?"

"Tim is dead."

Nick squeezed the phone in a white knuckled death grip and he camped his eyes shut as John continued talking. How could Tim be dead, he kept thinking. His best friend, closer than a brother. It couldn't be true.

"Wait a minute, John. Someone threw him out of an airplane?"

"Marie said that Tim didn't come home Friday night. He had left her a note saying he might have to go out of town for a client and that he would call her, but he didn't. He didn't even sign the note.

"Apparently, two guys were fishing in a skiff south of the Gandy Bridge yesterday morning. They were out there alone when they heard a sound like a shell exploding a couple hundred yards away. They went over to check it out and they found him."

"Dead?" Stupid question.

"I guess they took a few minutes getting him into the boat, but yeah. By the time they got him in, they said he was dead."

Nick heard Katy coming up the stairs but he didn't open his eyes. "They didn't see what happened?"

"They said they may have heard a small airplane a couple of minutes before but they're not sure. But when you're fishing in Tampa Bay a few miles from an airport that wouldn't make much of an impression."

"Were there any other boats around? Did anybody else see it happen?"

"You're thinking like a cop again, Nick. No people, no boats, and the water was too damned shallow for a submarine."

"Christ," Nick said, scraping his fingers through his hair. "I don't fucking believe this. There's no possibility they're wrong?"

"I guess the noise was pretty bad. Really big. Marie—" John paused, taking another breath. "Marie said she saw the body."

Neither man spoke for a minute. Nick blinked his eyes open and saw Katy framed in the bedroom doorway, wringing the apron in her hands. "Let me call you back in a little while. I need to sort this out."

He hung up the phone and turned to face his wife. Katy stopped moving and stared at a spot on the floor near Nick's feet. "Tim's dead," he said simply.

The words hung in the air between them, filling it with unspoken emotions.

Quietly she asked, "What are you going to do?"

Nick wanted to ask her, what are you so frightened of, but that was a different thing, he knew. "Something," he said. "I don't know what but I have to do something."

"As a cop, Nick?" She said the word bitterly.

"As who I am."

Nick wanted to stop talking, to pay some attention to the war of emotions taking place in his head. "I love you, Katy."

"I know," she said. "But I'm going to have to leave again, aren't I?"

Katy looked up and there were tears streaking down her cheeks. Without any more talking, they were both aware of something that neither of them had words for.

Nick stood and moved into the bathroom. A minute later, steaming water hissed from the shower and did not stop until a long time later.

Katy never moved.

* * *

The shower was numbing, as if it were cold, but billowing sheets of steam rolled over the curtain bar blanketing the bathroom with tiny moisture beads. Nick almost lost his footing on the slick porcelain as he got out of the shower and grabbed a towel from the rack. His body was on auto-pilot as, still naked, he walked out of the bathroom to the bedroom phone.

"John, I need an airplane."

"Nick? Is that you? Are you okay?"

"Yes, it's me."

"Are you alright? What are you going to do?"

"I'm fine, John, and don't keep asking me questions. Please."

After a silence Nick didn't have the patience for, John said, "Martin's a pilot, our database guy. I think he flies with a club or something out of Lakeland but I don't think he's been doing it long."

"Doesn't matter, I just need him to do it a little longer. I'll call him. Do one thing for me, will you? Tell Marie you let me know what happened."

"You're not going to call her then?"

"No more questions, John. I can't come up with the answers. Goodbye."

* * *

Nick got dressed and left the house. Katy had left some food on the table but wasn't in the kitchen. He knew he should eat something, especially after playing ball, but his stomach was rolled up like a frightened caterpillar. He picked up a dry erase marker from the counter and wrote a message to Katy on the magnetic board on the refrigerator and then left without looking for her or saying a word.

In the living room his wife sat on the sofa with an overstuffed pillow curled up into her legs. She heard the front door close and smeared the tears across her cheeks with her left hand. She stared at the saltiness glittering on the diamonds on her wedding band. "I'll put the eggs away, Nick."

In the kitchen, on the refrigerator, a sign said, "I love you so very much."

CHAPTER TWO

The drive to the Lakeland airport took almost 45 minutes. Sunday afternoon traffic should have been lighter but there was congestion at 301 where the State Fair had opened a week earlier. Nick's mind was turning thoughts over and over in his mind, all of them slippery things, none of them grabbing hold but always cycling back to the single question, "Why Tim?"

The airport at Lakeland was a large regional operation approximately forty miles away from Tampa International by air. Martin Cox walked out of a building as Nick pulled into a parking lot in front of it. The building was a large aluminum hangar with a sign painted in red and blue on its side: New Aero Training Center.

Martin raised his hand when he saw Nick and called, "Over here, boss."

Nick nodded and pushed a pair of sunglasses high up on the bridge of his nose. He followed Martin through a gate onto the tarmac in front of the hangar. Martin stopped in front of a beige and blue low winged Piper, looking uncomfortable. "I'm sorry about your friend, Mr. Kingman. It's a horrible thing. John said you were close."

Nick turned his head and held Martin's eyes through dark lenses. "You talked to John?"

Martin nodded and broke the eye contact, quickly moving to drain the condensation from the Piper's fuel tanks. "I don't know where you want to go, sir, but this isn't too bad for just two of us. It should do 85, 90 knots on a day like this."

"It won't work," Nick said. "The wings are low, I need to be able to see down. Straight down. We need a plane with high wings, like a Cessna. I should have mentioned it on the phone."

Martin's face took on a lost look, an expression that made him look much younger than he was. "Let me see about the 172. It's scheduled to be down for an annual but I'll see if they'll let us take it."

Nick nodded for him to go ahead.

Twenty minutes later the Cessna was fueled, pre-flighted, and Nick and Martin lifted off into the dense and humid air.

"I'm going to need to know where it is you want to go, Mr. Kingman." Nick refused a headset and Martin had to shout.

"West," Nick yelled back. "Head west. I want you to take me over the bay south of the Gandy bridge but not as far as the Pier."

Martin nodded and almost said, "That should take us about fifteen minutes from here," but didn't. Sitting together in the tiny cockpit they were a thousand feet above the earth and a million miles apart.

"How high do you want to go?" asked Martin.

"High enough," grunted Nick. High enough to die.

It wasn't long before they were over the grey-green Gulf of Mexico waters that Nick had described. They cleared the land and Nick told Martin to keep going and not circle. "Just stay over the water," he shouted.

Could you smell the ocean up here like I can, Tim? Did you know you were going to die?

The earth was laid out in front of them, flat, with the afternoon sun waning in their eyes. The perception of the horizon was lost to the moisture in the air, the range of vision stopped short of maximum. The air itself blocked the earth's edges. The airplane noise droned on, a repeating variance in pitch coming from the propeller, low to high. It sounded like kids in the park with those old motorized airplanes that flew at the end of thin ropes attached to a handle. The hypnotic sound grew louder and faded, grew louder and faded, as the propeller went round and round.

It wasn't an accident, was it, Tim? Your seat belt would have been on, the door would have been closed, but those things didn't help you. Why did somebody want to see you die, my friend?

Nick pressed his forehead to the clear plexiglass window on the door next to him and looked down at the water, away from the sun. He looked as straight down as he could, past the metal peg that served as a kind of step. It was welded to a strut that led down to the covered wheel. Beyond that, empty space filled the area between the plane and the ocean below. "Slow the plane down, Martin."

"Pardon me?"

"Slow the plane down."

Uncertainly, Martin reached forward and throttled back the engine, staring at Nick, not sure he had heard correctly but fearing to ask again. The altimeter read eleven hundred feet and they were flying west-southwest, on a line that led directly out to the Gulf of Mexico.

This whole scene was getting weird and it didn't start out too mundane, either. Nick Kingman and John Sanders owned and ran the software consulting firm where he had been lucky, he thought, to begin working after college. When Sanders had called him and told him that Nick would be asking a favor, a man whose best friend had just been killed, Martin had dropped his plans for the afternoon and was only too happy to help. Actually, he was thankful to be noticed. But he had no idea what was going on with the man sitting next to him. Kingman's face was tightly set, the muscles at the corners of his jaw rigid. This guy is losing it, Martin thought. Head out to the Gulf, fly 'high enough,' slow the plane down. A glacier was slowly working its way down from somewhere north and settling into his stomach.

Nick placed his hand on the door handle and turned it downward. The door didn't move, held closed by the pressure of the air flowing along the outside of the plane. "Slow it down more," he shouted over the noise.

Martin nearly swallowed his gum. "What—what are you going to do?"

"SLOW THE PLANE DOWN!"

For an eternity, neither man moved, the droning airplane sounds drilling into the heads of both men, the sense of hearing dominating all others. Slowly Martin reached forward again and throttled back the plane even more. The little Cessna shuddered as it began to stall and Martin quickly dropped the nose slightly then added a little more power to the engine. *What did I get myself into*, he thought furiously. *There is a crazy man in this airplane and I don't want anything to happen to him. I don't want anything to happen to me.* He concentrated very hard on the numerous gauges and dials in front of him, seeing them all and aware of none of them.

Nick pushed the door open. It resisted but he could do it with one arm. A foil gum wrapper rose off the floor and zinged past his ear into space. He was oblivious to the pilot as he unclasped his seat belt with his right hand. Now he could lean his head out the door and see the turquoise water shimmering below. *Is this what you saw, Tim? Was it green and pretty and peaceful? Did you remember all the time you spent fishing in the Gulf, the time spent here swimming and enjoying life? Is this what it looked like? Is this what you saw?*

He turned his body and swung his legs over the side of the seat hanging his feet eleven hundred feet above water as hard as concrete. Rushing air caught his sunglasses and ripped them from his face. Nick tried to watch them fall into the water but they blew backwards, toward the tail, and he lost sight of them almost instantly. *Surely it wasn't like that for you, my friend.*

Nick edged closer to the open door, extending one leg further into the airstream. There was constant pressure to be blown towards the tail and he held his leg rigid as he kept it in place. He leaned forward, left arm extended and elbow locked, forcing the door open against the air pressure. His right arm held him inside the plane as he leaned his body far enough outside the plane so that he could see the water laid out directly below his foot.

Holy Mary, Mother of Christ, Martin swore and shut his eyes. If we run into a thermal or hit some turbulence . . .

Martin banked the plane to left slightly in a subtle attempt to gently angle his boss back into the airplane. Nick's head whipped around and he looked at Martin for the first time during the flight. "Don't."

Martin automatically leveled the Cessna's wings and glued his eyes to the artificial horizon indicator. Silently, he began to pray, his lips moving. He wouldn't look at Nick again.

Nick turned back to the door and studied his foot hanging from the tiny airplane, a universe of empty space between it and the surface of the water below. He tried to get his mind around the concept of freefall and what it would be like to fall for the better part of an entire minute. To be perfectly fine and healthy, knowing with absolute certainty that you were going to die when your fragile body crashed into the water below, broken to pieces inside as your 120 miles per hour glide through the air was interrupted by a planet.

What did you think about, Tim? Were they the same things I would think about? Were you panicked? Were you accepting? God damn it, I want to know how you spent your last minutes of life. What was it like to be the target of such a slow bullet?

For long minutes they flew into the sun, neither man moving an inch, each held captive by their inner thoughts. I've never seen a man die, Martin thought, his eyes still glued to the panel before him. If he wants to jump, I can't stop him, not without crashing the plane. I won't watch him die. Oh God, why did he call me?

Nick sat stock still, legs hanging out of the airplane door, his body perched literally on the edge of his seat, left arm propping the door open, his right hooking him to the plane itself. *I can't do anymore, Tim. I can't know what you felt, what you thought. But I know it shouldn't have happened. Damn it, not to you. Probably not to anybody.*

He closed his eyes then very slowly pulled his legs back into the airplane. He let the door close itself against the fuselage as he swung forward in the seat and turned the handle upwards to lock it. "Martin," he said as softly as he could and still be heard over the airplane noise. The young pilot didn't move. "Martin," Nick reached over and put his hand on the other man's shoulder. "Let's go home."

Moisture salty as the ocean below glistened on Martin's face as he banked the plane around and left the open Gulf behind. Next to him, Nick fastened his seat belt around his lap. It would be a hell of a thing to fall out now.

CHAPTER THREE

The sunset turned the sky into an arrangement of surrealistic fluorescence, bright pinks and blues, reds and oranges, purples and yellows. It looks fake somehow, Nick thought, like a cheap painting in a bad frame. He squinted into the disappearing sun as the sky painted itself with the colors of its odd spectrum and slowly turned to dark. The gentle waves slapping the sides of the bowrider turned from silver to grey to black as the eyes gave up the ability to see the colors of the night.

Nick lay on the bottom of the boat, fingers clasped behind his head as he stared into the sky, propped up by a wedge of life vests. The smell of the sea was strong and if he breathed deeply it almost stung the inside of his nose. Glare from the nearby city took over the edges of the night sky and the sounds of rushing traffic carried from the distance across the water.

I don't know what to do next, he thought. I feel like I've been hit in the head and I'm wandering in a daze, not sure of where to go or what to do.

His mind drifted back to a summer from his college years, a few months spent exploring the myths of the Southern California coast lifestyle. It was in Hollywood, home of the stars, that he and Tim Clayton had met.

Traffic along Hollywood Boulevard had been brisk and the sidewalks were full of tourists and homeless people, sharing the glamour and the misfortune of the city. The lines of shops were mostly dirty, rundown dives offering sleazy tee shirts for three for ten dollars and electronic stores, the kind where you make a purchase and they keep the box for the next customer.

Nick was walking the sidewalk, reading the names of the stars embedded into the concrete sidewalk, fascinated by the history yet repelled by how it had deteriorated. It's not what they show on TV, he thought. Nick stopped at a star stained with something that had crept our from a recessed doorway and rubbed at it with his foot. The name on the star said Charles Chaplin. There was no one to look after him here.

It was in a little diner advertising vegetarian chili and fruit smoothies that he had met Tim Clayton. Nick had stopped in to try a "Malibu Sunrise" with mango slices and maybe a bowl of the chili. The diner was old, with sheets of dull chrome covering the tops and sides of the counter and tables. It looked like a restaurant from a Hemingway story.

After Nick ordered, he stood up from the counter and went into the bathroom. Two urinals, one vacant and one being used, were mounted on the wall across from the door. The one in use was mounted in a normal position maybe two feet off the floor. The empty one looked like something you might find in a circus. It was full sized but it could almost have been sitting on the floor it was so low, maybe two inches off the ground. Separating the two was a metal section of wall bolted into the tiles.

As Nick stepped up to the open urinal, the man using the normal one looked over his shoulder and said, "Hey, how's it going?"

Nick replied without thinking about it. "Not too bad." He looked down at the urinal and unzipped his fly. He kind of felt like he should say something, like it was his turn to make small talk. Thinking about the unusual plumbing fixture, he said, "Looks like I've got the small one."

The guy gave him an odd sort of look, nodded, and left the restroom after a quick stop at the sink. It took Nick a minute to realize what had happened. When two men are standing next to one another, even with a wall blocking each other from the elbows down, the last thing you say is "Looks like I've got the small one." At least it is when you each have your dick in your hand.

He washed up and left the bathroom shaking his head and feeling stupid. At least he was out of town and far from home.

The dining counter was shaped like a horseshoe with two ends extending out from the kitchen and meeting to form a generous "U" shape. Along one edge was the food Nick had ordered. Directly across from that was the guy from the bathroom. It was the middle of the afternoon and there wasn't anybody else in the place.

Well, isn't this awkward, thought Nick as he sat down and unfurled a napkin across his lap. Maybe we can compare sandwich sizes next.

The waitress, an unnatural blonde with hair of a shade not normally found in nature, stepped between them and asked, "You want anything else with that, honey?" Nick said no thank you and dropped a spoon into his chili. When the waitress moved away, the guy across from him was smiling. "I won't say anything about it if you won't," he said cheerfully.

Nick spread his hands open and smiled back, embarrassed. "I was talking about the urinal, you now, how it was hung so far down on the wall." Nick felt his face begin to turn red. "I didn't think about what I was saying."

The other man laughed out loud, a misplaced sound compared to the atmosphere on the street outside the door. "I know it. It took me a minute before I realized what you meant and I've been sitting here holding my breath trying not to laugh."

They both laughed then, draining Nick's embarrassment and putting him at ease. They introduced themselves and had an enjoyable conversation while they ate their lunch. The other guy's name was Tim Clayton, an engineering major from Pasadena, and about a year older than Nick. When they were through eating, they took a walk down to Graumann's Chinese Theater and Tim showed him where concrete impressions of Marilyn Monroe's and Jane Russell's hands were embedded in adjacent sidewalk panels in front of the theater. One of the actresses had written "Gentlemen Prefer Blondes" starting in one panel and crossing over to the other.

They talked about old movies, famous actresses, famous dead actresses, California, college, and careers. Both shared an optimism about the future, Tim because of the cutting edge engineering work he looked forward to being a part of, and Nick, who wanted a career in law enforcement because of the difference he thought he could make. And they became friends. They spent the last weeks of summer exploring southern California together, Tim as enthusiastic tour guide. When it was over, Nick had had enough "cools" and "groovys" and was ready to head back to his relatively laid back home town of Tampa, Florida.

Tim drove Nick to the airport and saw him all the way through to his gate. "Who knows," he said. "Maybe I'll end up in Florida one day myself." Which he did, three years later, when he transferred to Orlando in the employ of a major theme park corporation. They renewed their friendship and took frequent trips across Interstate 4, with it being Nick's turn to show Tim life on the "other" coast. Nick had graduated from the University of Southern Florida and had joined the Tampa police force. Both men had thought their lives were on track, headed in the direction they wanted.

That may have been true for Tim, who had a habit of sometimes drinking too much beer and proclaiming how life was being so good to him. His career had taken off, leading him into computers and information systems and new career paths that hadn't even existed ten years earlier. Things were a little different for Nick.

He had gotten married to a nurse he had met while delivering a pair of shot up pre-teen gang members to Tampa General one night. They fell in love and bought a house. But being a cop was hard, he didn't like seeing the worst part of the city he grew up in and thought he loved. Bad feelings grew in him and the longer he kept at it the more he hated the job and even the city itself. The stronger these feelings became, the harder he worked, as if the job was rotten because he wasn't trying hard enough somehow. His relationship with his new wife suffered and she left him when he didn't show up for a counseling appointment; he had fallen asleep in his car after working a hectic night shift. When one of the lieutenants in his squad retired after 22 years of sterling dedication to the job, drove home after a celebratory dinner in his honor, and 'ate his gun,' as they say, Nick finally walked away.

He took his wife, Katherine, on a cruise and they worked at patching up their young marriage. She forced him to learn how to relax and together they worked to restore his over stressed mind. A few months later, he proclaimed himself healthy, optimistic, and out of a job.

That's when Tim called and suggested he get out of Tampa for a while. "Come on up to O-town," he said. "The only thing up here big enough to take seriously is Disney World and how hard can that be?" Tim had set up shop as an independent consultant and had offered to teach Nick his field.

For three years Nick worked with Tim learning the business until Tim had developed a sort of pre-mid-life crisis of his own. He bought a 30 foot sail boat and took off, declaring that he wanted to discover the "rest of the things" Florida and the world had to offer. Nick moved back to Tampa and started his own business with a man he had met while working with Tim.

They kept in touch when they could, which meant Nick would get an odd post card here and there from some exotic port or island he had never heard of before. One day a letter arrived from Antigua with a wedding picture clipped behind the paper. On the back of the photo was scrawled, "By the way, you're going to love Marie." Six weeks later the couple had moved to a house in Sarasota, about forty miles south of Tampa and the two friends were reunited.

For Nick, business was doing good and growing, he and Katy were happy, and they had even talked about starting a family. He and Tim didn't see each other as often as they'd like, but each of them had been involved with some large projects at work.

And now this. A large single engine plane flew low overhead and Nick sat up in his boat. Suddenly, things had become very different.

He had no idea what Tim had been doing or who might have wanted to kill him. He hadn't even spoken with him for about a month. But Nick knew he couldn't just put on a suit and tie and go to work in the morning, trying to cope with the loss of his friend. He wasn't sure what he could do, but he knew it had to be more than that.

He drifted along the surface of the water for hours, ignoring the passage of time but unable to keep from feeling its weight. He wouldn't mourn his friend any more; he had done that earlier today in a small airplane at eleven hundred feet above the ground. He would miss him though, for a very long time, probably forever. Nick felt he owed his memory at least that much.

When dawn finally cracked the edges of the long night, Nick slapped a couple of handfuls of the bay onto his face and started the motor. It was time to move. He wasn't sure to where, but he knew it hurt too much to stand still.

CHAPTER FOUR

Monday turned out to be even warmer than Sunday, about 10 degrees hotter than usual for this time of year. Nick had returned home after taking the bowrider back to its slip and taking a shower at the marina. He was trying to stay away from home as long as he could. Familiar things struck him as oddly out of place and he wanted to keep moving, avoiding his daily routine.

Katy was gone when he got there, like he knew she would be. There was a note on the refrigerator board saying she went to stay at her sister's for a while. It was signed, "I love you—Katy." He picked up a paper towel and wiped the board clean without reading the rest of it. Some things would have to wait.

Nick called the police department and asked to be connected to Detective Hill's desk. He wasn't in and Nick left a voice mail asking Hill to meet him at the park with the basketball courts he had played at the day before.

Thirty minutes later, standing ten feet from a basket, Nick was mindlessly shooting free throws only vaguely aware of when the ball actually went through the net. It was close to two hours before Hill showed up, his partner Fetterman in tow like the day before. Both men walked up and stood behind Nick, not saying anything until Nick turned around. This wasn't unusual from Fetterman since he tended not to say much until Hill had said it first.

"I was sorry to hear about your friend Clayton," said Hill in a tone that didn't sound like it. "I'm sure he was a good man."

Like you would know, Nick thought. A cop with the emotional range of a reptile. He nodded back and led them to a playground scarred picnic table with attached benches. This wasn't a conversation he was looking forward to with these guys. They took seats around the table and looked at each other, Hill with his usual half smirking expression and Nick suddenly not sure of how to begin. He wanted to find out what the police knew about Tim's death and he knew Hill wouldn't make it easy. Still, he had sought Nick out yesterday here at the park, on a Sunday, and that didn't make sense unless there was something they wanted from him. Fetterman took a pocket knife from out of his trouser pocket and began to carve his initials into the table.

"So, Nick, after you quit the force, you never came around no more. We thought we might have done something, you know, to offend you or something." Listening to just his words, Hill didn't come off as an asshole. It was the way he said them, like there was a hidden meaning behind every sentence that only he knew, that made him so uncomfortable to talk with. Some guys just did that, found ways to get under your skin, like the more uncomfortable they made you feel the more at ease and in control they felt themselves. Which is just like a lot of cops, Nick thought. Not all of them, but too many were like Hill.

"When I left I was done with it all. I wouldn't have known what to say to anyone."

"Well, that's all right," Hill said like he was doing Nick a favor. "Usually when people just up and quit something like that it shows they probably don't have as much in common with the other guys as they thought." In other words, don't feel bad because you didn't belong, you weren't one of us. We understand and we'll still talk to you.

The only part about being a cop that still meant something to Nick was how close he had been to the other guys. They were all players on a team that forced them to depend on each other, sometimes for their lives. Nick had been as much a part of it, as much a part of the group, as anybody.

You're a real sweetheart, Hill. Take the good and make it bad as long as it keeps you feeling good. You small bastard. "I want to know about Tim."

Hill chuckled and hit his partner's biceps with the back of his hand. Fetterman's knife skipped out of the letter "B" and carved a new groove across the table. Looking at the initial, Nick realized he couldn't remember Fetterman's first name. He wasn't sure if he ever knew it. "So now you want to be a cop again, eh Nick, is that it?"

"I'm just trying to find out what happened to my friend." The way I'm feeling now listening to your shit I'd rather pull that gun out of your holster and blow your fucking teeth out of the back of your head. A pause and then, "Look, you guys are the only cops here. We both know I didn't stick it out."

Hill settled back, like Nick had surrendered something and he had just won a prize. The truth was, he didn't know why Nick had left the force. The other guys had seemed to like him and he had been a natural at the job. Maybe he was soft in his head or pussywhipped at home or something. Hill couldn't understand why anybody in their right mind would give up a job where nobody could tell you what to do. Except other cops of course, but that was different. Rank always has its privileges. Kingman must be some kind of outcast or something.

"Alright, Nick, we'll talk about it. But we don't know much." Next to Hill, Fetterman was scratching away on a new section of tabletop. He had finished with his initials and now it looked like he was working on a figure of some sort. Nick couldn't identify it but whatever it was, it was growing. Jesus, he thought, this guy is hard on picnic tables.

"What we do know is yesterday morning, at approximately 7:45 A.M., two brothers from Gulfport were in a fishing boat in the waters south off the Gandy Boulevard bridge. They claim they heard a noise they couldn't identify. A sound like a gun shot only louder, they said, that came from somewhere behind them. They may have heard a small airplane fly above a few minutes before, but they're not sure."

"I didn't know people usually fished in that part of the bay," Nick said.

"Yeah, we're checking out that part of their story. They may just be a couple of morons in a boat, like half the dickheads in Florida on a weekend. They said they never saw anybody else out there, not many boats, so maybe it was a good place full of fish nobody knew about." Hill scratched his forehead with dirty fingernails. "Maybe it didn't occur to them that they never saw anybody fish there because there wasn't anything worth catching. Anyway, it looks like they'll probably check out okay. The boat was full of tackle and fishing gear and they haven't been in trouble before except for a matching set of DWIs. Those they take turns renewing every year like library cards."

That's cute, thought Nick.

"They pulled in their lines and pointed the boat in the direction of the noise. About fifty or sixty yards away they saw something floating in the water. Evidently your buddy was wearing a windbreaker that had filled with air and was keeping him afloat." An ugly expression formed briefly on his face, then passed. "Weren't for that, he would've sunk like a stone, been down there a few days at least. Anyway they got to him and pulled him into the boat but he was already dead. Nothing unusual about the body except for some pieces of fried egg in his hair but we think one of the brothers probably puked on him and doesn't want to cop to it in front of the other one. I haven't seen the autopsy report yet, but cause of death seems to be consistent with a fall from a substantial height into the water. Or I guess at the speed he would have been going, it would have been 'onto' the water."

Good one, Hill. "What about this airplane they heard?"

"Well, they're not sure they heard one, but hey, the body had to come from somewhere, right? That's our assumption at this point although any plane would have had to fly relatively low to stay out of the TARSA." He looked at Nick who did his best to not show a reaction. "That's restricted the airspace controlled by the tower at an airport." Way to throw those acronyms around, Hill. "If they did fly into the TARSA, or if they had their transponder on, somebody may have picked up an ID on them."

Nick stood and walked in a circle, turning his back to the table so he could relax the expression on his face without showing Hill his distaste. Listening to him talk and looking at that smirk brought back a measure of all the stress and ill feelings Nick had walked away from years before.

"But why did all this happen? Why would somebody want to take Tim Clayton for a ride in an airplane over Tampa Bay and throw him out? I appreciate what you're telling me, but do you guys have any idea what kind of motive there might have been?"

Hill detached himself from the bench and stood up, stretching. He hated talking to someone who was standing while he wasn't. For that matter, he generally disliked people who were taller than him. "Well Nick, we may, but then again we may not."

What's that supposed to mean, Hill? What kind of game are we playing here?

"You see, we came out here yesterday morning to have a friendly talk, like we're having now actually, but you were a bit rude, Nick. More than a little, and you didn't even know why we wanted to see you." Shit, it is a game to you, you prick. "Now I could tell you some things that you probably want to know but they are of a somewhat confidential nature. Details of a pending investigation, you know. But I need a little help in return, Nick. We didn't come out here yesterday or even today just to give you a show and tell session."

And I yelled at you in public and in front of your partner and now you need to show me who's boss. "Alright. I apologize for yesterday. Okay? I didn't mean to make things hard on you guys. I'm asking you now, please just tell me, do you have any idea who killed Tim or why?"

"Geez, Kingman, slow down a little, will you? He just got himself killed yesterday. This isn't the only issue on the agenda here. There are other factors at play you don't even know about." Hill looked back at Fetterman who seemed oblivious to the whole conversation. His work on the table had grown in scope and was now swallowing some of the older carvings on the table. Nick still couldn't make out what it was.

"Okay. What did you want yesterday? When you came out here?"

"Well, that's a whole other thing, Nick." Back to his first name. "And it does have something to do with Clayton, although possibly not his murder."

"But it could, whatever it is?"

"Who can tell? But I don't know, Nick. Your best friend's been killed, you look like you haven't slept all night, you got to feel like shit warmed over. With your grief and all, maybe we should wait to talk about it until you get some rest, feel a little better. It can keep for a few days, can't it, Fetterman?" Fetterman gave a slow nod, hardly acknowledging the question and not breaking his rhythm with the knife.

Nick was too worn out to play any more. He sat down at the table again and said, "Look, Hill. You can keep filling my card but I'm not going to dance. If you've got something to talk to me about, do it now. Especially if it might shed some light on what happened to Tim. Just knock off the crap, okay? You're right, I feel like hell and I'm really not in the mood."

"Well Hell's Bells, Nick, you really do have some balls tucked away in those panties, don't you? Okay, let's not keep drawing this out. Here's the skinny. But I need your word, before I tell you anything more, that you repeat this to no one."

"Repeat what, Hill?"

"No shit, Kingman. I'm working an investigation and your buddy was helping me out. He's gone so now I've got to find some way to get out of the hole he left me in. That's what we came out here yesterday to talk to you about. But I can't let you, ex-cop or no, screw this up with any side investigations of your own. No loose talking with anything I might tell you about our little project."

"And this 'investigation' of yours that Tim was helping you with, you think that might have something to do with why he was killed?"

"I need your word, Kingman."

"Alright, Hill, you've got it. I'll play by your rules." Now tell me what the fuck you got my friend involved with.

Hill nodded and motioned for him to have a seat while he himself stood so he could look down at Nick as he spoke. "Have you ever heard of a business called the Walter Lankford Company?"

"Off of West Shore Boulevard on Cypress?"

Hill nodded. "That's the place."

"All I know about them is that Tim put in their network a while back." Nick thought about it for a moment. "I believe they had about seventy five or eighty computers they needed to connect as well as wide area connections to communicate with networks at other sites."

"Very good, Mr. Kingman. How come you're able to remember it so well?"

"Nothing spectacular, Hill. Tim stayed with my wife and I whenever he did a job in Tampa. It didn't happen that often so it's not terribly difficult."

"Okay, I can buy that. Anyway, you're right about it. It turns out these guys are big into their computer system, their networks. In fact, their whole business, from what we can tell, couldn't be run without it."

"That's not so unusual these days." *Even you should know that.*

"Well, it depends on the type of business that they're actually in, though."

"What does that mean?"

"Money laundering. They take in dirty money, invest it legitimately in hard to trace places, and return net worth to the original 'investor.' Keeping a little something for themselves, of course."

"Hill, that's about as unsurprising as their dependence on their networks. Finding drug money in Florida is like finding sunscreen on the beach."

"But there is something unusual about this case, Kingman. It's all mine."

"What about the feds?"

"There are no feds, not at this point. The problem is, I've got information but I don't have hard proof. If I give up what I've got now, I'm pulled out of the whole thing and this enchilada gets served up nice and warm to the FBI." He held up his hand before Nick could say anything. "Before you give me the rules and regs crap, I'm well within protocol to investigate my source, see if he's yanking my chain or what. Officially speaking, there's no evidence that the Lankford Company is anything other than what they say they are, a financial services and investment company."

Nick thought this out for a minute. "So you don't really have any proof they're doing anything criminal?"

Hill said, "That's right."

"So what the hell are you doing using a civilian to help you investigate a felony? Your investigation may have gotten him killed and you didn't even know if they were guilty or not?"

"Jesus Christ, Kingman," Hill yelled back. "If somebody farts on an elevator, you can tell something's wrong by the way everybody scrambles out of the fricking box when the doors open. You don't have to be plugging your nostrils with your necktie to believe it. You think I'm jerking you off or something? What the fuck do you think I'm doing here talking to you, you son of a bitch?"

Nick didn't know what to think at this point. He was feeling angry at everything and everybody. "Settle down, Hill. I'm just trying to see how this all fits in with Tim." He took a deep breath to calm himself down. He didn't want to completely alienate Hill at this point. "How did he actually get involved?"

"I'll get to that if you just shut up and listen. I'm trying to paint a picture for you here, before we get to the details. May I continue?"

"I'm sorry."

"Thank you very much. Anyway, it seems that the Walter A. Lankford Company *may* be involved with laundering money for a group of South American businessmen, possibly out of Venezuela, we're not sure yet. If the information we have is true, we can't just search their offices, tap their phones, and read through their garbage. We can't do all the normal crap we do. Care to guess why?"

"You tell me," Nick said.

"Because they don't talk on the phone, they don't throw shit in the garbage, and the only thing they do by mail is order fancy underwear for their girlfriends through Victoria's Secret catalogues."

Fetterman spoke for the first time, like Hill had set him up and it was time to deliver the punch line. "They do it all by computer," he said, then bent back to his work.

"That's right," agreed Hill. "So now you see what keeps this whole party going. But if they were just storing illegal data on their computers, that's no big deal. We could grab them and get that shit off, decode it or do whatever the hell we'd need to do, and we'd be good to go."

"And the problem with that is . . . " Nick prompted.

"The problem, Mr. Ex-cop computer nerd, is that what if there isn't anything stored on their computers or floppy disks? What if there's absolutely nothing on the premises physically linking them to any crimes?"

Nick began to see what Hill was getting at. "What you're trying to tell me is that they run everything through their computer networks."

"Everything. That's how they communicate with each other, how they move the money, how they track it, the whole deal. And none of it exists until Lankford links their computers to someone else's. They can start it up or shut it down as easy as turning on and off a light."

"Can't you go after the individual employees? Look at who's making more money than they should and focus on them?"

"They've got over two hundred people working there and most of them are normal working stiffs. They do a legitimate business. And even if there were some way I could get approval to go after each one of them, if one person finds out, the whole case is blown."

"What about wire taps?"

"I don't know what the hell to tap. But you're the expert, you tell me. How would you track it down?"

Nick thought about ways to hide your business on a computer network. The Internet is named for the word 'internetwork,' which is exactly what it is. An enormous number of government, university, medical, and private computers all electronically linked together to form a single, easily accessible network. A user in Baltimore can log on and swap electronic mail or files with a user in Switzerland as easily as he can with somebody two doors down in the same office building. Its potential for allowing global levels of mass two way electronic communication is enormous, creating the push for the development of the so-called 'Information Superhighway.' There would be countless ways to arrange something like this on the Internet, Nick thought.

Someone could access a remote database somewhere that was programmed to access another one somewhere else, and so on and so on, and that data could be sent to your network just like any other data. There would be no limit to how deep you could take an arrangement like that. Performance could be an issue, how long it would take to actually see a particular piece of information on your screen, but clever programmers could minimize that. The data could also be encrypted so that an electronic eavesdropper wouldn't be able to understand what he was looking at.

A computer could also be connected to the Internet wirelessly using radio or a microwave dish making it extremely difficult to trace.

"I see the problem," Nick said.

"I thought you might."

"What about the person who tipped you off to the whole thing? Can you get at it by going through the inside? That may be the only way you're going to find out what's going on with those computers."

Fetterman spoke again, this time without looking up from the table. His design had stopped growing and instead was taking on much more detail. "Can't do that. Informant's not talking anymore."

"Lean on him, then. I know you, Hill. There's not a lot you won't do to get a break in a case."

Hill looked back at Nick and didn't move. "Problem is,"

Fetterman went on. "The informant is not talking to anyone at all. At least not since yesterday."

What they were trying to tell Nick exploded across his brain. "You sons of bitches!" he said, rising to his feet. "You motherfucking sons of bitches!"

"Hey, calm down, Kingman," said Hill. "What exactly do you want us to do, huh? We didn't get his ass killed, he got that done by himself. We're trying to find out how it happened."

"How it happened is he was working for you and you fucked up and left him hanging. Tim wasn't a hero, he wouldn't have done anything like this on his own." At least not without talking to me first. God damn it, Tim, why didn't you come to me with any of this?

"Like it or not, Kingman, we didn't leave him anywhere. He left us. Isn't that right, Fetterman?"

"Yup. Yesterday was the second time."

Nick had difficulty believing what they were saying. "So why the hell didn't he come to me with any of this? That would have been more like Tim than to just go straight to your guys."

"Christ, Kingman, figure it out. You guys were like best friends, right? Two peas in a pod. He was best man or something at your wedding, wasn't he?"

Nick nodded.

"By the way, I never got my invitation. Anyway, you're his best pal who used to be a cop but you went a little nutso or something."

Nick looked at him sharply.

"Or whatever, but you lost your wife for a while, didn't you? Took a little trip to La La Land, someone called it." Hill had a 'don't blame me' expression on his face. "So here's your buddy, he knows about a crime, he isn't sure how you'd react and he doesn't want to cause you any heartache, so he takes it right to the cops. Which is what he should do anyway, according to the law. So tell me, Nick, just where exactly did he go wrong?"

When somebody killed him, you asshole. *Was that how it happened, Tim? Did you really think you were saving me from something by not coming to me first? Was it my fault in some way that this happened to you?*

"So now what?"

Hill put his foot on the bench across from Nick and leaned his elbows forward on his knee. "Well now it gets interesting, I hope. Really interesting."

As Hill spoke, Nick's eyes focused on the surface of the table where Fetterman was doing his carving. Without taking his eyes off it, he stood up and turned around so he could see it right side up. Under the scrapings and gouging of Fetterman's Swiss army pocket knife, the envy of any boy scout, was the image of a large evening sun disappearing behind a horizon made up of the sea. A small airplane was flying between two clouds and below it the surface of the water was disturbed by an incredibly detailed splash pattern that blossomed high above the waves. In the lower right corner were the initials 'FB.'

You are one sick son of a bitch, thought Kingman.

CHAPTER FIVE

Katy's sister answered the phone on the second ring. "Hello," she said.

"Rachel, it's Nick. I need to speak to my wife."

"Your wife, Nick?" She exhaled her disapproval into the phone. "Hold on, I'll get her."

When Katy spoke into the phone, Nick felt his heart begin to beat faster. "How are you doing?" he asked her.

"I'm doing fine, Nick. I'm thinking about you a whole lot, though."

He was afraid to ask, but he did anyway. "Good or bad?"

"Oh, Nick, you know I love you so much. There's not much bad. You know I—I just can't be around some things, you know?"

"Yeah. I do."

"Do you, Nick? You just get so involved with things and they smother everything. You take on these problems and split them up into tiny little parallel universes where only you can go. Then you can't deal with any of the others until you're through with them. You're like a damned puppy with a rawhide bone, you have to gnaw on it and gnaw on it until it's gone."

Nick swallowed. "I'm sorry, Katy, I—"

"No, Nick, don't apologize. It's the way that you are and I love you for it. It just is hard on me sometimes. Well, okay, a lot of times. I'm just not that way. I want to let things go for a while, spend time with my husband, the man I love, and maybe pick things up later after a break. It's not any better than your way, it's just different. It's slower." She paused. "I love you, honey."

"I love you, too."

"Tell me what you're going to do."

God bless her for taking control of this conversation. He couldn't have said what she did in a million years. "I met with a couple of the cops I used to work with. They think they know what happened to Tim. Or at least who was behind it. They want me to help go after them."

"And you're going to do it?"

"Honey, I don't know how not to. If these people out there killed Tim and there is something I can do to make them pay for it, how can I just walk away? I don't know what I would do tomorrow or the day after or any other day but I don't know how to let go of it and forget. I just don't. It's not like I want to, it's like I have to."

"You don't have to explain it, Nick. I'll be here for you when you're done. You just take care of you, huh? If somebody killed Tim . . ."

"Don't worry, love. Nothing's going to happen to me." That's easy enough to say, thought Nick.

"Do one thing for me, okay Nick?"

"What's that, sweets?"

"After all this is over, whatever it is, you put me in one of your little parallel universes and focus yourself on me for a while, okay?"

God, he loved this woman. "You've got yourself a deal," he said.

* * *

After the phone call with his wife, Nick went upstairs and collapsed into sleep. He dreamt of computer networks and airplanes but when he awoke, all he could recall were bits and pieces of scattered images. Nothing concrete, but he knew this case had been at the center of all of them.

As he took a shower and got dressed, he thought about what he needed to do. He hadn't wanted to discuss it with Hill, told him he had to think about it first, but he did have a few thoughts already. Obviously, there were two ways to go about getting at Lankford: go after the people or go after the computers.

Going after somebody actually involved with the company would be time consuming and risky. One word from them or one mistake and they would reveal the whole thing to the wrong people. If Hill had considered that a viable option, he would be pursuing it himself and he wouldn't need Nick. They couldn't consider going after whomever it was Lankford was communicating with because they had no idea whom they were or even where to look and even if they did, there was probably no way they could entice their cooperation.

So they had to go after the operation from the computer end. The network at Lankford was the one place they knew of where the information they were seeking actually went to, regardless of where it came from. Also, it was the only place they knew of where the actual information must be unencrypted and readable by a human. Somehow, Nick had to find a way to get access to that office. He had to get time on their system.

He left the house and started driving toward his office. From home, it was about a twenty minute drive but he did it on automatic pilot, his thoughts still focused on the Lankford Company. It was near midnight and the sky was a moonless black when he pulled into the parking lot outside of his building. He smelled a faint hint of salt water as he stepped out of the car and walked to the building. The bay was only a half mile or so to the west.

The building itself was a one story pre-fabricated concrete affair that was typical of west coast Florida office space. Kingman Sanders Inc. leased thirty five hundred square feet at the northeast corner of the building. This included a warehouse area in the back and two bathrooms, both of which were badly in need of redecoration. The previous tenant had marketed party supplies to private corporations and their taste had run to something that could have been called "early Carnival." One of the toilets was green and the other was yellow. Of the two, most people chose the green because the yellow one always looked like it had pee in it.

Nick unlocked the door and walked over to the console that controlled the burglar alarm. He did this out of habit, ready to key in his four digit security code within the allotted 45 seconds, but for some reason the alarm had already been turned off. Last person out forgot again, he thought, irritated. They had been robbed once before which had prompted the installation of the alarm system. He should probably leave a note on John's desk asking him to remind everybody to pay attention when they left.

He walked past the reception area and down the short hallway to his office. Halfway down the twenty foot passage he stopped when he saw a small light coming from his office. The lamp on his desk was turned on. He listened carefully but he couldn't hear anything other than the sounds of his own slow breathing. The alarm was turned off and somebody had been in his office. Or was still there. His mind jumped to Hill and Fetterman and he felt uneasy but wasn't sure why.

Just take it easy, he thought. There was no sound coming from the open door and no moving shadows in the light. Chances are John or one of the programmers had gone into his office for something and had simply left the light on.

Quietly, he moved forward and leaned the top part of his body around the door frame. The movement caused the person sitting behind Nick's desk to start, jumping literally inches out of his chair. His feet had been propped on the edge of the oak desk and a magazine had been in his lap.

"A little jumpy, aren't we?" said Nick. "No, no, don't get up," he added as the man started to rise. Instead the man bent down and picked the magazine he had been reading off of the floor. He was young, in his early twenties at the most and he smiled up at Nick as he sat back in the chair, startled but not at all bothered by the situation.

"You scared the hell out of me, man," he said.

"How about that," said Nick. "Who are you?"

"Cleaning crew. I'm new though, just been doing your building for about three weeks or so. You either work here or were sent by Mr. Farley, right?"

"Mr. Farley?"

"He's the guy that runs the cleaning company. They told me he sends people out sometimes to check on the new guys."

"No, you were right the first time, I just work here." Nick sat down in one of the two visitor's chairs he kept just inside the door. "What's your name?"

The kid looked more comfortable and said, "Reed Larson. I didn't mean to do anything wrong. I finished the cleaning and I was looking at some of the computer magazines on the desk." He held up the cover of the current PC Magazine.

"That's all right," said Nick. "Take them home with you if you want. I don't think I'll be getting to them any time soon." Larson was thin, slightly unkempt with a few days growth of beard, and Nick saw no reason not to believe him. "What do you know about computers?"

Reed flashed him a smile of naturally white teeth. "Not much, but I'd sure like to. I got into cleaning offices 'cause people leave you alone and they're easy jobs to get. Most of the people have daytime jobs and they quit as soon as they realize it's easier to suffer without the extra cash than to have to work fifteen hour days."

"So this is all you do?"

"This is it. At least right now. This your office?"

Nick apologized for not introducing himself and he stood up and shook the other man's hand. An idea had been forming in his mind. "Tell you what," he offered. "I'll tell you anything I can about the computer business if you'll help me out with the cleaning industry."

"The cleaning industry? Are you serious?" Nick nodded. "That's a little weird, isn't it?" Nick shrugged. "That'll be a short conversation on my end. What do you want to know?"

They talked for almost two hours, mostly as Reed had guessed, about the computer business. He didn't run out of questions but he was scheduled to clean one more office suite by morning. Nick asked for his phone number before he left and asked if it would be alright if he called him in a day or two. He might have a few more questions for him.

"Sure thing," Reed said. "You thinking of branching out or something?"

"Something like that."

A kind of friendship had taken root between them during their talk and Reed was grateful for the sort of information Nick had given him. It also didn't hurt, he thought, to make a contact in the business. They shook hands again and he left.

Nick sat behind his desk in the chair Reed had been sitting in. He wanted to take some time to think about the most important thing he had learned about the cleaning business: that with little or no supervision, workers were given a set of keys and passwords to the security systems of the places they were assigned to work.

CHAPTER SIX

Nick spent the hours between eight and ten at home making phone calls. He deliberately kept himself from dialing Marie Clayton's number, knowing from somewhere deep inside that he would not be able to talk to her. The more that he thought about what he could say the more numbing this inability became. The worst part, he thought, was that he didn't know whether or not he should be feeling ashamed of himself. There was no question he was feeling guilty.

Eventually he dragged himself upstairs and collapsed onto the bed, bothering only to kick off his shoes. He had been pushing his body, depriving himself of rest, wanting to get used to sleeping during the daylight. If things worked out as he was planning, he would need to be more alert at night.

At 3:00 P.M. he awoke, momentarily disoriented by an early morning time and a bright afternoon sun. He rolled off the bed and exposed himself to a cold shower before ambling down the stairs to the coffee maker in the kitchen.

Hill had called and left a message on the machine around lunchtime. Nick thought about calling him back but decided against it. He didn't want to talk to him unless he actually found something out or needed some help. He was pretty sure he was going to need to break a law or two in order to penetrate Lankford's electronic maze and he didn't want Hill to know anything that could come back at him later if he could help it. He would work with Hill but not for him.

Nick checked his watch and picked up the phone to dial Reed Larson. He had no idea if he would be waking him up or what his daily schedule was like but Nick had thought about how he wanted to proceed and was anxious to begin as soon as possible.

The phone rang just twice and Reed picked it up sounding as awake as he had been the night before. The fruits of youth, thought Nick. They exchanged small talk and Nick asked him if he had a name for breakfast at five in the afternoon.

"Pretty much MacDonald's is MacDonald's anytime," said Reed.

Nick chuckled and asked if he would care to join him at a place more familiar to Nick's own culinary disposition, a small cafe near the University of Southern Florida on Fowler Avenue. "There's something more about last night that I'd like to talk to you about."

"Sure," Reed told him. They had gotten along well when they had met and Reed appreciated the chance to talk to someone in the business that he himself would like to be in. Especially someone who owned his own company. "Name the time."

They hung up after another minute or so of talking and Nick poured some water into the coffee maker as he thought about what he would need to tell Reed. He needed the man's help but he didn't want to lure him into something potentially dangerous just because it was convenient for him. He found what was left of the fresh coffee and spooned it into a filter. How bad could things get as long as they had the cops on their side, he wondered.

Sitting on the edge of the counter waiting for the warm aroma of the coffee to find its way across the kitchen he wondered why that last thought didn't make him feel any better than it did.

* * *

James Rooker didn't particularly care for computers, any more than he felt any great connection to large kitchen appliances or digital stereo components. But he knew a money making opportunity when he saw one and in the early eighties he jumped into the personal computer revolution with both feet. In those days, anyone hanging a sign on their front door that said "Computers for Sale" had to be either a buffoon or a total idiot not to make at least some money. James Rooker was neither. He made out quite well.

In fact, James Rooker was a shrewd if somewhat less than totally honest businessman who took full advantage of his customer's lack of technical sophistication. They were coming to him for expert advice and that's exactly what he would give them. It didn't bother him that at all that his recommendations were carefully designed to keep his customers one step behind the industry's leading edge. If they bought for tomorrow as well as today, where would his market for upgrades go?

Now, unfortunately, the market was maturing and people were no longer buying the hardware at the breakneck pace of even a few years ago. And when they were, as often as not they were buying through the mail or at these electronic superstore monstrosities that had sprung up like weeds after a Texas rainstorm. Smaller companies like Rooker's just couldn't compete with the lower prices these stores could offer through their "volume purchasing." Also, the average user had gotten much smarter and it became harder and harder to talk even the dumber ones into buying something they did not need or want.

But, as he had heard somewhere, within every crisis there lies an opportunity. One just had to be smart enough to find it. Rooker recognized that once all these companies had purchased their computers, they would be searching for ways to network them all together. The profit niche for the smaller operations like Rooker's would be the consulting fees he could charge to peddle the expertise that would make this possible. But first, of course, he needed to acquire some.

He found that to be fairly easy. He could take these young kids and their diplomas fresh from the local technical colleges and use them for the grunt work. They didn't have to be paid much since the competition was fierce and they had no real world experience. The opportunity to be a professional and to gain that experience kept Rooker in a good supply of recruits. His turnover was inconvenient but that was a fairly easy price to pay.

The only remaining problem was one of attracting new customers. A sign on the door was no longer the most effective way of drawing in the desired clientele. And for some reason, word of mouth didn't seem to work for him the way it did for his competition. Questions concerning the quality of his work never entered his mind.

On the morning following the death of Tim Clayton, one of James Rooker's more prosperous rivals, he read the article written about the possible crime with a keen interest. Clayton had been something of a one man shop, he knew, providing the consulting services himself and contracting out any labor or installation work. It would seem, if viewed with the shrewd business-like mind of a James Edward Rooker, that a spate of potential customers had abruptly been made available. Deprived of their main source of data processing information, Rooker figured that he was ideally suited to pick up where the unfortunate Mr. Clayton had left off. All he had to do was come up with an angle for making them see that, too.

What a way to start your day. He felt a little sorry for Clayton, who wouldn't, but on the other hand, he hadn't known him all that well. They had come in contact mostly when Rooker was trying to sell to one of Clayton's clients. It had usually been unsuccessful. Actually, it had always been unsuccessful but that should all change now, he thought, if he could work quickly. He needed to come up with enough of a list of the orphaned businesses to give him a head start before they began looking elsewhere. If he did that, he should easily be able to double the amount of people currently on his client list, he was sure. Opportunities like this didn't present themselves to James Rooker very often and this was certainly one he wouldn't dream of letting pass.

CHAPTER SEVEN

"No shit, you used to be a cop?"

Nick took a sip of coffee and nodded. "Yup. And now I'm a computer nerd. If you don't believe me I can show you my pocket protector."

Reed laughed. "No, I'll take your word for it." He pushed his plate aside to make room for his elbows. "So how'd you get out of being a cop? And into working with computers? Or shouldn't I ask?"

"No, that's alright," Nick said, signaling the waitress for more coffee before he started. "I was rather hoping you would, actually." He waited a moment while the woman filled his cup. He thanked her before she walked away.

"I think most cops could probably tell you a story like this one. This is only unique because it's mine. There are a lot of cases that come out the way they're supposed to, where you solve the crime, catch the crooks, and whatever passes for justice gets done. But in the end, when it's finished, nothing seems to have been fixed or made right. A lot of things turn out looking a lot worse than they had been before.

"There was a couple from Michigan, the Bickfords there name was, that packed their two little girls into the family station wagon and drove down here for two weeks of vacation. They were going to do the beaches, theme parks and all the usual Florida tourist things. On their way down, they drove through an ice storm in Kentucky and almost slid into the side of a tanker truck filled with liquid petroleum. They were a little freaked out over how their trip had almost ended and they decided to lay over for a day and give the ice a chance to melt. Recover their nerves a bit. They arrived in Tampa a day late and since they had missed their check-in date, their hotel had given away their room."

"They never called the hotel, said they'd be late?"

"Harold Bickford told me later that they had been so flustered after their near accident that they never thought of it. At least not until they were almost there. Anyway, the hotel was full and the Bickfords hadn't confirmed their reservation with a credit card so they were forced to look for another room. It took several hours and since they were well into losing the second day of their vacation, they took practically the first thing they could find. It was two weeks after Christmas, prime tourist season and there wasn't a whole lot available." He paused, looking through the plate glass window into the front parking lot. "It would have been better for the Bickfords if the fricking city had been sold out."

"What happened?"

"Ramon Cruz and Bobby Padilla, two shit heels from Ybor City, decided to have a big night out. They scored a few rocks of crack cocaine, boosted a car, and for some unknown reason became fixated on Margot Bickford when they saw her sitting in the station wagon at a convenience store. Harold was inside paying for gas. They pulled up next to her and began propositioning her as if she were a hooker. When she told them she wasn't interested, Padilla told her that what she needed was a pimp and he dropped his pants and hung himself out the window so she could see his qualifications. The two little girls were asleep in the back seat but Margot was terrified that they would wake up. Harold finished paying for the gas, came out of the store, and Cruz and Padilla took off. The Bickfords drove to yet another motel, this time one with an open room due to a last minute cancellation. They didn't know that Cruz and Padilla had followed them there.

"The two of them sat in their stolen car, watching while Harold unloaded the station wagon he had parked in front of a ground level room. Margot put both girls to bed and began to undress so that she could take a hot shower before retiring for the night. You can probably guess where this is going."

"Not really. I'm trying not to think ahead."

"Are you okay hearing this stuff?"

"I'm not squeamish or prone to nightmares if that's what you mean."

Nick nodded and picked at the cuticle of his left thumb with his other hand. "Cruz and Padilla, each holding a pistol and one with an eight inch hunting knife, kicked in the motel room door a short time later. They bound Harold and the children with nylon rope Padilla cut from the window blinds. Over the course of the next several hours they repeatedly raped Margot on one of the double beds and forced her to perform a variety of sexual acts while her family, bound and positioned on the other bed, were made to watch. Whenever Margot tried to fight them, one of the men would take the hunting knife over to the children and comb through their hair with the serrated edge of the knife.

"After Cruz and Padilla had had their fun, they each took their pistols and shot Margot once in the head. One of them then shot Harold twice in the chest and the other one shot him in the groin. The little girls, although spattered with blood and pieces of their mother, were never physically harmed."

Nick stopped talking. Reed had slumped back into the booth and was slowly shaking his head.

And the children? He looked at Nick.

"The girls were six and seven," he said, reading the young man's mind. "You want to take a minute? Wash your face or something?"

Reed nodded and made his way off to the men's room to find a sink and some cold water.

I've put him into shock, thought Nick as he drank more coffee. The waitress appeared on her own with a refill. "Thanks," he told her.

A few minutes later Reed came back to the table, dabbing moisture from his face with a paper towel.

"Doing alright?" Nick asked him.

"I'm okay," said Reed. "You know, it's one thing seeing stuff like that in movies or even on the news but you were actually there. It's like I can feel it more somehow, listening to you talk about it." He reached for his own cup and took a long sip. "If that were me in that motel room, and two guys were doing that to my wife, and my kids . . ."

"You would have had to sit there and take it, just like Harold Bickford did."

"Man." Reed shook his head slowly and looked up at Nick. "I can't even imagine it. Not how I would feel. How did you deal with things like that?"

"That's the point of my story. I'm sorry, I should have thought more about it before I told it to you like that."

"No, it's okay."

"Then I may as well finish it. You deal with it by turning off part of you. You deaden inside. You stop feeling certain kinds of things."

"Like what?"

"Compassion, for one. You want to help the victims, but you really can't. You want to kill the asshole scumbags that do these things, but you can't. So you find yourself just having to accept that this is the way it is, the way it has been, and the way it always will be."

"But you're not like that anymore?"

"I try not to be. I noticed that ordinary people, people who weren't cops, could still go to sleep at night not overly troubled by what kind of stink hole we've turned this world into. And I didn't think I could make that change, I couldn't make it better. I decided I wanted to be like everybody else. Right about this time, something else happened.

"There was a detective that had been around forever. Eddie Rossenburg. We all liked him, looked up to him, really. He hit retirement, went home, and two weeks later killed himself with his own gun. He'd been shot at lord knows how many times but never once in all those years had he ever been hit or wounded. Until he did it himself.

"All those years on the job, you think he makes it and just like that, he pulls his own curtain. Game over. It shocked everybody. We talked about it for weeks, wondered why he did it, went through the whole nine yards. But nobody seemed to catch on. Except me. At least I thought I did. I told myself I knew exactly why he did it. And I knew that even at my relatively young age, I had already had enough."

"Are you okay with that now? Or are there parts of it you miss?"

"I don't like quitting. I didn't get into it on a lark, I got into it because I believed in the job, I respected it, like most of the other guys. The going got a little tough for me and I left, but everybody else stayed. They took it. I don't know how to explain it, but quitting was both the hardest thing I've ever done as well as the most necessary, for lack of a better word."

"How about now? How are you today?"

"I'm happy, I live a reasonably normal life. There's still a chunk missing, I think, something I'll never get back. And every couple of days I need to spend a little time pushing some of the old things back into their little holes. I'll ever read a newspaper again."

They sat in silence for a few minutes, Nick sipping his coffee, Reed gazing through the window at the small clouds of fog forming over the water filled ditch along the highway.

"So tell me what ended up happened to Cruz and Padilla."

"They plea bargained down to avoid the chair. They're in for life. 'No possibility of parole.'"

"I can't believe it can be that easy for them. How about the family?"

"That's harder." Nick thought a moment before he answered. "This sounds cold but I don't know and at this point especially I don't want to know. I can tell you the facts of the case, I can tell you how it happened, but there's no way I can make you understand how it felt to be part of it. The anger, the impotence, all of it just gets so big, makes you feel so ineffectual . . .

"The pressure is enormous. You can't sleep, your health goes to hell, and you go on a diet of straight Rolaids. But always, deep down at the very heart of it, you know that no matter how lousy, how ugly, how bad you feel about all of it, it's nothing but a small pimple on a fly's ass compared to what Harold Bickford and his daughters had to see."

Nick turned to look out the window. "If that had been me, if that had been my wife, the last thing in the world that I would have wanted was to have lived through it."

Nick slowly took another sip from his cup. He was drinking the coffee out of blind habit than from thirst. The act of picking up the cup and putting it back down was a thin tether to the present. When he spoke again Reed could barely hear the words. "I can never think about the daughters. I push them off into a dark place and I don't think about them. They were never there, they couldn't have existed."

Reed wouldn't have spoken then, but Nick looked at him, gray eyes staring as if asking, is that so terrible? "Maybe that's just sane," he offered.

Nick let his focus sink downward into the table then somewhere beyond. As Reed looked dumbly at the top of his head, he heard, "Maybe it is."

They sat that way for a much shorter time than it seemed, just a minute really, before Nick straightened his back and raised his hand to signal the waitress. Reed could see new lines on his face that he hadn't noticed there before. "You still live this stuff, don't you?"

"First half of show and tell is over. I"ll buy you a piece of Key Lime pie and tell you the other part of the story."

"I hope this one has a happier ending."

Nick spoke to the waitress for a moment than she was gone. "Actually, Reed, it doesn't. This is what I really wanted to talk to you about. My best friend was killed last weekend."

Reed stared at Nick, waiting for some kind of punch line. After a minute he said, "You're serious?"

"Yes, I am."

"Holy shit."

"I'd like to tell you about what happened to me after I quit being a cop, how I got into the computer business. At the end of it I'm going to ask you two things, neither one dependent on the other."

"What's that?"

"I'm going to ask for your help about what happened to my friend, and I'm going to offer you a job."

"A job? But I haven't learned enough about computers yet."

"I'll teach you. You can come work for me and we'll see how you do."

"I don't know what to say. I'd love it. And of course I'll help you with—what happened. Just tell me what you want me to do."

Two slices of fruitless pie and plastic whipped cream arrived at the table as Nick told Reed all about Tim Clayton and what he had meant to him. He told him about the murder and his later conversation with Hill and Fetterman. At the end of it, pie untouched, Reed said, "I'm hooked. I don't know why you picked me or what I can really do for you, but I'll do anything you think that I can."

Nick reached across the table and slapped Reed in the shoulder. The gesture was in some way both a thank you and an acknowledgment. "Wait until you hear what I have planned first."

"Just tell me I don't have to do something like dress up as a woman. I'd really hate that."

Nick smiled back. "That's in Plan B. Let's just hope that Plan A is the one that works."

CHAPTER EIGHT

The air temperature was in the low seventies, barely warm enough for natives to take their shirts off. On the beach, where the heat reflecting off the sand made it hotter, bright red and white islands of tourists burned slowly throughout the morning. A group of frolicking Canadians were the only ones enjoying the water as the Gulf of Mexico was still cool, just beginning its springtime climb. In a few weeks it would become nearly eighty degrees.

"Oh my God."

"What is it?" Nick asked. "You got something?"

"We're gonna need wider angle lenses on these things."

"What are you talking about?" He reached over and took the binoculars from Reed's eyes. "Let me look."

"Do you see her?"

Nick worked the focus knob with his finger. "Oh my God."

In the binoculars was an enormous woman wearing green pants and a short sleeved shirt. She was pointing with one arm and seemed to be giving directions to the person she was speaking with.

"She has the enormous biceps of the truly fat."

Nick studied her carefully through the binoculars. "You don't see many people of that size in Florida."

"That's because animals that big generally became extinct about 250 million years ago," said Reed. "Hell, you need to put down the binoculars and back up a ways if you want to see all of her at once."

Nick started walking toward the beach. "Not if we want to talk to her. Try to be nice. Or I'll tell her you don't have a girlfriend."

Reed jogged a little in the sand to catch up. "Wait a minute, you mean that's who we're looking for?"

"It's a little hard to tell, but I think so. If it is, she's put on a lot of weight. But I think it's her."

They made their way across the sand from the wooden hut that served as refreshment stand, gift shop, and changing room for the south end of Clearwater Beach. Both men were wearing shorts and carrying their shoes in their hands while black headed laughing gulls swooped and glided at eye level all around them. "I'm always worried those things will fly into my head," Reed said. "That's why I never buy food here."

The woman was spreading a double sized bed sheet across the sand, weighing the corners down with items taken from a large canvas beach tote, as they approached. When she saw Reed and Nick, she immediately dropped her massive body into a sitting position on the center of the sheet and clenched a meaty forearm around her bag.

Nick slowed his pace as he approached the edge of the sheet. "That's you, isn't it, Lu?"

She looked up at him and shook her head slowly. "Last time they took me out of here when I didn't want to go it took twelve of them and a flatbed truck. You two don't look like you got that much firepower."

Reed looked away to keep from showing her his grin. Now that she was sitting down, he thought, how could she possibly get up at all without that much help?

Nick dropped down to his knees so the woman wouldn't have to squint into the sun. "Relax, Lu, we don't want to take you anywhere. We just want to talk to you for a minute."

"Yeah, I've heard that one before." She made a snorting sound through her nose. A sea gull landed on the beach next to Nick and began to walk along the edge of the sheet. "I know this game. Just what is it you want?"

"Well, the first thing is I want to know if you remember who I am."

She wrinkled her forehead in mock surprise and waved the back of her hand at him. "Remember you? You're some cop, aren't you? Or isn't that right? What's your name?"

"Nick—"

"Kingman," she said, raising her voice and nodding her head. "I do remember you. It's going back a few years but yeah, you're the same guy. I heard you quit being a cop, though. What's the deal?"

"I'm not a cop any more, that's true. And neither is my friend here. We really do just want to talk to you."

Reed nodded to her in what he hoped was a reassuring way. He couldn't get over the size of the woman's neck; it was as big around as one of his thighs.

"Well, hell, as long as you're not going to bust me for anything, have a seat." She waved Nick down. "But you," she said to Reed. "Sit over here a little closer." She patted a spot on the sheet next to her and smiled sweetly, all traces of her suspicion melting away into the sand.

Reed wasn't sure what he should do. Was she serious? The woman didn't even know him. He looked at Nick who nodded at him, then moved to take the offered seat.

Uncomfortable, he sat down next to the large woman, carefully avoiding any contact with the spread of her body. Maybe this won't be so bad, he thought. I just don't want to have to touch her.

Without warning, Lu unwrapped her left arm from around her bag and swung it out and backwards toward Reed's head. He ducked as fast as he could but the meaty hand caught him squarely above the right ear. If he hadn't seen her swing and start to move, the blow would have taken his head off. As it was, his movement plus the contact sent him rolling off the sheet and into the sand. His ears were ringing as he sat up holding his head.

"Tell your boyfriend, Kingman, that it's not a good idea to laugh at people where they can see you. I'm fat, I know, but I'm not blind. Or stupid. Now tell me what it is you wanted to talk to me about or leave me alone."

Nick looked over at Reed who was sitting slumped forward, a look of painful surprise still on his face. "He's sorry, Lu, he just doesn't know any better. Do you, Reed?"

"Obviously not," he heard himself say through the background noise in his head. "I apologize, ma'am, for my lack of sensitivity as well as for my poor manners."

"Nice comeback," she told him. "Go ahead and relax, I'm not going to hit you again." Reed told her thank you and sat back in the sand, careful to be at least an arm's length away. He was going to have to be gentle for the next week whenever he used a comb.

"I need to find someone with the particular skill set you used to employ in your work," Nick said to the woman. He was trying to be tactful; he needed Lu to put aside her natural distrust if he had any hopes of her helping him.

"Uh huh," said Lu. When they had met, Mary Lu Bates, now known mostly as "MamaLu" Bates, had been scraping out a living for herself picking the pockets of the tourists that annually peppered the sands of Clearwater Beach. It hadn't been something that she'd get rich at. In a beach setting, there sometimes just weren't that many pockets to pick. Still, she had skill and she could afford to be a regular at most of the restaurants near the beach where the tourists went to spend their money.

She hadn't been all that ambitious, and that's something that helps in any line of work. She liked the beach and if she became too prolific she'd attract too much attention, something a lone pickpocket tended to avoid. She merely worked enough to support her relatively modest lifestyle: A single bedroom efficiency apartment one block off the beach and freedom from the stress of deciding what she would do if she chose to make an honest living.

All that had changed one day when she met Carl Pantucket and fell in love. Carl was a visionary, she thought, a self-styled entrepreneur with small dreams and a big mouth. To his credit, the fact that he hadn't been able to cut it in the professional world did no damage whatsoever to his self-image, which consistently buoyed his ego with pictures of a misunderstood man who's time was simply yet to come. Carl's belief was such that when he inherited $150,000.00 of his mother's estate, he merely considered it as part of that time coming due. Justification for a life of meaningless failures. So he graciously accepted the money and did what he thought a great man like himself should be doing. He bought an imitation Italian suit and opened a donut shop on the beach.

The shop was on the same block as MamaLu's little apartment and one day, when she stopped to buy an eclair, they struck up a conversation and eventually, after many more, fell in love. He was the only man she had ever told about what she did for a living. This intrigued Carl because lately the donut shop hadn't been doing too well. Business decreased dramatically in the winter months which unfortunately coincided with the operation of Tampa Bay Downs in Oldsmar. With his newfound money and lifestyle, he had quickly developed a love for fast horses. It was his misfortune that he only bet on the slow ones.

After an intense period of romance, which included all the free donuts either of them cared to eat, Carl one day was forced to declare himself bankrupt. A donut shop without customers and a bookie with a mean streak forced Carl to realize that, while it had looked promising for a while, his time had not yet come. He approached Lu with the idea of her picking pockets again, maybe bankrolling a franchising venture for a string of Carl's Deluxe Donut Shoppes up and down both sides of the peninsula. Lu finally admitted she knew a loser when she saw one. It just took her longer sometimes with people she cared about.

She threw him out. It hurt, but she knew it was for the best. Carl accepted it stoically, as if he'd been through something like it before, kissed her on the nose and announced that he would be moving to Minneapolis. She said, why Minneapolis, and he said he'd heard they had good welfare and unemployment programs up there and it was important for him to make a positive start.

Months of depression followed. Lu had never been in love before and she had no idea that the fallout could sometimes be more intense than the passion. Like a lot of people, she turned to the solace she found in the refrigerator. Already blossoming after spending months in a donut shop, things for Lu went from bad to worse. It became evident that a person of her newly acquired stature simply didn't fare well in an illegal occupation that depended on one's ability to be quick and sure with one's movements. She had sized herself out of the market and now she needed a career change.

The beach itself provided the answer, as MamaLu had come to believe it did for most things. She became what she liked to call a professional beachcomber. Rather than scavenge the sands for interesting shells or misplaced pocket change, she developed a talent for observing beachgoers and the vehicles they arrived in. She would wait for them to put their money and keys in their shoes and then go swimming or walking down the beach. She would switch the keys with a dummy set and then raid the car. It required the development of a new set of skills but she was proud that she could teach herself some new tricks at this particular stage in her life.

She was doing well, actually, a lot better than when she had picked pockets. People tended to leave more in their cars than they brought with them down to the beach, especially in the way of ladies' purses. She didn't have to pull as many jobs as she used to in order to make her quota.

Life was getting better in these post-Carl days, she thought. Until now anyway, when an ex-cop turns up on her figurative door step asking her questions. He had busted her once when she worked a Buccaneer game at the stadium in Tampa during one of her rare forays off the beach. He had been decent enough about it at the time, she remembered. But a cop was still a cop. And what, if anything, did he know about her current activities?

"Why are you coming to me?" she asked Nick.

"I need some help with a problem I have. You were, or even are for all I know, a professional pickpocket. I need to find someone with those skills."

"Is there money in it?"

"Of course."

"How much?"

"Well, that depends," Nick told her, "if you're interested in the job yourself or if you've got somebody you're going to recommend."

"Just what is this 'job' you're talking about?"

Reed looked at Nick and wondered if it was a good idea to tell this woman anything. Although he had faith in her ability to beat the hell out of anybody foolish enough to get within her reach, he just couldn't imagine her being subtle enough to take somebody's wallet out of their pocket without them being aware of it. It's Nick's call, he thought. He edged another few inches away, just in case she decided she knew what he was thinking again.

"I need someone to lift a set of keys off someone who cleans buildings," said Nick.

The truth be told, MamaLu had serious doubts about her own ability to perform like she had in the past. But a set of keys? Hell, that's how she'd been making her living the past six months.

"Then they've got to be put back," Nick added.

That's a little different, she though, but still she should be able to figure out something that wouldn't be too difficult. "So this is like some janitor, huh? Where does he keep the keys, in his pocket, on his belt, or where?"

"We don't know yet, but we'll find out and tell you before you actually have to do the work."

"What happens to the keys before they get put back?"

"We make copies of a few of them."

MamaLu laughed and shook her head. "I never thought I'd see the day," she said. "Did you figure out a way to beat the system, or what? Why does an ex-cop want to take off a building with the help of a professional thief? What's the big score here, Kingman?"

"Uh uh," he told her. "There's no score other than the keys, and the why is not part of the deal. If you're interested, tell me how much it will take."

No score. Yeah, right. This guy's boosting keys for the fun of it. He must be on to some seriously big shit, being an ex-cop and all. "Five grand," she said.

Reed almost gagged and laughed despite himself. Five thousand dollars? Maybe she could do the job but for that kind of money they ought to be able to figure out something cheaper. He watched Nick, who hadn't flinched. He must know what he's doing, Reed thought.

For the next five minutes, MamaLu and Kingman dickered over a price. They finally agreed on a sum of two thousand dollars for one night's work. MamaLu also agreed to make the copies herself. It had become a recent hobby of hers, she told them, she'd be glad to do it.

She held her hand out to Kingman, who reached forward and shook it. Reed stood up and began walking away. There was no way he was going to let her grab hold of his hand. She blew a kiss at the back of his head and called, "See you around, sweetie."

Nick told her they'd be in touch in a week or so and hurried to catch up to his friend. "That's done," he said.

"You trust that over-inflated Rocky wannabe to do this thing right? You think she's capable?"

"I think so. The money should be good for her and I haven't been able to figure out a better way to get at those keys. Back when I knew her, she could do some amazing things with those hands. By the way, how's your head?"

On the beach, MamaLu peeled off her shirt to reveal a massive yellow halter top. She laid back on her sheet and thought about taking the day off. These guys had to be after something big. They had to. Ex-cops wouldn't just turn into felons without looking at a huge payoff. And who better to get away with a crime than a criminal who used to be a policeman? Yes, sir, today was definitely going to be a vacation day. She had some serious planning to do.

* * *

An hour later, Nick and Reed were sitting in Nick's kitchen sipping fresh squeezed orange juice from a container in the refrigerator. "So the next thing we've got to do is get me inside Lankford's office," Reed said.

"Right. And I'm hoping that won't prove to be too difficult. The more legitimate we can make it appear, the better off we'll be if something goes wrong. I have no idea how many times we're going to need to be in there."

"But if they don't store any data there, what is there to go after?"

"Even if we assumed they did store their actual data there, we probably wouldn't want it. They probably use an encryption scheme that we couldn't break and we'd just be wasting our time."

"The cops can't bug the phone lines that connect them to the Internet?"

"They could probably tap into that, but you've got to remember that they have a couple of hundred computers in the place, all doing the things normal computers in brokerage houses do. All that traffic across a network cable is broken up into many, many tiny little pieces. We'd have to locate the ones we're interested in, find a way to string them together, and even then I assume the data they contain could be encrypted."

Reed pulled a chair out from the small kitchen table and sat down. "So what do we do?"

"Well, think about it. Where is the one place on the computer that whatever you're working on is displayed for you, completely undisguised, in plain English?"

Reed arched his eyebrows. "The screen?"

"Usually referred to as the monitor, but yes, the screen. You've got to remember, the computer itself provides the security measures, human beings aren't that smart. And if I'm going to tell the computer to do something, how do I do it?"

"You type it in at the keyboard."

"Exactly. *After* you type it in, the computer can encrypt it or translate it or do whatever you want. But I'm willing to bet that they type their information in the way the see it—in plain English."

"So how do we get at it?"

"In a way, we're going to bug the monitor and keyboard. People always move to safeguard their computers, they rarely if ever think of the peripherals. At least that's what I hope."

"Do you know how to do that?"

Nick nodded. "The keyboard, yes, the monitor, not yet but it shouldn't be too difficult to figure out. What we've got to do in the meantime is get you in at Lankford's so we've got the physical access we need."

Reed tried to stifle a yawn. It was barely one in the afternoon but his normal said he should still be sleeping. "So I quit my job and then what? Apply at, what is it, 'Bay Area Cleaning Service?'"

"That's it. That part of it is all up to you."

"Well, like I told you, it shouldn't be hard to catch on with them doing something. Cleaning services are almost always short-handed, people just up and quit all the time. It's not that easy being a vampire when everyone else you now lives their lives during the day. But there's no way of knowing how much work they'll give me, or where it'll be."

"That's alright," said Nick. "Just beg off Wednesdays and Fridays if you can. That's when Lankford's offices get their weekly cleaning."

"How'd you find that out?" Reed asked.

"It wasn't too difficult," Nick told him. "I went to their office and saw the decal on the door for their security monitoring company. I called them up, told them I was a cop investigating phony cleaning service break-ins, and they told me. If you know how to make people think you're a cop, they'll tell you anything."

"Phony cleaning service break-ins?"

"Get out of here so I can take a nap. I want to do some work tonight and Tim's funeral is tomorrow in Sarasota."

* * *

Technical expertise had never been one of James Rooker's strong points in business. That honor would have to go to his silver tongue and his willingness to manufacture the truth whenever he needed it. With these skills, he felt he was ideally suited for the consulting business.

He had been able to compile a list of eight companies he knew had been clients of the late Tim Clayton. This morning he had begun visiting all of them in person. He found that it was much easier to feign sincerity when you were actually face to face with people. Rooker considered that a lesson to be learned by careful watching of interminable hours of political election coverage on television.

So far, it had been a good day. He had been to two of the companies on the list and both, after expressing disappointment and sorrow at the news of Tim Clayton's death, had promised to call Rooker the next time they needed something done. He had no reason to doubt their veracity but he figured he would find out if they meant it when the virus he had left behind on their systems kicked in.

The third place on his list was called The Walter Lankford Company. They were into financial services or stock brokering or something, he didn't care what it was. He presented himself to the receptionist and asked if it would be possible to speak to the network or computer administrator. Before she had a chance to discourage him with their 'No Soliciting' policy, he added that he was with the company that had installed their computer network. She thought it was odd that she hadn't seen him before and that Rooker didn't know Mr. Darwin by name, but she'd let Darwin deal with that. She wasn't paid to be anyone's bouncer.

Ronald Darwin appeared from around a corner made by an arrangement of those modular walls that were used to create small cubicles for the lower level employees. He was smartly dressed and he came straight to Rooker and held out his hand. Rooker shook it while introducing himself.

"What can I do for you, Mr. Rooker?" asked Darwin.

"I wonder if we could go somewhere and sit down. I have some news concerns about your networks that I'd like to share with you."

Darwin motioned to two chairs set along the wall next to a cherry coffee table with a grey marble top. Rooker estimated that the chairs couldn't have cost less than five hundred dollars apiece. He wouldn't even guess at the table. "Does this have something to do with the death of Tim Clayton?"

So they were already aware of it, Rooker thought. That should be alright, as long as they hadn't already found someone to replace him. Rooker nodded and began to explain how shortly before his death Tim had approached Rooker about the possibility of combining their two companies for the sole purpose of offering a stronger, more competitive service. He had felt that the two of them each brought different things to the table and thought that it would be beneficial to the existing customers of both companies for this merger to take place.

"Tim never mentioned anything about this to us," said Darwin.

No, he wouldn't have. They had both been waiting until they had worked out all of the details. Unfortunately, their conversations had been interrupted by the unwelcome and untimely event of Tim's death. A terrible, terrible tragedy.

"Do you have any idea why this would have happened to Tim?"

"Me?" said Rooker. "I have no idea whatsoever. This whole thing comes as quite the shock. He was a good man. One of the absolute best." As far as Rooker knew. He'd only met the man once in passing. Darwin seemed satisfied with the story he had told him.

"What can I do for you today, Mr. Rooker?"

Here we go, thought Rooker. He explained why he was there this morning, at no charge of course, to take an informal survey of the computer networks and systems that had been installed by Tim's company. Then, in the future, should The Walter Lankford Company require additional services, Rooker would be in the best possible position to efficiently accommodate their needs and requests. It would just take a few minutes and all he would need was the supervisor's password to the network and an open terminal.

Darwin agreed. He wasn't sure he completely believed the man's story, he seemed too showy where Tim had been down to earth, but he would watch him closely and see what he did. He led Rooker past the receptionist to his own cubicle, a tidy arrangement of technical manuals and trade magazines. He indicated that Rooker should use his own chair and parked it in front of the computer monitor on his desk.

From his briefcase, Rooker removed a form he had generated last night on his laser printer and proceeded to fill in the appropriate blanks. He entered several commands into the computer and was disappointed to find a very effective anti-virus program. The little trick he had played on his first two stops this morning wouldn't work here.

The man Darwin was standing over his shoulder and watching him like a hawk. If Rooker had any chance of winning their business, he would have to appear competent at the keyboard. He began to move to different areas of the network file server's hard disk and call up lists of the individual files. "Just checking out the directory structure," he said to Darwin.

He was about out of things to do when he noticed something strange. There was a directory entry that appeared empty yet at the same time the computer was showing it as occupying some space, as if it contained some files. Ah, now this is clever, he thought as it dawned on him what someone had done. This entry that appears as a directory with no files is really a file by itself. It's not a directory at all.

Darwin was still in the cubicle but had stepped back to have a conversation with someone who had come looking for him. Rooker quickly slipped the blank floppy disk he usually carried in his shirt pocket into the drive on the computer. Within twenty seconds he had made a copy of the file and returned the disk to its home in his shirt. Rooker just couldn't resist anything this clever. Something worth hiding was usually worth money.

He glanced over his shoulder. Darwin was still speaking with the other person and had been joined by another. Rooker deftly typed in a command that displayed the contents of the mystery file on the screen. It was a short list of four names followed by twelve digit hyphenated number that he hadn't seen before.

"Are you almost through here, Mr. Rooker? I'm afraid I have to get back to work."

Rooker cleared the screen and swivelled around in the chair. If Darwin suspected anything untoward, he gave no sign. "Of course. I've got what I need, Mr. Darwin." He stood and handed the man another business card. "If anything comes up in the future, I look forward to the opportunity of serving your needs." They shook hands and Darwin showed him to the door.

Outside, in his car, Rooker sat and adjusted the air conditioning so it blew across his face. For some reason he tended to perspire when he got excited. He had only had a quick look at the names in the computer file, but something about one or two of them had struck him as familiar. He touched the plastic disk in his pocket to make sure it was still there.

Obviously, someone had tried to disguise the existence of this file. If he hadn't been so familiar with how some viruses make files appear after they had been infected, he never would have noticed it. Had it been Clayton? And if so, why? Rooker put the car in gear and slowly began to drive. Somehow he had to find a way to identify those four names.

CHAPTER NINE

The church parking lot was full but not overflowing. Nick sat in his car and watched the people entering through a set of iron bound doors with inlays of stained glass. He recognized a lot of them as people he knew, although most not well. It was amazing how many friends a good man has when he dies, he thought. He wondered how many would show up at his funeral.

He wasn't ready to go inside yet. Funerals were for the living, not the dead, and whatever catharsis they provided he had gone though during the flight of a small airplane and a night spent on his little boat. Still, he wasn't ready to say goodbye, not while whoever had killed his friend went unaccountable. You don't just walk away from something like this, smooth the hurt over with a funeral service and a wreath and get on with your life. At least Nick couldn't, not in a situation like this.

He thought about Tim's wife, Marie. He still hadn't spoken with her since the murder but he knew he would have to today. God, what she must be going through. Nick felt a little guilty for not spending some time with her, but he knew she was being well taken care of. And although he hadn't spoken with Katy since that night when he called at her sister's, he knew that his wife would have taken the time to get down here and see Marie.

"Fuck it," he said angrily and reached forward to start the car. He drove slowly out of the parking lot. It's Tim I want to see, not his family and a bunch of his goddamned friends.

His mood, not good to begin with, turned bitter and dark as he drove toward the cemetery where Tim's body would be buried. Alone with the demons in his mind and the ghosts in the ground, he would wait until everyone else showed up.

*　*　*

The cemetery itself was an old one, but it was nice. Nick wondered if there was such a thing as a new cemetery; he had never heard of someone buying land and starting one.

Large oak trees provided a measure of relief at sporadic intervals from the Florida sunshine. The plot awaiting Tim Clayton touched a small patch of the shade offered by an ancient scarlet oak. Not mindful of his black cotton suit, Nick sat with his back against the trunk of the great tree, careful to check for fire ants. Surprisingly, there didn't seem to be any.

He sat that way for two hours, his mind drifting over mostly nothing as he contemplated the hole in the ground that would accept the body of his friend. Absurdly, he wondered what they did with the soil that would be displaced by the presence of the casket.

Eventually the long train of cars arrived and quiet mourners began to make the slow sixty yard walk along a gravel path toward the plot. Pallbearers carried the casket from the hearse and placed it on the belts that would lower it into the ground, to be buried beneath sandy dirt and bittersweet memories. Nick stood and brushed pieces of dried grass from his trousers. Without removing his Carerra sunglasses, he moved to the rear of the gathering crowd and tried to disappear.

It didn't work. A gentle pull at his elbow and he turned to find the veiled face of Marie Clayton looking up at his. "Nick," she said.

Around them, the other mourners eased away slowly, allowing the two of them the grace of some privacy. "Hello, Marie." He reached for her and she came into his arms for a brief embrace. They held each other for several breaths until Marie backed away and took hold of Nick's wrists.

"I was going to call you," he said.

"I know you were. I talked to Katy, she said you were taking it hard."

"All of us are, Marie." Nick couldn't help scanning the crowd.

"She's not here. She said she didn't want to get in your way. Are things okay with you two?"

Good God, Nick thought. With all her problems she's worried about my marriage. "We're doing fine, Marie. Really we are."

She nodded and looked down. "I looked for you at the service but I didn't see you. It was beautiful."

"I'm afraid I only made it as far as the parking lot."

"Oh, God, Nick," she said and moved herself closer again. Her hair smelled like salty tears and lilacs. "What happened?"

What could he tell her? Instead of talking, he concentrated on holding her tightly.

"I know you want to ask," she said into his shoulder. "And I want to tell you. But if he was in any trouble, he never mentioned anything to me about it. Nothing at all. I have no idea why anybody would have wanted to do this to him."

Nick shushed her, told her she didn't have to say anything. "I'll be alright," she said. She let Nick go and stepped backwards, dabbing her eyes with a balled up handkerchief. "He loved you, you know. He said you should have been brothers."

Emotion welled up in Nick's eyes and he struggled to contain it behind the lenses of his glasses. We were brothers. Marie reached forward and held one of his hands. "I have to go," she said. "Promise me you'll come down to dinner soon."

Nick tried his best to manage a nod.

"Promise," she repeated.

"Yes, I will," he half croaked. Marie nodded and turned to make her way to the side of the casket which hung, poised for eternity, above its grave.

Somewhere in front of him, a priest from the church began a prayer. Without listening to the words, he let his mind slip into the cadence of the speech as the rest of the group joined in.

His peace only lasted a few minutes. A gruff whisper erupted in his left ear. "Something wrong with your phone you don't return your calls, Kingman?"

"Hill." Nick turned his head and looked at the detective. There was an egg stain on his tie but at least he had managed a black suit. Fetterman stood behind him, an indecipherable grin plastered across his lips.

"We're not too happy about this lack of communication. I thought we had an understanding going, that we're working on the same team."

"Take it easy, Hill." He stepped away from the funeral so as not to disturb the ritual with their conversation. "Things have been a little hard lately. It hasn't been all that easy to concentrate on things."

"And in the meantime you want us to sit back and wait for you to feel all better before we move ahead on this thing."

"Give me a fucking break, Hill. This is the goddam funeral of my best friend and you're here busting my balls. If you were a little more human and not so much of a baboon , you might understand what the hell I've been going through."

That had the effect on Hill that Nick had been trying for. The detective looked at his partner then brought both hands up to his throat to fix an imaginary problem with his tie.

"All right, Kingman," he backed off. "But better sooner than later, you know what I'm saying?"

Yes, I know what you're saying, Nick told him. I've been working on a few things but I need some more time to put them together. When I do I'll call you so we can talk about how to use them to get at Lankford.

"You sound just like your dead buddy. Just be sure to call soon. We've got some other avenues we're looking into."

"Do you have more clues?"

Hill sent a thin stream of saliva squirting through the space between his two front teeth into the soft grass between his own feet. "Not really. We cleared the brothers who found the body and we haven't been able to track the plane. Might have been a smuggling plane on its way out of the country. Who knows?" He motioned to Fetterman with his head and they started to walk off toward the lines of parked cars. "We'll be waiting for that phone call. See you at the reception."

The burial ceremony broke up a few minutes later, most of the words had already been spoken at the church. Several people found their way to Nick and they shared their condolences and asked if he would be going to the reception after the service. It was being held at someone's house in Bradenton and was on Nick's way back to Tampa. "No," he told them. He wouldn't be going to any reception. He had work to get to. He didn't speak again to Marie.

On the ninety minute drive back to Tampa, he found himself thinking about Hill and Fetterman. If you don't have any new clues, he thought, just what 'other avenues' are you pursuing?

There was a message from Reed on the answering machine when Nick got home. He had gotten the job with Bay Area Cleaning but he wouldn't find out what they wanted his schedule to be for another day or two. He'd check back later to see what Nick wanted him to do next.

Nick pressed the button to reset the tape and walked into the room he used for an office when he worked at home. So far, so good, he thought. But the next step is up to me.

He hung his jacket over the back of his chair and removed his tie as he waited for his computer to boot up. He had a lot of programming to do before they were ready for Lankford and even then it would be a crap shoot. He had no illusions about what they were doing. Whether they were successful or not he knew what the consequences would be if they were caught. He wondered if Tim Clayton had, too.

* * *

Writing a computer program can be a grueling, demanding task that often requires long periods of solitude and intense concentration. It is an uncommon mix of technical skill and artistic creativity that turns long hours into brief minutes, drawing the programmer deep into a place far separated from the world around him.

Alone in his home office, Nick had tapped into this electronic Nirvana and for the first time in days had not been consciously aware of the terrible events that had recently affected his life. The afternoon had raced by at light speed, blurred but productive, and he had made good progress on the program he needed for Lankford's.

The phone on his desk rang just after seven o'clock. Nick's mind jerked back to real life as he reached for a pencil and wildly jotted a note to himself so he wouldn't lose his current thought. He picked up the phone on the fourth ring and said hello.

"Hey, bud, it's me." Reed. "What's up, were you sleeping?"

Nick rubbed his eyes as if he had been. "No, I'm just here programming away."

"Good, I'm glad to hear I'm not the only one getting things done. How was the funeral?"

"Fine," he said. He told him he hadn't seen much of the ceremony, but he had put in an appearance and spoken to Tim's widow. That was enough. "Hill and Fetterman were there, too."

"Your two cop friends?"

"Yeah. They were leaning on me pretty heavily to tell them what I was doing for them. They don't know about you and they certainly don't know about Lu, and that's the way I want to keep it. I didn't tell them much."

"How come? They're going to get at you sooner or later, aren't they?"

"You've got to think about what we're doing here. Not only are we talking about breaking a couple of dozen state and federal laws, Lu Bates is likely violating parole and I'm paying her to do it. If somebody at Bay Area Cleaning or, heaven forbid, Lankford's came across what we were trying to do, we'd be so far up Shit Creek we wouldn't need paddles because there wouldn't be any point in trying to go anywhere. Hill and Fetterman may be cops, but that doesn't automatically qualify them for the Nice Guy Hall of Fame. My gut tells me that the less they know, the better this thing will go. For all of us."

"What about if something goes wrong and we need their help?"

"Ask me that again if something goes wrong and we need their help."

"I get your point." Nick couldn't tell if Reed was bothered by his opinion of Hill and Fetterman but there wasn't anything he could do about it. Reed would just have to trust him. "Did you get the message I left earlier? I got the job with the cleaning company."

"Yes, I did," said Nick. "Congratulations."

"Thank you very much. They are a little shorthanded, which means the owner and his wife are having to go out and clean the buildings themselves, so they loved me. They'll come up with a schedule for me tomorrow, probably."

"How about not working Wednesdays and Fridays?"

"I asked, but they said they couldn't promise. I didn't want to push it too hard. I'm the new low guy on the totem pole, remember. We should talk about what you want me to do next."

Nick's stomach had begun to let him know what it wanted him to do next. "I want you to pick up a couple of large pizzas and a six pack and get over here. We can talk more about it then," he said.

* * *

It took Reed an hour to get the food and appear at Nick's house. Nick had taken a shower and changed clothes, having somewhat reluctantly powered off his computer. It was hard to walk away from a program once you were heavily into it. Leaving it behind became easier when you were nearly finished and most of what was left was filling in the cracks and tweaking the small details that were necessary to present a finished product. That was the grunt work of computer programming and Nick had never met anyone who enjoyed it.

They watched the Orlando Magic play the Chicago Bulls on a televised basketball game while they ate. "I'm not much of a fan," Reed said.

"Hell, without basketball, there'd be no reason for cable TV," Nick told him.

"Not counting the Playboy channel, you mean."

Nick smiled. "Of course." Reed had a knack for keeping a conversation light, a talent Nick admired. The more he got to know the young man, the more he liked him. That led him to think about the situation at Lankford's and what they had ahead of them. "We need to talk about where we go from here."

Reed knew instantly what Nick was referring to and washed down the last of the pizza with a mouthful of light beer. "Okay, let's hear it," he said.

Nick used the remote to lower the volume of the TV. "There are a number of things that we could try to somehow break into Lankford's computer system and look for evidence we could use to bring them down, maybe find out what happened to Tim. But what you have to understand is that where computers are concerned, no matter what we do, we're going to leave traces of ourselves behind. That's just the nature of the beast. So the trick is to try something they probably haven't thought of, something outside normal security precautions that they might not notice."

"How could they overlook something that could cause them so much damage?"

"Good question. Remember that they are supposedly doing everything illegal over something called a 'wide area network.' This is what you call it when you link one computer network to another over a phone line of some kind. From their point of view, security mostly means protecting how that connection is made and to whom the connection is with. Since they don't store any of this information on their own computers, they already feel very secure every time they simply turn off their computers. It's the equivalent of hanging up the phone."

"And we're going to ignore all that, for the reasons we talked about before?"

"Exactly. Even if I could think of a good way to do it, we'd be dealing with all kinds of legitimate as well as illegitimate data, cable taps, and last but not in any way least, encrypted data that would probably be impossible for us to read. So we'll be taking a different approach."

"Through the monitor and the keyboard."

"And that's why I need you at Lankford's. No matter what we do, we're going to need physical access to the computers. We need a key, we need the pass code for their security system, and we need to establish a semi-plausible excuse for one of us to be in there after hours."

"You would be referring to me. And my mother thought I wasn't going anywhere when I became a cleaning person. How exactly are we going to do all this?"

"We need to find an excuse for you to go to Lankford's while the regular cleaning guy is there. Somehow, you need to find a way to get the security system pass code from him. I also need to know the exact brand and model of the keyboard in Walter Lankford's office. We're going right to the top."

Reed reached for another beer as he thought about this. He wanted to make a joke of some kind but he knew that Nick was being very serious now. "I'm sure I could find a reason to stop in. I could show him I'm from Bay Area Cleaning, tell him I'm new and my girlfriend moved out and took all my garbage bags, or something stupid like that. I'm on my way to do my buildings and could I grab a few bags from him so I don't have to stop at a 7-11 and spend my own money."

"How did you know to stop there, at the building he was at?"

"You mean how did I know he was from bay Area, too?" Nick nodded. "I saw a list of clients when I was hired and the name of that one stuck in my mind?" This was a question.

"You saw the list and you remembered that one because your aunt married a man named Walter Lankford back home in Baltimore, or wherever your back home is. That should sound like a strange-but-true coincidence and he won't think past it."

"Okay. That gets us some free garbage bags, but then what?"

"How strange would it be for you to show up the next time he was there and show your gratitude by helping him do the cleaning?"

"I don't know," Reed said. "He'd probably love it. He'd be able to get out of there in half the time."

"That's what I was thinking. And then while you're there, you need to find Lankford's office and flip his keyboard over. There should be a label with the information I need. Write it down and get it back to me."

"What about the pass code?"

"That's a little harder. The only thing I can come up with is if you can manage to be watching him while he punches it in. What do you think?"

"Beats me, I've never tried it before. I guess that would work unless he's some kind of anal retentive security type and won't let me stand behind him. When do we put this glorious plan into action?"

"I want you to go over there Friday night, if you can. We need to get this moving so we can get something to Hill and Fetterman before they come looking to us. If you can borrow the bags Friday and be grateful next Wednesday, then I think that's about the best we can do."

On the TV, the Bulls had taken a two point lead with just over a minute left in the game. Nick turned the sound up and motioned for Reed to watch as a slow motion replay of a slam dunk was shown. He wanted to relax the mood. "Hugh Heffner could never do this," he said.

Reed laughed. "But how much do you know about Miss September?"

* * *

Nick made good progress on his programming task. He had figured out a way to capture the signals being sent to the monitor from the computer and store them in a computer file. There were still significant things to be worked out, but the next thing he planned to do was create a routine that would take that file and create an image on the monitor. He would then have the two main components of his monitor bugging program and would have to find a practical way to implement it at Lankford's. Which in this case meant as undetectable as possible.

Saturday morning Reed called with news of his stop at Lankford's the night before. "It went great," he told Nick. "The guy's name is Ray Alvarado and he gave me half a box of fifteen gallon two ply poly garbage bags. Said he was glad to help. Real nice guy. He looks like he's about thirty five or thirty six years old and he's married and has three kids. He works days at the dog track in St. Petersburg."

"Great going. So you spent some time with him, got to know him a little bit?"

"Yeah, we shot the shit for about a half hour before I left. I didn't want to hold him up so when I go back Wednesday he wouldn't have a bad association with my face. Most cleaning people want to get done and out of there as soon as possible."

"We'll make a spy out of you yet. Anything else happen?"

"I got the keyboard for you."

"Get out of here. How'd you manage that?"

"It was almost Ray's idea, the way it worked out. Turns out the man likes to fish and he asked me if I did, too. I told him not really, and he said I didn't know what I was missing, especially living here in Florida. So he takes me into this plush office and shows me a stuffed tarpon or something that's hanging on the wall. Very few people caught these fish from shore, he said. He hadn't done it yet, but he got close twice last year." Nick heard Reed yawn on the other end of the line. "I'm sorry, I still need a few more hours. I'm losing my train of thought."

"You were telling me about the keyboard."

"Yeah, the keyboard. I admired the fish, whatever the hell it was, and I put my hand on the desk behind the keyboard next to the cable. I tried to point at some part of the damn fish and would you believe, I somehow managed to accidentally pull the keyboard off the desk. Of course when I picked it up, I couldn't help but turn it over and look at the label."

"Of course you couldn't. What did it say?"

"It said, 'Keymatic' for a brand name, and after where it said model number it had the numbers '5251.' I didn't have time to get the serial number."

"No need. What you got was perfect."

"Well I'm going back to bed, then. What's up next?"

"Sleep until noon. I'll pick you up and we'll go shopping at the computer store. We'll come back to my place and we can play Humpty Dumpty with a keyboard."

In the middle of another yawn Reed said, "I can't wait." Nick smiled and hung up the phone. The kid was coming through. They just might have a shot at pulling this off.

* * *

They went to the computer superstore that was in Tampa, near the stadium, and found the exact keyboard they were looking for. "It's extremely popular as a replacement model," said a salesman who looked too young to remember a time when there weren't such things as personal computers. They agreed and paid forty five dollars for it and brought it back to Nick's house.

"So what exactly are we going to do with this thing?" Reed asked Nick. "I assume we're going to bug it somehow and pull a switch with the one in Lankford's office. Am I right?"

Nick had the keyboard upside down on his desktop as he pawed through the drawers looking for tools. "Close, but not quite. Switching the keyboards themselves is too risky. It would be too easy to notice the difference. Not only would the new one be cleaner and look different, it would probably have a different feel to it when you typed on it, even though it's an exact replacement. We're just going to use this one to practice on." He found a zippered vinyl pouch and opened it to reveal an assortment of tools. Nick extracted a small

Philip's head screwdriver and began to remove the tiny screws from the bottom of the keyboard.

"Practice on it how?"

"You need to know about how a keyboard works. Every time you press a key it sends a code to the computer."

"What if I type an 'A'?"

"The keyboard would send a 65 if it were upper case, or a 97 if it were lower case. The computer deals with these numbers, not the actual letters on the keys. What's important to us is that it sends these numbers to a certain place in the computer's memory called the keyboard buffer. When the computer itself wants to know what you've typed, it looks at the numbers stored in the buffer. This buffer is only big enough to hold a few keystrokes and it constantly overwrites itself as you type. And when you turn the computer off whatever is in the buffer fades away."

"How does this help us?"

Nick held up a small computer chip and a round silver disc. Reed stepped closer and looked at the objects in Nick's hand. "That's a camera battery, isn't it?" asked Reed pointing to the disc.

"That's exactly what it is. And this is a memory chip." Nick extracted a small collection of tiny wires from another desk drawer. "We're going to connect them both with this thing and wire it into our new keyboard here. Every brand is a little different but once we know how to do this one right we'll install it at Lankford's. Then, whatever gets typed into the keyboard will be stored in the memory chip and the electricity from the battery will keep it from discharging when the power is turned off. We pull the chip and the battery, read the codes, and we should have the user ID's and passwords that we'll need to access the network."

Reed sat down in a chair across from the desk. "I'm impressed," he said.

"No matter how hidden your password, how difficult you make it to get into the system, you still have to type the secrets into the keyboard to make it work. So that's what we're going after. This whole concept was originally an idea of Tim's that he developed when he was hired by a bank to check their security."

"It's only right for him to be helping us out with all this." Reed thought about what he had just said and jerked his head up abruptly. "I'm sorry, Nick. I didn't mean to make a joke about your friend. I—"

Nick looked into Reed's face. "Don't worry about it," he told him. "You didn't dishonor his memory or anything like that. You didn't offend me. Believe me, it would take a lot more than that from you. Helping me go after these bastards means more to me than I can tell you." He waved for Reed to move closer to the desk. "Now come here and I'll show you how this is done."

CHAPTER TEN

MamaLu Bates lay back on her sheet and closed her eyes against the afternoon sun. She felt the heat on her skin that let her know it was past time for an application of sunscreen. She preferred the spray on kind best because she could cover her entire body in about a third the time it took her with a cream or lotion. Also, she didn't have to get her hands all greasy, which was an important consideration for someone in her line of work.

She'd get up in a minute and make her way down to the beach stand on the other side of the food grill to see what they had. Right now, she just wanted to take a second to relax. It had been a good afternoon for her. She pulled one job on a German couple that showed up in a rented mini van and scored big. Big enough to stop for the day. She had even managed to return the keys after she had finished with the van.

The guy had put the keys in his shirt pocket and then stripped down to nothing but those disgusting bikini briefs that these Europeans all seem to wear. I swear, they're like Madonna they think they look good no matter what they wear, she thought. Belly fat rolling down almost covering the little pouch that held them in. Didn't they know what they looked like?

It was such a double standard, she thought, and she was as guilty of it as anyone. People with a weight problem just weren't treated the same as other people, especially on the beach among all the 'beautiful people.' But that would change for her, she knew. With the five hundred bucks she just took out of Mr. Bikini Brief's wife's purse, she would pick up the key cutting machine from the CashAmerica pawn shop and be ready for the job with that cop, Kingman.

That would be the big score, she thought. It had to be. An ex-cop wouldn't risk getting busted and getting his cop ass sent to prison without a very, very good reason. A reason MamaLu could cash in on if she was just smart enough to do it.

She pictured herself with a swollen bank account and some time on her hands. First thing she'd do, she'd fly out to California, find one of those fat farm places that took people like her and worked and massaged her down to what she still considered to be her 'normal' size. Then maybe she'd dress up like Madonna and take a trip to Europe, show those foreigners what a good looking body really did for a bikini bottom.

Maybe she could even find someone who wasn't as much of a loser as her Carl had been. Maybe settle down, start up a family. Life had finally smiled on her for a change when that cop showed up. All she had to do now was take advantage of it.

* * *

Rooker wasn't having much luck with the names in the computer file he got from the Lankford Company up in Tampa. It was frustrating because he was sure that one of the names, Ricardo Rivera, was familiar to him but he couldn't figure out how. He didn't even know if the names were important, and he had no idea what those funky numbers were for. Or if they represented anything meaningful.

He sighed and tossed his reading glasses onto the paper printout of the names. Maybe he was hallucinating, making it all up. These four guys in the file could just be four guys in a file. But somebody went to some trouble to hide that file, not just protect it with a password or something that you can do with a word processor. Somebody wanted those names hidden and they didn't want anybody else to find them.

But Rooker did. And whether or not he could parlay that into some form of profit or not, he didn't know. How could he, until he found out what the names in the file meant? All in all, it was a very frustrating situation.

After he had driven back to his office from his visit at Lankford's, he printed out a copy of the file and asked his secretary if she knew anything about a Ricardo Rivera. Maybe he had even been a client or something. But she just shrugged. Only thing the name reminded her of was some drug guy that got busted in Tampa a few months back. Wasn't that his name, she had asked. That rich guy, was supposed to have a bunch of money nobody could find?

Rooker didn't know. He always thought his secretary was a little wacky anyway. Besides, in Florida what drug dealer didn't have a pile of money stashed somewhere? They wallpaper with the stuff down in Miami.

Still, though, the more he thought about it the more the notion stuck in his mind. Maybe he had seen this guy Rivera's name on TV or something a while ago. He could almost picture the connection but wasn't quite sure of himself. Every time he tried to concentrate on it, his mind would conjure up an image of his secretary with her 1950's brunette bee hive hair-do saying, 'I don't know, wasn't that the name of the drug guy in Tampa?'

What the hell's a 'drug guy?'

Let's say Rivera was this person. Who did the other three names in the file belong to? Were the four of them connected? He tried to think of them as missing persons, people he knew but that had disappeared. What did one do to find a missing person, he thought. Call the cops.

Something turned over in his mind. The cops. Didn't he just meet two cops at the reception after Clayton's funeral? Of course he had, the one guy who looked like he used his tie for a napkin and his partner, the one who didn't say much. Maybe they could help him out, give him a few ideas. They wouldn't have to know where the file had come from.

First thing, though, he had to remember their names. He hadn't paid much attention to anyone's names; he never did unless they were a potential client. The one with the tie, he was drawing a total blank. But the other name, there was something it reminded him of, something from history maybe.

Fetterman. He didn't remember a first name but he was sure the last was Fetterman. The same name of some dumbshit army officer in the mid 1800's that thought he could whip all the plains Indians by himself. He went after a small group of warriors one day and against orders followed them too far from the fort, right into a full-scale ambush. His entire party had been massacred and then mutilated. Rooker smiled and reached for a Tampa phone book. He had gotten out of college with a degree in history and for the first time it had actually done him some good.

He dialed the number for the Tampa police department and asked how he could get in touch with Detective Fetterman. The woman put him on hold and a minute later a man's voice come on the line. "This is Hill," the voice said.

Hill. That had been the other cop's name, the one that did all of the talking. Rooker put on his best salesman's voice and told him who he was.

"You're who?"

Rooker told him again. "James Rooker. We met briefly at the reception following Tim Clayton's funeral. Terrible thing, that was." Rooker caught himself and quickly added, "Clayton's death, I mean. Not the reception. That was lovely."

Lovely? Hill didn't like to have conversations with grown men that used the word 'lovely,' especially when he didn't remember who the hell they were. He wrote the name 'Rooker' on a sheet of paper and turned it towards his partner who was seated at the desk across from him. Fetterman, who was in the middle of sharpening a pencil with one of the tools from his pocket knife, read the name and shook his head. He didn't recognize it, either. Hill didn't try hard to mask his annoyance.

"What can I do for you, Mr. Rooker?" he asked with an edge to his voice.

Rooker picked up on the Detective's mood and tried not to let it sway him. He made up what he hoped was a somewhat realistic story of coming across a list of unidentified names at one of Tim Clayton's old clients. Their computer had apparently been affected by a power surge or a lightning strike or some damned thing and the names had been part of a file that had become corrupt. Of course, since Tim was gone, they had called in Rooker as their new consultant.

It was very important that his client identify these names so that certain accounts and records could be restored to order. Rooker was just wondering if maybe Hill and Fetterman, in honor of the late Tim Clayton, might be able to offer some suggestions as to how he might go about finding out who these men were.

When he was finished, Hill couldn't help but laugh. "You're kidding me, right? We solve murders here, Mr. Rooker, not run errands for local businessmen. Call a private detective if you want to find somebody."

Rooker didn't want to give up yet. Private detectives cost money. "Maybe you'd just let me read you the names, okay? I have reason to believe one or all of them could be from Tampa. You just might be familiar with them." Without waiting for an answer Rooker read the four names into the telephone.

There was a long moment of silence on the other end. Rooker wasn't sure if he had angered the policeman or if something maybe had gone wrong with the telephone connection. Finally, Hill spoke again, but this time the edge was gone and there was something new there.

"Mr. Rooker? Maybe we can help you out after all. Why don't you tell me where we can find you. I think we need to get together in person."

Rooker smiled. Something in his story must have worked, or maybe the Detective did recognize some of the names. Whatever the case, he was pleased that he was able to make something happen.

CHAPTER ELEVEN

Wednesday night at Lankford's went smoothly. Ray Alvarado happily accepted Reed Larson's offer of help, though he assured him it wasn't necessary, he'd been happy to help the new guy out. But if he really wanted to help clean tonight, Ray would be grateful for the company. Some guys actually brought their wives or girlfriends along to help them clean buy Ray wouldn't even consider that. Trini took care of the kids all day and kept up their own house. Let her relax a little when the sun goes down, Ray thought. It's my job to bring home the paycheck.

They worked fairly quickly, Reed going from office to office removing the half full garbage bags and replacing them with empty ones, Ray pushing a vacuum cleaner across the carpet in each room. There used to be two of them assigned to clean this place, Ray said. Now it was just himself but that was okay since this was the only building he had to do two days of the week.

After Reed had hauled all of the garbage outside to the dumpster, he washed the dishes stacked at the sink in the little kitchen and scrubbed the insides of the microwave oven. It was amazing the messes people were willing to create at work that they wouldn't tolerate for a minute inside their own homes. After he was through there, he joined Ray and together they dusted the table and television in the conference room, as well as the computer monitors on each desk.

"That's about it," Ray announced after the last screen was clear. "We can go home." Maybe you can, Reed thought, but I still have to clean three office suites downtown.

They made their way through the building turning off the lights and meeting again at the front door. "Don't move," Ray told him and pointed at the motion detector mounted on the wall. Ray was standing at the security system keypad and Reed was slipping on his windbreaker by the front door. The receptionist's desk and twenty feet separated the two of them.

Shit, Reed thought, I fucked up. There was no way he could see the keys that Ray was about to push from where he was. Damn it! Nick was counting on him and here he was, sleeping at the wheel. He should have been paying more attention to what Ray was doing. Without hesitating he started walking toward him. It was his only move.

"Hold it there," Ray said, holding up his palm. "I can't turn this thing on if you're moving."

Reed stopped at Ray's gesture; there was nothing else he could do. If he pushed it any more Ray would be suspicious. He wondered how pissed Nick was going to be.

Ray entered five numbers into the keypad and motioned Reed toward the door. "We have to leave within sixty seconds." He motioned Reed to follow him out.

Ray took a set of keys out of the back pocket of his jeans and locked the front door. What the fuck am I supposed to do now, Reed thought. At least I see where he keeps his keys. Got that one right.

They walked down the short sidewalk to their two cars. Reed had parked his beat up Toyota next to Ray's pickup and as they got there Ray stopped and offered Reed his hand. "I want to thank you very much for your help," he said as they shook. "You didn't need to do it but I am very grateful that tonight I can go home early."

Reed gave him a genuine smile. "You helped me out last week, remember? I'm just glad you let me repay the favor. It was good to meet you, Ray."

"I enjoyed meeting you, too," he smiled back. "You'll have to stop in again and we'll talk some baseball. The season's almost here. And maybe one day I'll even get you out fishing."

Better that than baseball, Reed thought. Or maybe not.

Reed didn't think a lot happened in either sport. In any case, Alvarado was being polite more than anything else. "Sure thing, Ray. See you around," and he turned and walked to the driver's side of the Toyota, deeply disappointed with himself. The point of being there tonight was to get the security passcode but he hadn't even come close. He had let Ray catch him off guard and he had failed.

He opened the door and climbed into his car. Next to him, the gray pickup truck started with a rumble and slowly backed away from the curb. Angry at himself, Reed reached into his pocket and dug for his car keys.

Somewhere behind him, Ray changed gears and began to move forward out of the parking lot. Reed jumped out of his car and ran after the pickup. "Ray!" he shouted, waving his arms. "Hold up a second! Ray!"

Alvarado heard him and halted the truck. He rolled down his window as Reed caught up to him. "What's wrong?" Ray asked. Concern showed at the corners of his eyes.

Reed shook his head, mocking himself. "Like an idiot, I think I left my car keys inside. I took them out of my pocket when I was cleaning the kitchen and I never picked them up again. I need to get back in. Just for a second."

"Okay, I'll park the truck."

"Hell, Ray, that's okay. Just give me the key and I'll run in. I know right where I left them."

Ray sat forward and extracted his key ring from his back pocket. It would be alright; they were both professionals that worked for the same company. "It's this one," he said, holding the ring out by a single key. Reed took it and said he'd be right back.

When he was several yards away, Ray called out. "You will need the password for the burglar alarm."

"Oh, yeah," said Reed turning back toward the truck. "Almost forgot."

"No problem. It is '84841' to get in, '84842' when you leave."

"Got it," Reed said and turned to jog back to the front door.

He got it alright, and he wasn't going to lose it. Inside his left pants pocket, his car keys made chinging sounds as he ran. He slowed down to a fast walk so that Ray wouldn't hear the noise.

* * *

"Are you sure we need the fat chick? I mean, I had the keys in my hands. If I could do that again, maybe switch them—"

"Hold on," Nick interrupted. "It's not your job to get the keys. If something went wrong, not only would we not have the keys, at the very least you'd be out of the game. I need you too much to risk that. If Lu blows it, all we lose is a little time and we can try something else from there."

"You'd still be out your two grand."

"Believe me, the last thing in the world I'm worrying about right now is money." Nick moved the phone to his other ear and said, "You just don't like that woman."

"Anybody hits me upside the head like she did generally doesn't leave a very good impression. No pun intended."

"You deserved it and you know it. Anyway, you've got the passcodes so I'll head out to Clearwater and find Lu. Do you see any problem with her going to work Friday night?"

"You mean as far as with Ray? No, I think one day's as good as another as far as he's concerned. But I'm supposed to work four buildings tomorrow."

"That's fine, I don't want you anywhere near Lankford's when this goes down. We'll leave this all up to Lu."

"Oh. Okay." He sounded disappointed. "Just tell her that there are two keys she'll need to get. One for the front door that says 'Schlage' on it, and one for the president's office. That one says 'Uniface.' There are two or three other Unifaces on the key ring, though. You'll have to handle that somehow."

"I was going to have her copy all of the keys, just to be sure. Go back to sleep and I'll get back to work. Thanks again, Reed. I don't know what I'd be doing without you."

"Sure." Reed said it sarcastically but Nick was being serious and he felt complimented. "Give my love to your beach buddy and I'll talk to you later."

Nick said goodbye and hung up the phone with a guilty tear at the corner of his conscience. He walked into his office and set his keyboard in his lap. Reed had really come through for him. Just don't fuck this up, he told himself. You've lost one good friend already, you don't need to lose any more.

* * *

There he is, MamaLu thought as she watched a pair of headlights turn into the parking lot in front of the Walter A. Lankford Company. From where she was, a hundred yards away and across the street, she couldn't be sure it was the right vehicle, but the timing was about right.

She walked around the corner of the building she was using for cover and worked her way behind the wheel of her extended cab pickup truck. She'd give him a minute then cruise the street and make sure it was really him. Then she'd get the truck ready and go into her act.

Lord, please help me to not blow this thing, she prayed as she pushed the power button for the stereo. She spent a few minutes fidgeting with the controls, picking up one country music station after another until she forced herself to sit still. The twangings of a slide guitar slid through the air around her but she didn't pay attention. This was a very important job and she hadn't done this kind of work in a very long time. That made her nervous and that was a bad thing. Nervous in her profession meant mistakes and there weren't too many ways to explain the presence of your hand in someone else's pocket.

Damn it! Stop shaking, she told herself. This could be her ticket to a new life, away from the petty crime and beach cops in short pants and bicycles. A turning point, that's what this was. A way to go back to being pretty Mary Lu Bates from Alabama, not

MamaLu or Mama anything, just a sweet little Southern girl from the panhandle who liked the beach. A girl who used to have a weight problem and a questionable past perhaps, but now was blossoming into a strong, independent woman of means. She was a butterfly ready to leave behind her cocoon.

But only if she worked this right. She took deep breaths as she started the truck and slipped it into gear. She didn't really have to figure out everything the cop was doing, just enough so she could hold it over his head. If she got in there, worked it out, and walked away with whatever prize Kingman was after, great. She'd be in control. But other than that, she planned on making herself a new partner in his enterprise. The threat of blackmail or exposure should be enough to bring them to a satisfactory middle ground. An arrangement that would get her off the beach and into a new life. First stop, the Malibu Health and Weight Loss Retreat in sunny Southern California. First stop to a new Lu, she thought. She liked that.

She drove her truck slowly down the street and got a good view of the vehicle parked in front of the Lankford Company. The magnetic sign on the driver's door said, "Bay Area Cleaning Service." That's the one, she thought and pressed down on the accelerator. She forced herself to keep taking deep, slow breaths. It wasn't time yet. First, she had to get back to the interstate, get the truck going good and hot, and then she'd be back. She had a plan to stick to and the night was young.

* * *

Ray Alvarado had just finished emptying the last of the executive garbage cans when he heard the front door open and close. He had never been in the habit of locking the door once he began cleaning, he went out to his truck too much, but his heart always skipped a little if someone walked in during the night. It was usually just some employee picking something up he had forgotten, something like that, or occasionally even someone stopping to ask directions to a night club somewhere. He put down the garbage can he was holding and walked toward the front.

"Hello?" he heard someone call softly. It sounded like a woman's voice, unusual out here at this time of night. He walked around the partition into the receptionist's area and there she was. A woman, yes, and what a woman. Ray wasn't a big man himself, maybe a hundred and forty five pounds after a big meal, but she looked to him like she could easily go double that. There was a worried look on her face, almost as though she were about to cry, Ray thought, and he asked her if she needed some help.

"Something's wrong with my truck," she said. "I was driving down the street and all of the sudden a bunch of smoke came pouring out from under the hood. And there was some kind of funny smell. I didn't know what to do. I saw your lights on and pulled in."

Ray gave her a reassuring smile and stepped up to the front door. "Is that it there?" he asked her. Parked next to his own was a purple and black pickup truck with an extended cab and tinted windows.

"Yes," she told him. "That's it. I don't know what to do. I don't really have anyone I can call."

"Would you like me to take a look?" Ray offered.

"Oh, would you mind? I would really appreciate it. All I know about cars and trucks is how to fill them up with gas and drive them away. I have some money, though. I can pay you."

Ray extended his arm and held open the door for her. "Don't be ridiculous," he said. "Let's go out and take a look." They walked down to the end of the short sidewalk, Ray in front of the woman. There wasn't enough room for them to walk side by side and not step in the grass. "This is a nice truck," he told her. From up close, the custom paint job and windows gave the vehicle a sleek, menacing look.

"Thank you," she told him.

Ray knelt down and poked his finger into a greenish puddle that was still collecting under the truck. "This is your engine coolant," he told her, sniffing at the glycol. "Why don't you get in there and pop the hood for me?"

MamaLu did as he asked. Alvarado lifted the hood and held it while a last steamy cloud found freedom and escaped. He propped the hood open with a metal rod and peered at the engine for a moment, then went to the rear of his own truck and plucked a disposable flashlight from a utility box.

MamaLu got out of the driver's seat and stood on the curb behind Ray as he inspected the engine. "Here's your problem," he told her. "The hose for the antifreeze has come loose from the reservoir." He held the loose end in his fingers so she could see. MamaLu placed a hand on his lower back and bent forward to look but slipped off the curb. She had to grab Ray with both of her arms around his middle to keep from falling into the truck. He tried to support her weight as they performed an awkward dance in a slow circle around each other. "Are you okay, miss?" Ray asked as MamaLu regained her equilibrium.

I'm perfect, she thought. You've got a dummy set of keys in your back pocket and I've got the real ones clutched in my left hand. That wasn't so hard. Like riding a bicycle, she still had the touch. "I'm okay, thank you. I didn't mean to be so clumsy. Did I hurt you?"

Ray smiled because the lady so easily could have. "No, no, I am fine. Let's get your truck back together and you can go on your way."

"You can fix it?"

"Yes. Just let me get some water and I'll fill the reservoir until you can replace it with real antifreeze and then you'll be fine."

* * *

Ray was even more surprised when the woman walked into the building the second time. He had been finishing up the vacuuming when he felt someone tap him on the shoulder. He hadn't heard the door and he must have jumped a foot off the ground when she touched him.

"Mother of Christ," he breathed as he turned around to face her.

She took a step back, a worried look on her face, but he held out a hand. "No, no, it's okay. You startled me a little is all." He felt his heart thumping in his chest. "Is everything all right with your truck?"

MamaLu returned his smile and produced a fruit basket she had been holding behind her back. "The truck's fine. I just brought this for you for being so nice to me." She jiggled it once in the air. "Here, take it."

"That's not really necessary. I am only happy that I was here and was able to help you out."

"No no no. I'm not going to argue about it. It's just a silly basket of fruit and I absolutely insist that you take it." She thrust it at him again. "Go on. It doesn't mean we have to get married or anything."

Embarrassed, Ray ran his fingers through his thinning hair and reached out for the basket. No sooner did he take it then MamaLu stepped forward and crushed him in a mammoth bear hug.

"Thank you again," she said. She embraced him warmly and lifted him several inches off the ground. Ray was powerless to do anything about it. He couldn't have hugged her back if he had wanted due to the fact that both of his arms were pinned to his sides.

"Uh, you're welcome again. My wife and I will enjoy your gift very much, I'm sure." It was all he could think of to say and he hoped the mention of his wife would help to mellow the woman's feelings of gratitude.

"You do that," she told him and with both hands grabbed hold of his butt and squeezed. Oh my God, he thought, swearing again. He felt his keys pressing into his right cheek as she released him. I am helpless in front of this woman.

Lu backed away and said with a different voice, "I'd give you a kiss but you probably couldn't stand it, sweetie. See you around." She turned and ambled out of the building. It had taken her more than an hour to copy the keys back at the motel room she'd taken, but it was done and now she had returned the originals. The night had gone very well, she thought. I've still got it.

As she drove her truck to the 24 hour restaurant where Kingman was supposed to be waiting, Ray went to the front door and locked it with his key. He had been happy to help but he just wanted to finish his cleaning and go home. The big woman had turned so aggressive. He hoped that she was done with him now and would not come back. He set the basket on the edge of the receptionist's desk and looked at the assortment of apples, oranges, bananas, and kiwis wrapped in translucent cellophane. Where had she gotten a fruit basket at this time of night?

* * *

Rooker was feeling decidedly uncomfortable. These two cops, Hill and Fetterman, weren't treating him as he'd hoped and he was now beginning to feel as if maybe he had stumbled into something by mistake. Something the Tampa police didn't like and by extension, something he would rather have left alone.

The tail lights of the brown sedan he was following flared and veered to his left, off the pavement and onto a gravel road. The moon was barely half full and Rooker had to strain to see enough of the road to stay on it. Fortunately, the two cops weren't in a hurry and were making it easy for Rooker to follow. A mosquito buzzed in his ear as too late he rolled his window up against the insects and the tangy smell of the swamp after dark. Spanish moss hanging from the branches above the road swept over his car as he crept along the winding trail.

They had driven east out of Sarasota, turned north at Myakka City and out of the county altogether. Where the hell were they taking him? Maybe they were going to show him something that would answer some of his questions, instead of just asking their own, like they did back at his townhouse where they had met. He wasn't sure he cared any more. At this point, he was wishing he'd never found the file with those names in it at Clayton's client's office. Or a t least that he hadn't had the bright idea of asking the police for their help. What the hell could they show him out here, anyway?

The road seemed to have ended but they picked their way through the trees without it. Fifty yards or so ahead of him, the brown sedan stopped at the entrance to a slight clearing, big enough for three or four cars to park side by side. Rooker pulled up behind the sedan and shut off his car. This better be good, he thought as he opened the door and stepped out into the soft sand.

He could hear water sounds coming from somewhere in front of the sedan. A narrow river cut its way through the land just ahead. He stood impatiently, trying to control his annoyance as Hill and Fetterman took their time getting out of their car. This whole night has been bullshit, he thought. Somewhere down river a night bird or frog made a reptilian croaking sound that made him jump. Wild Florida. Bug and creature capital of the world.

"What the hell are we doing out here?" Rooker demanded. The damp, heavy air muted his voice and he didn't sound nearly as authoritative as he wanted. Being this far removed from civilization made him nervous.

Detective Hill answered him with a crooked smile. "Why Mr. Rooker," he said. "We just came out here to continue our little exchange of information. That's what you wanted, wasn't it? I mean, that's why you originally called us, right?"

Fetterman scrounged a fallen stick from the brush next to where they had parked and brought out his pocket knife. He moved to a position a step behind Rooker and began to slowly whittle the dead branch. Rooker felt little shavings bounce off the backs of his legs as something different bit him on the ankle. He danced a little as he rubbed at the spot with his other foot but didn't say anything. Something definitely was not right with this situation. His annoyance evaporated into something much more disturbing. He began to realize that he was afraid.

"Now I don't want any more crap, I don't want any more stories. I want to know why you have those four names and I want to know how you got them. I want you to tell me all this now."

Hill stuck his face half a foot in front of Rooker's. "All of it. Right now."

Rooker said nothing for a moment as he considered what was happening to him. Would these men actually hurt him, cause him pain? They were policemen, officers of the law, for Christ's sake. As a taxpayer and a citizen they worked for him, didn't they? He may have been unethical, certainly unprofessional, he knew that, but James Rooker was no threat to society. That ought to count for something. "I told you already, back at my home. I don't know why you have to hear it again." A small warm spot of artificial courage settled into his stomach. Rooker slapped at a mosquito on his cheek. The bugs were eating him alive.

Hill looked over Rooker's shoulder at Fetterman. It seemed to Rooker that he was the only one moving as he waved at the unseen cloud of insects swirling around his head. Something else bit him on the same ankle as before.

After a long minute, Hill said to Fetterman, "Do you believe him?"

Fetterman's knife made a slow rasping sound as it cut through another layer of stick, then stopped. "Not with that face, no."

"Let's try another one, then." Hill brought up a meaty fist and stepped forward as he drove it into the center of Rooker's face. Blood exploded from a fractured nose as Rooker's world went dark and light at the same time and he sagged backwards into Fetterman's arms.

Hill wiped at his knuckles with a handkerchief taken from his back pocket. "How about now?" he asked his partner.

"Yeah, I think he's starting to look more sincere." He took a step back and let Rooker fall the rest of the way to the ground.

Hill bent down and peered into Rooker's damaged face. "How about it, Rooker? Do you have anything else to say?"

Rooker's mind was in shock and all he could manage was a kind of groan that formed bubbles of blood on his lips as it left his body. His eyes gazed feebly back at Hill, who straightened up and said to Fetterman, "Bring him over here."

Dragging Rooker by walking backwards with his hands in

Rooker's arm pits, Fetterman followed Hill a few yards on a short trek toward the river. Hill stopped in front of a mound of white sand that rose like a miniature volcano almost a foot out of the ground. Similar mounds, separated by at least twenty feet from each other, punctuated the landscape made dully visible by the soft reflected light off the half full moon.

"I hate these damn things," said Hill. "How about you, Rooker? Do you hate these little guys? Why don't you say something to them about it." With the bottom of his foot, he swept away the top half of the mound revealing a dark, writhing stain. "You know what a quail is, don't you Rooker? You know, the bird." He knelt down to where Fetterman still held Rooker's upper body off the ground and gave him a light slap across both cheeks. Rooker squirmed and made groaning noises while blood continued to flow downward onto his chest. Hill took Rooker's chin in his hand and turned it so the wounded man's eyes were looking into his own.

"Quail lay their eggs in little holes they dig in the ground, not in a nest up some goddamned tree somewhere. Problem is, these little guys over here," he motioned toward the half-mound with his hand. "They moved up here from South America and just like that, there went the neighborhood. At least for the quail. A colony of these critters move through a quail nest for breakfast. Leave behind nothing but pieces of dried up eggshells and tiny little quail bones. What do you think about that, Rooker? How do you think it would feel to be picked apart and eaten by a couple hundred thousand hungry little insects? Find yourself a new spot on the local food chain, what do you think?"

Rooker's eyes fluttered several times and three nasally syllables escaped through lips thick with crusting blood. "Arr ess mee."

Hill released Rooker's chin and stood up. "Arrest you? Mr. Rooker, we can't arrest you. You haven't broken any laws that we know of. Besides, we're only two counties away from our legal jurisdiction." He looked up at Fetterman. "Hey, how're your arms holding out? You been holding him up a few minutes now."

"He's starting to get a little heavy."

"Set the man down and get yourself a little rest. You've been working too hard." Hill reached down and took one of Rooker's arms while Fetterman shifted over to the other. They flipped Rooker over so his stomach was on the ground and held him just above the mound.

Thick drops of blood, black in the moonlight, spattered the sand below him as Rooker shook his head feverishly from side to side. "Remember the quail," he heard Hill say. Then they dropped him on his face.

Bright lights illuminated the inside of his skull as the impact on his damaged nose drove a shock wave of pain backwards into his brain. He tried to lift his head off the ground but for some reason he couldn't. His mouth was full of sand and other things as he spit and struggled to breathe through the dirt. As the pain from his nose subsided he became aware of a tickling sensation on the rest of his face, his neck, and even the inside of his mouth as he maintained his struggle for ragged breaths of air. Burning pricks of fire followed, first a couple, then a few, then hundreds and even thousands more as the angry colony began to attack and feed on the body of the intruder.

Rooker flailed his arms and legs wildly, trying desperately to push away from the fire ants and protect his face at the same time. Hill waited for a full two minutes before lifting his foot from the back of Rooker's head. He rolled away and scrambled wildly, clawing at his face as his momentum brought him dangerously close to another mound. He spit with every breath, trying to clear his mouth and throat. In one motion he pulled his shirt off and over his head and flung it to the side.

The two police detectives stood side by side, watching impassively. "Would you look at that," Hill said. Rooker was using the little fingers of both hands to dig the tiny red ants out of his bloody nostrils. He couldn't see as his eyes swelled shut with pain, tears, and the effects of formic acid.

"You know that's gotta hurt," said Fetterman.

Nick stood as MamaLu entered the restaurant and approached

his booth. "A gentleman," she said and worked her way into the seat across from him.

"Coffee?" Nick asked as he seated himself and picked up the pot he had been nursing.

"No thanks, don't drink the stuff." She pushed aside her cup and plopped an oversized purse on the table between them. "Let's get this over with."

"How did it go?"

"Beautifully. He never had a clue. He had a nice butt, though."

Nick let that one go. "So you got the keys?"

Lu took her hand out of her bag and slid a ring of keys across the table to him. "Hot off the press. That'll be two thousand dollars, please."

He deposited the keys in his jacket pocket and took a plain white envelope from his briefcase and handed it to her. He waited while she held it in her lap and counted the bills. Looking up she said, "I'll need fifty bucks more for expenses."

"Expenses? What are you talking about?"

"A motel room. I had to have some place to cut the keys, didn't I? Here, I brought you a receipt." She handed him a piece of paper from a place called the All American Motel on Kennedy Boulevard. He had never heard of it. Nick took his wallet out of his pocket and took out the money. He wasn't about to argue over fifty dollars.

"Thank you very much," she told Nick and started to ease sideways off the bench. "It was a pleasure doing business with you." And it was. She was still high from the buzz she got after she had put the original keys back into Alvarado's pocket without being caught. She had her touch back and it made her happy to know that. If she thought about it, this had probably been her happiest night since she dumped Carl.

She stood and said goodbye to Nick. He got to his feet and said, "Thanks for the work." MamaLu gave him a smile and then turned to leave. You'll be seeing me again, she thought. Don't think you won't.

* * *

When he could speak again, Rooker pushed some sounds upward through his burning throat. "They were eating my face." He worked his eyelids and tried to see the two cops standing somewhere in front of him. "They were eating my face," he repeated.

"I know," said Hill.

"We saw," said Fetterman.

Rooker wailed, "Oh my God," and collapsed backwards onto the ground in a sitting position.

"I don't think I'd sit there if I were you. That's a little close." Hill poked a finger in the direction behind Rooker. "You're on another mound."

Rooker rocked wildly forward and swiped manically at the seat of his pants with both hands. In the dim light, his bare chest was the same pale shade of gray as the ant mounds around him. His face looked ruined, a grotesque image of what it had been. The man was broken and all three of them knew it.

Hill stepped forward. "Okay, Rooker. I'm tired of feeding the animals but you need to know I've got all night if I need it. So do you, incidentally. But as soon as you tell me the truth about those names, this thing can be over. Now what do you say?"

Rooker reached forward and tried to feel where the man was standing. Hill didn't move as Rooker's hands found his face and then his shoulders. "I'll talk to you. I'll do anything you want."

"Of course you will," Hill told him.

* * *

Later, when it was over, Hill asked Fetterman what he thought about Rooker's information. "Do those numbers he gave us help?"

Hill shrugged. "They're something, I guess. But they're just account numbers. Without passwords . . . " Hill didn't bother to finish.

Fetterman nodded. "We've still got Kingman."

The two men climbed into their sedan and carefully backed up and turned around in the clearing. As they drove out toward the gravel road, the reddish glow from their tail lights cast an eerie pallor on the naked body of James Edward Rooker. His broken form lay spread eagled face down across an angry nest of swarming fire ants, still lips parted slightly as if offering a silent and unheeded apology to the creatures whose nest he unknowingly disturbed.

CHAPTER TWELVE

Saturday morning dawned brightly across the Florida sky, improbable colors gradually turning to more common shades of blue. A light veil of fog hung over the ground, hinting at a heavier blanketing outside of the city. Nick stood on the balcony adjacent to the kitchen and thought of his wife. *She's still at her sister's, safe and away from all this. Whatever this is. At least her life can stay close to normal.*

So far they hadn't accomplished much by way of finding out who had killed Tim Clayton. All they really had was Hill and Fetterman's view of what had happened and some of the tools to allow them access to the Lankford Company.

He kept thinking in terms of 'us' or 'we,' counting more than himself, and that was a concern. How much should he allow Reed Larson to get involved? He knew as he asked himself what his answer was. He was going to find out who killed Tim and why, whatever it took.

The phone rang around ten in the morning. As expected, it was Reed checking in, calling to see how it had gone the night before.

"Lu Bates came through," Nick told him. "We're in."

"That's good," said Reed. "I feel better with her out of the picture. She is, isn't she?"

"You're just afraid she'll hit you again."

"Wouldn't you be?"

Nick laughed. "That's beside the point. But yes, she's out of the picture."

"Good. What do we do next?"

"I want you to take me in to Lankford's tonight. We'll make sure that the keys work and I want to check out a few things on their computer system. We'll bring Lankford's keyboard back here and install our memory chip, then we'll switch them back."

"You don't want to install the memory there, at his office? Wouldn't that save us a trip?"

"I'd rather risk getting caught twice doing nothing obvious with a legitimate employee of their cleaning service than getting caught once with a dissected computer and a soldering iron. That's a little bit harder to explain."

"That's why you make the plans, boss."

Nick told him to come over that evening. They'd have some dinner and go over to Lankford's later. By the day after tomorrow, Monday night, if everything worked as it should, not only would they have access to the building itself, they'd have the password to the computer network as well. And if they've got any hidden skeletons in their electronic closet, Nick thought, we're going to find them.

* * *

The night was long but uneventful. They went in at midnight and checked the keys made by MamaLu Bates, which worked perfectly. Nick verified that the physical layout of the computer network was what he expected, based on his familiarity with Tim's work as well as on his conversation with Hill. In Walter Lankford's office, he powered on the computer and watched as it booted up and eventually paused, prompting for a network user name.

"Are you going to type anything in?" Reed asked.

"No. This just tells us that the first thing he enters when he boots up is his log in name. The next thing the computer will ask for is his password."

"Are you sure? Can you test it?"

"Yes, I'm sure, and yes I can test it, but we don't want to. The system could be logging failed attempts to access the network and somebody might check it out. We don't need to risk it." Nick turned the computer off and bent down to unplug the keyboard from the back of the machine.

"Monday night, after the computer has been used for a day, I'm going to ask you to come back here and remove the memory chip. Then we'll dump what it's got into a file on my computer. I've got a program that will translate the digital data in the file into the proper alpha-numeric characters and all we'll have to do is read the first thing that was typed before the 'Enter' key. That will be the login name."

"And the second thing will be the password." Reed looked down at the computer on the floor as Nick put the keyboard into a gym bag. "I know we've gone through a lot to get here, but somehow all this seems too easy."

"You've got to remember what I said about computer security. There's no such thing. When personal computers were designed nobody dreamed of the kinds of things we'd be doing with them today. Nobody knew how clever we could be with them. As far as the machine itself goes, anything that we can think of to secure the data, we can think of ways to un-secure that data. We can't outsmart ourselves."

Nick took the keyboard they had brought from home and set it on the desk where the original had been. "Let's get out of here and get this over with. The night is not so young."

"And neither are you," Reed joked.

Nick socked him in the upper arm. "I don't need that from you. Let's go."

* * *

Hill called Nick at eight o'clock on Monday morning, getting him out of bed. Staying on his late night schedule, Nick worked on the software program that would record the signals sent to Lankford's computer monitor until early in the morning. There was one part of it that needed to be completed and he hoped to finish it in a few more hours. After he spoke to Hill, he knew he would get it done that day no matter what.

"So what you're telling me," Hill had said, "is that in a week you haven't done shit on this thing. Is that right?"

Nick swallowed his response as it started to rise from his throat. Whatever he got out of Lankford's, he wanted to have it for some time before he gave it to Hill. He needed to give him a reason for the delay without telling him what he was really doing. "No, that's not right. I think I may have found a way into their network but it is going to take a little time to set up."

"Oh, yeah? That sounds like a good thing. Tell me about it."

"They're connecting their network to others through the Internet, right? Most businesses aren't connected directly to the Internet unless they're providing a service on it. What Lankford does is use a service provider for their connection."

"And what does that mean?"

"Just that rather than have special systems set up just for the Internet, Lankford uses their own equipment to dial into the service provider, who offers the actual connection. I think I have a way to penetrate the connection from the provider itself."

"So you'll be able to follow what they're doing on the network?"

"If I get in." He didn't want to sound like he had anything substantive yet that would bring Hill closer. "It looks good, but I won't know until next week."

"What the hell, Kingman. If you can break into this provider's network next week, why can't you just do it now?"

"Because I'm not breaking in at all. A year ago, I worked a contract with the same company that provides Lankford's service. I tried to break into their network from the outside, to show them how it could be done so they could plug the security holes. I think I can convince them I'm doing some kind of follow up work so they'll let me do some more poking around. That's how I think I can get at Lankford."

As a lie it may not have been great, but he just needed to convince Hill to hold off for another week or so. By then, Nick hoped, he'd at least have something off of Lankford's system tying them to Tim's murder. He wanted to deflect Hill's attention so he asked, "Once I get on, is there some kind of specific information you think I should look for?"

Hill grunted into the phone. "Yeah, there are a few things I can give you. You just get hold of me when you get your access."

So he did have something else, Nick thought. Apparently Hill had his own secrets to keep.

"Tell me this, Kingman. You working with anyone else on the this, someone we should know about?"

Shit. Could he have found out about Reed or MamaLu? "Who do you mean, Hill?"

"I'm talking about another computer consultant, a person who knows networks, someone like that. If you are, Kingman, I've got to know about it."

If they knew about Lu Bates, she'd probably be back in jail. He could check that out. And if they knew about Reed, they'd know he wasn't a computer pro, that he was more or less just some kid Nick had come across. Was Hill on a fishing expedition or did he have a specific reason for asking?

"What are you talking about, Hill? My own company doesn't even know what I'm doing. As far as they're concerned I'm just taking time off. No one else knows what I'm doing."

"Alright, Kingman." He seemed to be satisfied. "Keep it that way. But you let me know as soon as you get into that network. Then we're going to have a little meeting."

Nick told him of course he would. He couldn't wait.

* * *

Monday night was their busiest yet. Nick went with Reed on his cleaning assignments to get them done and out of the way as early as possible. It was just after ten o'clock when they were ready for Lankford's.

"All you want me to do is remove the memory chip you installed in the keyboard and bring it back?" Reed asked Nick. "You don't want me to anything else while I'm there?"

"No, that's it. Just be very careful not to break the connection with the battery. If you do, whatever is stored in the memory will fade away and we'll have to put it back in for another day. The whole operation shouldn't take you more than fifteen minutes."

"No problem. I'll be back at your house in an hour."

Nick waited until Reed had driven out of the parking lot in his old Toyota, with mop handles, broom handles and a vacuum cleaner all visible through the windows from their positions in the back seat. If Hill and Fetterman knew about Reed, they most likely had seen him at Lankford's or had seen him with Nick. Which would mean they were either watching Lankford's building or watching him. There hadn't been any sign of them doing either. Nick started his own car and pulled out after Reed. It wouldn't hurt to make sure.

He picked up Reed's tail lights before he hit the interstate and followed him to the West Shore Boulevard exit. Reed went south a quarter of a mile then turned off at Cypress. Nick kept going for a few blocks before circling back and slowly driving down the street containing Lankford's building. Reed's was the only car in any of the parking lots that he could see. Satisfied, at least for now, he turned around and headed home.

Half an hour after he got there, Reed pulled into the driveway, a characteristic grin stuck across his face. "How's this, boss?" he said as he held out the memory chip wrapped in a paper towel. The battery was still attached and the entire assembly looked exactly as it should.

"Perfect," Nick told him as he carefully picked it out of Reed's hand. "Let's go see what this baby has to tell us."

He led the way into his office where his computer sat on top of the desk, its cover removed and on the floor. Two thin wires, extending from somewhere inside the computer, were draped over the side of the case. Carefully, Nick connected these to the memory device Reed had brought him and powered on the computer. When it was finished booting up, Nick typed in the name of a program and a second or two later, numbers and letters began to scroll across the screen. "Looks like it's working."

The scrolling stopped and the prompt reappeared as the last set of characters dissolved into nothingness. "Cross your fingers," Nick said as he typed something else into the keyboard. The screen turned blue and an orderly set of words and sentences, as well as groups of numbers, were displayed in small white letters.

"Did we get it?"

"Right here." Nick pointed to the upper left hand corner of the screen where the letters 'WAL' were displayed followed by the word 'ENTER' in square brackets. "This file shows everything Lankford typed into the keyboard, followed by the enter key, which shows up like this." He moved his finger to the word in the brackets. "Any time you see something in these brackets, that's where he pressed a key like enter, backspace, or an up or a down arrow."

"Something that doesn't represent a letter or number."

"Or punctuation. Exactly. Now look up here." Nick pointed back to the letters 'WAL.' "Remember that the first thing he needs to enter is his login name. After that he enters his password." Nick dropped his finger down to the next line where the word 'LIBRA*NOIR' appeared.

"That doesn't make sense," Reed said.

"Sure it does. It's actually a very good password. It's made up of two words, one of which is French, as well as a non-character symbol. Most people use the names of their spouses or children or something that anybody who knew them could guess easily. By using a foreign word and an asterisk, he protects the password from a hacker who could use a computerized dictionary to run through the entire English language to find it."

"Clever." Reed moved in closer and examined the figures on the screen. he could imagine Walter Lankford sitting at his mahogany desk entering all of his secrets into his computer, taking it for granted that he was the only one who would be able to see them. "I feel like a kid reading my sister's diary," he said.

"Only your sister didn't murder anybody, I hope."

"If she had, it probably would have been me." Reed turned and faced Nick. "When do we go back to Lankford's?"

Nick picked a diskette up from the desk and waved it at Reed. "How about now? We've got the password and there's no reason to wait." He didn't want to tell him about the pressure from Hill. "You drive, cleaner man."

Approximately twenty minutes later they pulled into the parking lot at Lankford's. Nick told Reed that he should park around the corner of the building, out of sight from the street. Reed did this and they walked along the sidewalk back to the front door. As they entered the building, Nick told him how the monitor bugging program worked.

"There are three parts to this it," Nick began. "One part captures the information sent to the monitor, the second part is a file that holds that information, and the third part is the program that reads the data file and shows us what Lankford's screens looked like. The program we're going to install here will load itself every time he turns on his computer."

"Won't he be able to tell that it's running?"

"Not unless the program itself does something to make him notice. Although if somebody calls up a list of everything that's in memory, or if they look at the configuration file that loads all of the device drivers, they'll see it on the list. We just have to hope they won't do that. Or, if they do, that they won't have any reason to check out what it's doing."

"How likely is that?"

"It's a pretty good bet. Your typical computer today will automatically load several program that are built like this, sometimes more. Once they're installed there isn't any need to do anything more with them. Just let them be. Your average user has never even heard of them."

"Good. Then I don't feel so dumb," Reed joked.

They had turned off the alarm system, re-locked the front door, and had now just entered Walter Lankford's office. Before they turned on the lights Nick crossed the room and rotated the rod that closed the Venetian blinds. "Make sure we remember to open these back up when we leave."

"Got it."

Nick moved to Lankford's desk and turned the computer on. When it asked for the log in name and the password, Nick entered the initials and the words they had read from the keyboard file. He was rewarded with the familiar operating system prompt, a letter followed by a colon and a greater than symbol. "We have access," he told Reed, who was smiling.

Sitting down in the chair behind the desk with Reed watching over his shoulder, Nick copied the file from the diskette in his pocket to the computer's hard disk drive. He removed the floppy when it was finished and began typing commands into the keyboard. "As far as being discovered is concerned, I'm more worried about the file that will hold the information that we capture."

"Why's that?"

"Mainly because it can get fairly large. See, the video card in the computer is continually sending signals to the monitor and if we tried to capture everything it sent, we'd fill up the hard disk in a matter of minutes. I wrote the driver program to capture data every few seconds, and then only to save the data that has changed since the last capture. That way we don't save multiple copies of the same image. But still, even though I'm compressing the data to save space, I'm limiting the size of the file that gets created. I'm afraid if we let it get too big, Lankford will run out of disk space and get somebody in here to investigate."

"But doesn't that mean we won't be getting everything?"

"To a certain point. But we don't have any idea how much data we need to get. We may get everything we need, who knows. We'll just have to hope what we do will be enough."

After a few more minutes, Nick was finished installing the program. He spent another fifteen showing Reed how to move the holding file off the hard disk and onto a series of three and a half inch diskettes. When Reed declared his confidence, Nick switched off the computer and the lights. Reed moved to the windows and opened the blinds. When the office was physically as they had found it, the two men left the building.

During the short ride home, Reed said to Nick, "I want you to know that I'm taking all this very seriously."

"What do you mean?" Nick turned to face him.

"Well, you know, sometimes I make jokes about things when I probably shouldn't. In case you haven't noticed, I have a habit of usually saying whatever pops into my mind without questioning it. I just don't want to give you the wrong impression. This is the first thing I've ever done in my whole life that means anything to anybody. If these guys are involved with drugs and killing people, I want to see them go down, just like you do. I want to help. It makes me feel like I'm doing something worthwhile, something more than emptying other people's garbage cans. I just want you to know I'm glad you feel that you can trust me like this."

Nick turned back and stared through the windshield at the white lines painted between the lanes on the highway. He thought about Tim Clayton's body being thrown out of an airplane, Tim's wife Marie at her husband's funeral, his own feelings of guilt for not even having been aware that his friend, his brother, had been in danger. After a few long minutes, he said to Reed, "Just be careful." He didn't look at him.

The atmosphere in the car changed with the shift in Nick's mood. "Just be what?" Reed asked, trying to loosen it up.

"Shut up and drive."

* * *

Marie Clayton called Tuesday afternoon shortly after Nick had finished eating breakfast/lunch. Damn it, I'm an idiot, he thought as he heard who it was. He hadn't forgotten about their conversation at the funeral, but he hadn't made the time to call her, either. Not yet. And now here she was having to track him down. "I'm sorry, Marie," he told her. "I should have called you by now."

"That's okay, Nick. Really. How are things going for you?"

What stupid questions we all have to ask each other at times like these, he thought. We have to ask them to show that we care and we're concerned, but how are we really supposed to answer them? I'm fine. I'm okay. I'll survive. I've changed. I'm bitter. I'll never be the same. I'm still pissed. I'm going after the guys that did this and I'll see them pay.

"Going okay," he told her. Stock answer.

"Good," she said. "I'm glad to hear that. I really am."

There was an awkward pause as Nick refused to give in to the urge to ask her the same question. It wouldn't matter how she answered, they both knew how she was feeling. There weren't any good words for that.

Finally, Marie said, "I was wondering when we could get together for the dinner we talked about. There are a few things I'd like to ask you about, if it's okay."

"Of course it is, Marie, you know that. Is there anything you want to talk about over the phone?"

"No, no. Just a couple of things I want to go over with you. I don't think it's anything to worry about."

Nick didn't have any idea about what she could be talking about. "Any time you want, Marie. Just pick the night."

"Thanks, Nick. I was thinking maybe you could come down Friday night? There are still some other issues I have to see to."

"Friday night's fine. I'll pick you up and we'll go some place quiet."

"You can bring Katy if you'd like."

Nick sucked a long, deep breath through his teeth. "I don't know, Marie. Katy's staying at her sister's right now. She's giving me some space I need, and it's hard on both of us. I don't think it's quite the time yet."

"You know, Nick, during things like this, most people need somebody they can be with."

"Marie—"

"That's okay, Nick. I already talked to Katy, she said you had some things to work through. I just don't want to see anything bad happen to you two. Tim used to tell me you carried a lot of baggage from your past and some things were hard for you. I just want you to know that I love you both."

"We love you too, Marie." That was safe, and he said it quickly so he didn't have to think about comforting words from a woman who had just lost everything. What gave him the right to feel so bad compared to her?

They held on for a minute in a silence that was more comfortable than the one before. Marie said she'd see Nick on Friday then breathed a goodbye and hung up.

Nick put down the phone and thought about his wife as he looked up at the battery powered clock hanging on the kitchen wall. She'd still be at the hospital working the day shift in the emergency room. He missed talking to her, hearing her voice, telling her he loved her. Marie was right. He did need somebody, only now was not the time. Not for him.

CHAPTER THIRTEEN

That night, Nick went with Reed to clean more buildings. There were three of them and they started early, impatient for the time when Reed would go to Lankford's and retrieve the file produced by Nick's bugging program, which was how they thought of it. An electronic snoop on Lankford's digital dealings.

When it was finally time, Nick told Reed to be careful, that if someone at Lankford's had in fact noticed something wrong with their system, it was conceivable somebody might be there waiting. They agreed that Nick would take his car and drive past Lankford's building while Reed waited in his Toyota a few blocks away. Nick would meet him there and tell him if it looked clear.

Reed halfheartedly balked when Nick suggested he unload his cleaning supplies and carry them into the building to keep things looking as routine as possible. If he were to get caught, he would just be the cleaning guy. If whoever caught him knew Reed was there on an off day, he could claim a scheduling problem or something had caused him to come a day early. "That's just a lot of extra work for nothing," he complained.

"Think of it as a favor to me," Nick told him. The two men left Nick's house shortly after eleven thirty. Forty five minutes later Nick told Reed it was okay to go in. He would stay there, on the corner where Reed had been waiting while he did his drive-bys.

An hour passed until Reed pulled his Toyota up next to Nick's car, facing the opposite direction and aligning the driver's side windows so they could talk. "Got it," he told Nick. "It was as quiet as a tomb in there."

Nick had been fiddling with the radio, advancing the tuning dial click by click, momentarily listening to each station as it grew from static to intrusive music or speech , and then back to static. He had found it difficult to concentrate while Reed had been gone. Now all he felt was relief. "Given the circumstances, can't you come up with a better simile than that?"

Reed shot him a grin through the open windows. "Let's head back to my house," Nick told him. He began to relax as he pulled out of the parking lot and turned toward the highway. He hadn't been aware that he had grown so tense.

When they arrived, Nick announced that he had decided to get some sleep. He'd start with the file first thing in the morning. If Reed wanted, he could sleep on the couch rather than drive home.

"How can you just go to bed without looking at what we've got?" Reed asked him. "I thought you were going to devour this thing. Bloat yourself on coffee and pull an all nighter."

"I thought about it, but I'm already tired. That file is huge and it's going to take hours to go through it and I don't want to risk overlooking something important. Besides, we're going to get a file like that every night and there's going to be a lot of material to go through."

"Do you mind if I look? I'm still kind of jazzed after going in there tonight."

"Not at all," Nick said. He led the way into his office and restored the file Reed had backed up onto six diskettes. Then he entered a command and a new image appeared on the monitor. He stood up and Reed took his place at the desk. "Every time you press enter, the computer will show you the next screen image that was captured. Press the escape key when you've had enough."

"And what exactly is it that I'm looking for?"

Nick gave him a shrug and a yawn. "We probably won't know it until we see it. All we really have to go on is that somewhere buried in that file may be a reason to kill someone."

With characteristic humor, Reed asked, "Doesn't it give you nightmares to talk like that right before you go to bed?"

"You have no idea how many things give me nightmares, pal. I'll see you in the morning."

* * *

Reed was asleep on the living room couch when Nick came downstairs after his morning shower. It was a little after ten and Nick decided to hold off on breakfast so he wouldn't disturb Reed. Instead, he headed for the office and Lankford's computer file.

The bugging program he had written captured the equivalent of an image of the screen every few seconds as long as there was some activity on the computer. Scanning through the resulting file was tedious, Nick thought, like reading a boring novel or reading statistics. Some parts were kind of interesting, some were just boring, and just when you were ready to put the whole thing down something would happen that would hold your attention a little while longer.

Nick found that extrapolating what had occurred during the brief intervals between the screen captures was mildly addicting. The jumps between screens were sometimes confusing, but on the whole he believed he could follow what was going on. After an hour or two of viewing screen after screen after screen, he felt that he would in fact be able to reconstruct the activities of Walter A. Lankford on his computer.

When Reed walked in with a tray full of peanut butter and jelly sandwiches, Nick had totally lost track of the time. "It's past noon, man. This was all I could find in the kitchen."

Nick forced his mind to break free of the rhythm of the flickering monitor and rubbed at the back of his neck. "Mine was starting to hurt last night when I turned that thing off," Reed said. "Have you come up with anything yet?"

"Not yet," Nick said as he bit into a sandwich. There was more peanut butter than jelly and he scraped at the roof of his mouth with his tongue. Reed laughed at him and said he liked the sandwiches that way.

"So does my wife," Nick managed through the stickiness. "She thinks peanut butter should be fun."

"Don't you?"

"Maybe not on a sandwich. How long did you stay up last night?"

"Too late. Even after I wanted to quit, I kept pressing that damned enter key, looking at just one more screen. It was like being hooked on some incredibly boring video game. I kept thinking, 'Just one more and I'll go to sleep.' I didn't have any clue what I was looking at but it was hard to make myself stop."

"You didn't see anything that looked interesting?"

"Not to my untrained eye."

They finished the sandwiches and Nick focused his attention back on the computer. There was nothing suspicious that he could see. He worked through the entire file once, broke for a trip to a fried chicken franchise with Reed, then went through it all again. The day had long since been over when he turned off the computer and rubbed his tired eyes.

Reed put down the magazine he was reading and rotated into a sitting position on the leather couch. "Anything?"

"No. It's like you said. It doesn't look like there's anything wrong there, but I'm not sure I'd be able to recognize it if there were."

"Maybe they only break the law on Wednesdays."

"You're a real help, aren't you? I guess we'll find out if you're right. We should probably give your buddy Ray a couple more hours before we send you to get today's file."

Reed studied his watch for a moment then said, "We could probably check it in an hour or so. He should be out of there by then."

"Sounds good," Nick said as he stood and stretched. "I'm going to drop some Visine in my eyes and lie down on the other couch. Are you going to stay awake?"

"I've napped on and off all afternoon."

"Then wake me if I doze when it's time to go. We'll work it like we did last night."

* * *

Thursday and Friday were virtual repeats of Wednesday with Reed going into Lankford's and copying the file and Nick spending the next day studying it. He had been keeping a list of items he thought might be questionable, things he wanted to go back and look more closely at, but so far nothing had come remotely close to looking like an illegal activity. During another fast food lunch on Friday afternoon, Reed asked him what he thought this meant.

"I'm not sure," Nick told him. "It could be a number of things. Possibly Lankford himself is clean and somebody else in the firm is doing the dirty stuff. Or maybe it's just been an off week for money laundering, I don't know. Maybe every transaction we're looking at is bad and we're simply too ignorant to see it."

"But you believe that Lankford has to be in on the action."

"It makes the most sense. In a firm that size, with the president and sole stockholder actively running the business himself, if he isn't doing it he knows it's going on. I just can't believe an employee can pull off a scam like this and remain invisible. Lankford has to know where the money's coming from and where it's going."

"But if it's not him, say he's given this department to someone else, how do we find that person? We can't bug all the computers, can we?"

"We probably could, at least for a while, but we wouldn't have a prayer of being able to read every file we get. That's not the answer."

"So what is?"

"I'm not sure. Hill said that he had something that would help us. I was hoping to come up with something first, before we went to him, but it's probably time to give him a call."

"I get the feeling that you really don't trust this Hill guy."

"No," Nick said. "That's not it, exactly. Saying that I really don't like him would probably be more accurate. I just don't want to put ourselves in a position where we have to trust him. We're better off if we can stay a little bit in front."

"You're being a control freak, huh?"

The telephone rang and Reed reached behind him and picked up the cordless phone from the kitchen counter and tossed it to Nick. He caught it with one hand, extended the antenna and pushed the talk button. "Hello," he said.

"Kingman," came the single word.

Nick move the phone away from the lower part of his face and mouthed, 'Speak of the devil.' "I was just thinking about you."

"Don't even tell me," said Hill. "My knees go weak. I need to know where we are with this thing."

Nick swore to himself. Reed could see that he wasn't happy. Nick had wanted more time to figure out exactly what he was going to tell Hill and now he had to wing it. He started with, "I'm making some progress."

Hill jumped all over that. "What the hell does that mean? How much progress?"

Nick had a sinking feeling that told him he wouldn't be able to control this conversation. He felt like a child about to be caught in a lie to his parents. He tried to change the direction they were going. "It means that I would like to know what I need to look for on Lankford's network. You said you had something that would help."

"What we've got won't do you a bit of good until you can actually get on that damned network." Hill paused for a moment. "Son of a bitch, Kingman, is that what 'making some progress' is? Did you get access to their network without letting me know? Tell me, goddamn it, and tell me now."

Boom. Just like that Hill had laid it open. "I was able to get on for a while today," Nick surrendered, trying to remain consistent with his earlier story. "Just for a short time. I need to know from you what to look for the next time I get on."

"Why the hell didn't you call me, Kingman?" Hill exploded into the telephone. "I've been sitting on my ass all fucking week waiting to hear from you. What the fuck are you trying to pull? I've got a goddamned investigation I'm trying to run here."

I'm sorry, daddy. It won't happen again. "Give it a rest, Hill. I'm not trying to pull anything. I told you, I was just about to call you when the phone rang. I can get on the network and watch what's going on. Now it's time to tell me what it is you've got so I can check it out."

Nick stopped talking after this last statement. He knew that Hill wasn't used to having someone stand up to him. Hill was a boss and a bully, he told people what to do and he beat down any resistance as hard and as fast as he could. That was how he got things done as a cop, and that was a fundamental reason why Nick had never gotten along with him. There was no room for other people, be they innocent or guilty, victim or bystander, help or hindrance. There was only Detective Hill, who always did what he needed to take what he wanted. When it coincided with the job, he could be an effective policeman.

"I need to know exactly how you get on that network," he said after a minute, with an edge to his voice.

"No way, Hill. I have access, and that's all I'm going to tell you about it. I don't want this going back against anybody." He wanted it to sound like he was protecting somebody.

This time, he got an unexpected laugh. "Nick old buddy, I sometimes get the feeling you don't have a lot of faith in me."

Imagine that. Nick said nothing.

"Got a pen handy?"

Nick stood and walked to the dry-erase board on the refrigerator. Uncapping a black marker from the counter, he told Hill he was ready.

"I'm going to give you four names. I need to know every scrap of information you can come up with connected with any of them. And I mean everything, even if you find something that doesn't seem to make sense to you. It might to us."

"Because you've got the bigger picture?"

"Always."

Hill dictated the names of four men while Nick wrote them on the board, then told Nick to call him after the weekend on Monday. He said they would need to keep in closer contact from now on.

Nick pushed the talk button a second time to end the conversation. Reed was sitting at the tiny kitchen table, looking at the names Nick had written but not sure of everything that had just happened. "So how're we doing, Boss?"

"You never know with that guy," Nick told him. "I'll fill you in later. I've got to get ready for tonight. I'm driving down to Sarasota to have dinner with Marie Clayton."

"That's right. I forgot that was tonight. What about today's file from Lankford's?"

"You don't need me. Just be a little extra careful and do a drive-by before you go in. You know what's up."

Hill hung up with Nick and related their conversation to Fetterman who was sitting at his usual place across from Hill at his own desk. "Uh huh," Fetterman said when Hill had finished.

"I think we may have been a little too loose with our Mr. Kingman," Hill added, his voice low. "I think maybe we need to start checking out some things, make sure nothing's going on that we should know about. What do you think?"

Fetterman looked back at Hill with the same unchanging expression he had worn as long as the two of them had known each other. "No time like the present," he said.

CHAPTER FOURTEEN

MamaLu Bates sat in her truck and watched car after car slowly leave the parking lot of the Walter A. Lankford Company. She'd been watching every night this week and by far this had been the most rapid exodus. She glanced at the dime store clock stuck to her dashboard with an adhesive strip. 6:05 p.m. Thank god it's Friday, she thought. Yuppie go home.

She waited another fifteen minutes until there were only three cars left in the lot. Two of them she recognized as having stayed late every night, usually leaving close to six thirty. She dropped the truck into gear and glided across the street and parked next to the one closest to the front door. As she worked her way out of the truck, she could see some activity inside at the reception area. Better hurry, she thought. Don't want them to leave too soon.

From the bed of her truck she plucked an ancient Hoover vacuum cleaner, easily lifting it with one arm. With the other she scooped up a box of garbage bags and a collection of spray bottles she had scrounged from the maintenance closet of her apartment building. Thus armed, she made her way up the short sidewalk and kicked at the front door three times. Inside, one of the men who had been standing in the lobby moved to open the door.

"Hold that for me, will you, sport? Thanks." MamaLu waited for him to walk all the way out of the building and hold the door from there before she went inside. The lights had been turned off and three people, two men and a woman, looked to be in the final stages of wishing each other well for the weekend. Got here just in time, MamaLu thought. All three watched her enter the building and drop her supplies at their feet.

"Are you here to clean this place?" one of the men asked, trying and failing to suppress a grin.

That's not obvious? "I didn't come here to have you guys invest my vacuum cleaner," she told him. "Bay Area Cleaning Services." She had gotten that from the magnetic sign on Ray Alvarado's truck. "I've got a scheduling conflict tonight so I have to start a little early."

"Where's the regular guy?" asked the woman.

"Ray? He'll be here in a while, help me finish up." He'd be there in a while all right, but she planned on being long gone by then. She picked up her stack of garbage bags and started to move around the receptionist's desk away from the front of the building. If they were suspicious they'd come after her, ask her more questions. If not, they would probably just leave.

She saw a room in the back with a small kitchen that she thought must have served as the company break room. Since she didn't know the first thing about cleaning buildings, let alone a fancy office suite, she thought she could go in there and bang some dishes around until the people up front left. As far as she was concerned, they had served their purpose. She had gotten into the building without having to know the password for the security system.

After five minutes, when nobody had followed her to the back, MamaLu returned to the front door area. Her vacuum cleaner and spray bottles were as she had left them but the building itself was otherwise clear of people. They had even been so helpful as to have locked the front door, trusting that she had her own set of keys.

She dropped the garbage bags on the floor next to her other things and fished in her pocket for her new key ring. Kingman had said that the two most important keys for her to copy were the one for the building and the one for the president's office. She'd locate that and start there.

It should be three or four hours before Alvarado showed up, based on when he had arrived last Friday as well as this past Wednesday. Still, she didn't want to cut it that close. Even though she had no idea what she was looking for, whether she found it or not she'd still be talking to Kingman in the morning. She looked around at the framed artwork on the walls, the expensive wooden furniture. This place was obviously prosperous and that suited her.

That's the magic word she thought as she tried a key in the locked door: Prosperous. Whether she figured out what Kingman and that kid were after or if she had to resort to blackmail to get some of it, that's where she was headed. MamaLu Bates had a date with prosperity.

* * *

It took Nick nearly an hour and a half to drive the seventy miles to them Clayton home in Sarasota. Save for the long bridge over the bay the drive was long and flat, scrub swamp lands lining each side of the highway. So far, at least, this part of Florida had been mostly spared from the ravages of the developers and their bulldozers.

Images of captured computer screens flickered through his mind as he drove, a montage of meaningless names and numbers. After studying a four day supply of information from Walter Lankford's computer, he had yet to find anything suggesting money laundering. He was primarily looking for the transfer of large amounts of money out of the country.

For a foreign drug cartel operating in the U.S. it is very difficult to move their huge profits safely out of the country. The ideal method is to find a way to get it into the banking system where it can easily be converted to other currencies and transferred somewhere else.

A number of things make this difficult. With a million dollars in twenty dollar bills weighing a hundred and twenty five pounds, physically moving the money poses its own challenges. To get that much money into a bank in any form would require the filling out of a CTR, or Cash Transaction Record, paperwork the government requires for deposits greater than ten thousand dollars. The system is designed to leave a trail.

So far though, Nick hadn't seen any signs of it, which was not to say they weren't there. There was always the possibility of smurfs, people used by the drug lords to open accounts with smaller, less noticeable sums of money. Even in that case, he should be able to see traces of it leaving the country after it was in the system.

Then there were the four names Hill had given him. He'd have to go through all that data again to look for their presence. That might be something.

Nick found himself aware of the fact that he had entered the subdivision where Tim had bought a house upon his return from the islands. With a dock behind it on the Gulf of Mexico, he and his bride had never been far from the sea that had brought them together. Until now.

He pulled the car into the driveway and parked. He had many memories, many associations with this place, and he could feel the anger and frustration inside him kindle themselves into a burning fire. *God damn it, Tim. Why didn't you tell me any of this had been going on? I could have helped.*

Things could have been different.

A light came on over the front door and Nick quickly stepped out of his car. He was here for Marie and he refused to let her see the pain he was feeling. She had enough of her own.

He met her at the door where she appeared wearing a pair of simple slacks and a white blouse with large padded buttons. They embraced for half a minute before Marie broke away, pulling the door all the way closed and leading Nick back toward the driveway. "I was going to invite you in," she told him. "But I just want to get the hell away from here for a while."

They were quiet as they drove to the restaurant. The dinner rush was over and the dining room was mostly empty as they were seated at a table in the corner, over the water. Half of the room was built on a wooden platform that extended over the slow current and brown waters of an estuary leading to the Gulf. A fine screen mesh made up the walls and chirping insect sounds passed unfiltered into the restaurant. Enclosed candles were the only source of light, one per table. An intimate atmosphere for lovers and secrets, Nick thought.

"I want to thank you for coming to see me, Nick. You don't know how much I appreciate it."

Nick made an awkward gesture in the air above the table with his hand. "Don't thank me, Marie. It wasn't a favor. I came because I wanted to see you."

"You're sweet, Nick."

A waiter appeared at the table and Nick ordered a carafe of red wine for the two of them. He returned a minute later and Nick dismissed him by telling him he would pour. He filled two glasses and placed one in front of Marie. When he was done, he stared at the reflection of candles on the outside of her glass and wondered how far the light reached into the wine.

"I wanted to ask you about some business things that have come up since Tim's death."

Nick kept staring at the wine glass until a delicate hand lifted it from the table, paused, then gracefully put it back. He realized that he was about to talk about Tim's death and that made him sad. "What are you going to do, Marie?"

"There are some things that need to be settled. Then I think I'll leave for a while, get out of Florida. If I sit in that house and do nothing I'll lose my mind in two days. I need to move around, see things go past me. Remind me how to live life."

He sat listening to the wife of his murdered best friend and knew that he had nothing to offer. He sipped his own wine and said nothing.

"My mother lives in Vermont, did you know that?"

Nick shook his head.

"I've never been there before. I miss seeing mountains. You almost forget they exist, living here. Everything is so flat."

She slid her cloth napkin out of its plastic ring and twisted it around her fingers. "There are a few things that need to be taken care of, though. I want to ask you what you think I should do with the business."

The waiter reappeared and quietly stood beside the table. Nick noticed him and the man began to recite the evening's specials, all of which featured a seafood entre. Marie tried to say she wasn't hungry but Nick told the waiter to bring them two of the broiled grouper specials. "You have to eat, Marie."

She nodded as she continued to play with her napkin, not wanting to lose her train of thought. "I didn't know if—" She stopped herself then began again. "I don't know if you have any desire to take over the business. I need to ask you that."

This came as a total surprise. "Is that what you want? Do you want me to take it over?" He hadn't given any thought at all to what would happen to Tim's business. Mentally he kicked himself. The business hadn't ended with Tim, it had passed to Marie and she would need to deal with it.

"Well, no, I'm not asking like that. Ron Pauley made me an offer to buy the company. He says that there's a lot of value in the maintenance agreements Tim had as well as in the work in progress. I don't really have any idea what he's talking about. I just want to do what's best."

Pauley was a local Sarasotan that periodically worked for Tim on a contract basis. Nick knew him and respected his work. "Sell the company, Marie. Tim would have approved and it is probably the best thing for the customers. If that's what you want to do."

"I think so. The offer is fair and I just thought I should check with you to see if, you were maybe interested in taking over. I didn't know if this was something you had thought about."

"I have a business in Tampa. Tim's clients would be happier with someone closer, I'm sure." Nick reached across the table and squeezed her hand, the one without the napkin. "Take the money, Marie. It's okay."

"Thanks, Nick. Tim had insurance, and I'm going to sell the boat, but the money will help."

They sat alone in the near dark, breathing the humid air and listening to the night's sounds. The water beneath them made almost no noise as it slowly passed beneath their feet. In a little while, their food arrived and they began to eat.

During the meal they spoke lightly of Katy, Marie respecting the unspoken situation between her two friends. Nick answered her questions but didn't offer more, himself not comfortable talking about it. When the waiter returned for their empty dishes and dessert orders, they both declined more food and asked for coffee instead.

"Thank you for the dinner, Nick. The food was wonderful. I didn't realize how hungry I really was."

"I'm glad you enjoyed it."

"You know," she said, wrinkling her forehead. "There's something else I can ask you about, if it's alright. Of course, if I sell to Ron this would become his problem but I'm not sure there's anything to worry about."

"What is it?"

As the coffee arrived, Marie asked, "Have you ever heard of a man named James Rooker?"

Nick thought about it for a moment, then said, "No, I don't think so. Who is he?"

"He was a consultant like you and Tim, I guess. From Sarasota. A couple of days after the funeral, several of Tim's customers called the business number. They were very nice and very sweet, but they all wanted to know about this man James Rooker. It seems he was going around to some of our clients representing himself as Tim's partner, someone who was taking over the company. They wanted to know if it was true, if he was who he said he was."

"Do you know him?"

"I met him at the funeral otherwise I never would have known who they were talking about."

"What did you tell the customers?"

"The truth. That I had no idea why this man would be telling them this and that it wasn't true as far as I knew. I don't think Tim ever met him."

Nick sipped at his own coffee, then slowly shook his head.

The things some people will do to make a buck, he thought. Let the body grow cold, for Christ's sake. "I'll talk to him, Marie. I can put on my cop act and tell him to back the hell off. I'm just sorry you have to put up with this kind of thing."

Marie shook her head. "That's just it, Nick. I don't. He's dead. It was in the paper this morning."

"He's dead? What happened?"

"Apparently he was murdered. The paper said he had been badly beaten but they didn't know the exact cause of death yet."

"No, they'd have to wait for an autopsy. Who did they say did it?"

"They don't know."

Nick listened carefully as Marie recounted as much of the story as she could remember. When she was through, Nick sank into the back of his chair. The mortality rate for computer consultants in Tampa Bay was going through the roof, he thought. He poured another half glass full of wine for himself and Marie.

If this guy had been low enough to try to steal a dead man's business from his widow, he had probably had other enemies as well. Provided this wasn't some random killing, the police should be able to find whoever did it. Usually if the victim provoked enough rage in his antagonist to get himself beaten to death, the path back to the killers was reasonably clear. "What was he like at the funeral?"

"Oh, I don't know. He didn't make much of an impression on me although I wasn't exactly in the best state of mind. I saw him with the two policemen from Tampa that are investigating Tim's death so I wondered if you knew him."

Nick straightened in his chair. "Say that again."

"I saw him with the two detectives from Tampa that are investigating Tim's death." Concern wrinkled her features. "Nick, what's wrong?"

"Something, maybe. I don't know." It had struck him when he heard her make the statement about the Tampa police. It was at the edge of his thoughts, flitting like a firefly, visible during the occasional spark. Marie stayed silent as she watched Nick. His forehead was creased and he was staring at a spot on the table between them.

What had Hill and Fetterman been doing with another computer consultant? Had they had someone else working on the Lankford case or did their knowing each other just happen to be a coincidence?

"Marie, was one of the companies that called you about this guy the Walter A. Lankford Company?"

Marie's face took on a nervous look in the candle's light. "No," she said. "One of them was from Tampa but they were an office supply wholesaler or something. The others were all in either Sarasota or Bradenton. I have a list back home if you want to see it."

"No, that's alright." He reached forward and squeezed her hand again. "Don't worry. I just think too much, sometimes." Still, something was tugging at him and he didn't like it. "Would you excuse me for just a minute? I need to find the bathrooms."

She gave him a nod and an uneasy smile as he stood and walked out of the dining room to the front of the restaurant.

There were pay phones located just outside the doors leading to the bathrooms and Nick stepped up to the first one, lifting the handset to his ear. He punched in his credit card number followed by his home phone number and waited until his machine answered the call. His own voice asked him to leave a message and after the tone he said, "Reed, if you're there pick up the phone." A pause. "Reed."

Nothing happened.

He repeated the question and hung on for a minute longer, willing the phone to answer him with Reed's voice. Then he hung up and dialed again, this time trying Reed's number. There was no answer there, either.

He stood by the phones, unsure of what he should do. As far as he knew, there was no connection between this Rooker guy and the Lankford Company, no real reason to grow alarmed. On the other hand, there was a definite link between Tim, Rooker, and

Hill and Fetterman. What did it mean that the two cops were the only ones still breathing?

Fuck it, he swore to himself and went back to the table. He had to do something.

Marie hadn't moved. She was still sitting in her chair, staring patiently into the flickering fire dance of the candle, imagining herself as a stick of wax, half of which lay in molten pebbles piled around its base. "I want to go home," she said to Nick without looking up.

Wordlessly, Nick left enough money on the table to cover the check and led Marie by the elbow out to the car. As he opened the door for her she broke the uncomfortable silence by saying, "I just can't get away, can I?" Without waiting for an answer, she lowered herself gently into the car seat. Nick didn't know what to tell her.

* * *

Nick was tense during the long drive back to Tampa. When he thought of Marie he felt guilty, upset with himself that he had been unable to provide a quiet, relaxing evening for her. There was just too much going on, it seemed. Too much at stake.

He checked his watch for perhaps the twentieth time, then looked at the speedometer. Tampa was a lot closer at ninety miles per hour but it would still take him over an hour to get there. Traffic was almost nonexistent and he knew that if he came across a cop he'd be pulled over and ticketed in a heartbeat. He didn't want to lose that time.

Hill and Fetterman hadn't told him everything; he knew that. But he also knew that he hadn't told them everything, either. The question is, had what they kept from him caused the deaths of two men? He remembered Hill asking him if he was working with somebody else who knew computers. The thought chilled him as he considered it what Hill may have meant.

He needed to find Reed, that much he was sure of. Find him and regroup before they moved ahead any further, possibly walking into a situation they couldn't walk out of. He wondered if that had been what happened to Tim Clayton and James Rooker.

He looked at the time again but it didn't help. He had no idea if Reed had already gone to Lankford's, if he hadn't been there yet, or even if he was there right now. There was just too damned much he didn't know and he gripped the steering wheel tighter and watched the speedometer needle as it edged further to the right, his knuckles throbbing with his frustration. If something happened to Reed because of Hill and Fetterman . . .

He let that thought trail off in his mind. It was not a possibility he was prepared to allow to happen. If Hill and Fetterman were setting him up, if they had had something to do with the death of his friend, he would find a way to make them accountable. It may be melodramatic, he thought, a bad cliché out of a Hollywood movie, but he would find a way to make them pay.

Somewhere behind him, a lonely woman sat on the deck of a sail boat tied to a dock behind her home, and cried.

CHAPTER FIFTEEN

Once he hit Tampa, Nick had to force himself to slow down as he turned off the freeway. He had been speeding for so long that traveling at the speed limit felt as though he were hardly moving.

The moon was a mere sliver and spray from overnight sprinkler systems peppered the windshield making the night seem darker than it was. Nick rolled down his window and felt the warm humid air cover his face like a mask. He wanted to have a clearer view as he drove by Lankford's.

He turned right onto Cypress and kept the car moving at a steady speed five miles an hour slower than it had been. Lankford's was dark, the parking lot empty. There was no sign of Reed or anyone else.

He drove further to where the street ended at the bay and slowly turned the car around. If anyone were to see him, he was just another out of state transplant who had turned down the wrong street. As he drove past Lankford's building again, from the west this time, he had a brief view of the lot where he had told Reed to park. It was also empty.

Okay, he told himself. He's not here but there's no sign of anything wrong, either. He headed back for the highway and accelerated toward his house.

The driveway was empty and no lights were on. Same story as Lankford's. Still, he left the car in front of the garage and went inside, hoping to find a message or some kind of sign.

The light on the answering machine was blinking once. He pushed the play button and walked into the kitchen as he heard his own voice speak to him from the tape. He flicked the light switch and as the fluorescent lights flicked on overhead, he saw that the dry erase board on the refrigerator was blank. He turned to walk out of the room then froze. Hadn't he left the four names from Hill on the board?

Nick took a step toward the refrigerator then stopped. No, he had erased the board after he had copied the names onto a legal pad from his office. Calm down, damn it, he told himself as he turned off the light and left the kitchen. It doesn't help if I get so damned jumpy.

He passed back through the living room on the way to his office, the only other place in the house that Reed might have been. It too was empty and there was no sign of anything wrong.

Picking up the telephone, he dialed Reed's number again. After the fifteenth ring he hung up. Where the hell could he be? Without a clear plan, Nick took a felt tip pen out of a drawer and wrote, "Reed—If you get here, stay here!" on a sheet of paper and tore it from the pad.

He found some tape in another drawer and took a piece from the dispenser, attaching one end to the paper. He went back to the living room and slid a chair to a position across from the front door and posted his note so it wouldn't be missed by anyone coming in. The he left, jogging out to his car in the driveway.

The only thing he could think to do at this point was drive to Reed's apartment, make sure things looked alright there. The problem is, he thought, I don't know where the hell it is. All Reed had told him was that he lived somewhere in Town and Country. That wasn't a great help.

Nick slipped the car in gear and backed out of the driveway. He was going to make another run past Lankford's when something occurred to him. He had given Reed his duplicate key ring, a set of spares he kept in case something happened to his own. That meant that Reed would have access to Nick's office as well as his house.

It was an easy twenty minute drive that Nick made in twelve. As he turned into the familiar lot of Kingman Sanders Inc., he could see Reed's Toyota parked lazily across two spaces in front of the building. Son of a bitch, Nick thought as he parked and hurried to the front door.

It was locked and the lights were out. Nick unlocked the door and strode directly down the short hallway to his office. The green shaded lamp on his desk was on, much like it had been the night he had first met Reed.

This time he wasn't in the chair behind the desk. He was lying in a curl halfway to a fetal position on the couch that Nick used when he entertained customers. Nick slapped hard at the bottom of Reed's feet then stood back near his desk. Reed jerked awake, startled, until he saw Nick and standing in the light. "Don't do that, man. You'll give me a heart attack or something."

"Better you than me. I've been trying like hell to find you."

"How was dinner?" Reed rubbed his eyes and yawned.

"Terrible. I'll tell you about that later. Did you get to Lankford's?"

Reed looked at his watch. "Oh, man. Not yet. I mean, I went there once but I didn't stay. I came here to wait for a while and I guess I fell asleep. Did you go?"

"Just to look for you. Why didn't you stay?"

"There was a car in the parking lot and some of the lights were on inside. I didn't see anybody but I didn't know the car, so I backed off. It wasn't Ray's. What's up?"

Nick related what Marie had told him about James Rooker, Rooker's connection to Hill and Fetterman, and what he feared it all might mean. When he was finished, the two men sat quietly for a moment, considering.

"So you raced all the way back here to see if I was okay?"

"Amazing, isn't it?"

"Well, thanks anyway." He shook his head like a wet dog coming out of a bath. "So what are we going to do next?"

"You're going home. I want you far away from this until I know more about what's going on. I'm going to make one more trip to Lankford's and disable the bugging program for the time being. Beyond that, I don't know yet."

"I don't want to run out on you like this."

"You're not running out on me. I'm asking you to walk away from it."

"Same difference." Reed strafed through his hair with his fingers. "I'm not trying to argue something with you, I just want to let you know that I don't want to do it. I don't want to run or walk away like I'm scared because I'm not. It doesn't feel right."

Nick stood up and held the chain that would turn off the desk lamp between two of his fingers. "Tell you what. For now let's get ourselves over to Lankford's and finish up there. We can talk about this later." Reed stood up and Nick pulled down on the chain. There was enough brightness from the lights in the parking lot coming through the windows to allow them to see their way out.

On the ride over to Lankford's, together in Nick's car, neither man had much to say.

* * *

Nick unlocked the door and Reed walked in ahead of him and turned off the alarm. Without switching on the lights, Nick waited and followed Reed to Walter Lankford's office, which he also opened. Once in, Reed moved to close the blinds and Nick went behind the desk to the computer.

He seated himself in the brown leather chair and reached for the power switch on the computer, housed on the vertical case beneath the desk. He pushed the button until it clicked then pulled his hand halfway back. "This is odd," he said.

"What is?" Reed asked. He walked around the desk next to Nick and looked at the computer monitor.

"Not there," Nick told him. "Down here." He motioned toward the space under the desk with a nod of his head.

"What? All I see is a garbage can."

Nick pulled the small plastic container out from under the desk and looked closely at the contents. Then he picked it up and held it out to Reed. "What's that?"

"The obvious answer would be 'garbage,'" Reed said. "And since it is lying in a garbage bag in somebody's garbage can, I'd pretty much have to go with that." He reached into the container and withdrew his hand, a brown Snicker's wrapper pinched between two fingers. "Or am I missing something?"

"The whole point," said Nick. "What happens here on Friday nights? On Wednesday and Friday nights?"

Reed cocked an eyebrow. "Oh."

"If Ray Alvarado cleaned the office, which would have included emptying the garbage cans, who—"

"—threw away the candy wrapper," Reed finished. He handed the garbage can back to Nick who returned it to its place under the desk then placed a diskette in the drive and began the process of removing the file containing the screen information that had been captured that day. After a minute, he removed the diskette and replaced it with another. He hit a key on the keyboard to continue the process. Reed hadn't moved.

"When did you see that car tonight?" Nick asked him. "Was it before Ray would have been here, or after?"

Reed didn't hesitate. "It was after. Definitely after."

Nick thought on that for a moment, again switching diskettes when the current one became full.

"What do you think it means?" Reed asked.

Nick shook his head slowly. "I don't know. Maybe nothing. Maybe Walter Lankford stopped by before we got here. Maybe Ray got hungry while he was cleaning and popped a candy bar."

"But these things don't worry you."

"No, they don't. What worries me is that there are too many things going on here that we don't understand. The more things we find, the more nervous I get." He swapped another diskette out of the drive. "On the other hand, it could be I'm just being paranoid. What do you think?"

Reed moved around the desk and sat in one of the two chairs that were facing it. "I don't know, boss. You're in charge here."

Nick shook his head again and another few minutes went by

as he continued the removal of the computer file from Lankford's machine. When he was through, he sat up in front of the monitor and rapidly typed in a new command. He told Reed he was disabling the bugging program. He wanted to figure more of this out before they exposed themselves in Lankford's office again.

"Sounds like a good idea."

Nick turned off the computer and the monitor and Reed moved to re-open the blinds. As they were leaving the building, Nick stopped him. "What kind of car was it that you saw earlier?" He was thinking that it shouldn't be too difficult to find out what kind of car Walter Lankford drove and they could reconcile this latest coincidence that way.

"It wasn't really a car," Reed said. "It was a pickup truck."

Oh no, thought Nick.

"I didn't see the make or model or anything, but it was one of those extended cab jobs."

"What color was it?"

"Purple and black. Really slick looking. I think the windows were tinted but I'm not sure, it was too hard to tell in the dark. Why?"

Nick didn't answer the question. Instead, he swore softly, almost to himself.

They were outside the building walking through the parking lot to Nick's car. Reed took hold of Nick's upper arm, making him stop. "What is it?" he asked. "What's wrong?"

"I know that truck."

* * *

They drove to Clearwater, to the beach where they had first found MamaLu Bates. They had no idea where she lived and no clear idea where to begin looking.

"It's almost 2:30 in the morning, Nick. How are we going to find her?"

"I don't know," Nick said as he pulled over and parked at a meter on the side of the street. "But we've got to try."

They walked along the sidewalk fronting the public beach, stopping at the pay phone kiosks as they went. There was plenty of artificial light shining down from the street lamps and the motels across the street. A mole cricket scurried across the sidewalk under their feet and made a sound like a flash bulb popping when Reed stepped on it. "Whoops," he said.

The first kiosk had a short length of frayed cable swinging back and forth carelessly in the ocean breeze. No phone books. The second one had a copy of just the yellow pages, and the third one had both. Nick snatched them up and balanced the hard plastic cover on his knee as he looked up the name 'Bates.'

After a minute, he let the books drop and resume their dangle at the end of the cable. "Nothing," he said and turned toward the ocean. They couldn't see it from the sidewalk, a rolling mound of sand was between them, but the white noise of the waves washing onto the shore filled the air like the mist from a dense fog.

Nick led Reed back to the car. They drove through the streets near the beach until fatigue was mixing with futility and Nick turned the car toward home. It was an absurd hope, he thought, trying to find her truck.

They decided to leave Reed's car at Nick's office for the night and drove directly to Nick's house. As they pulled into the driveway, not long before the appearance of the sun, Reed asked, "Do you have any idea what's been going on?"

Nick shook his head no. "I wish I did." Those were the first words he had spoken since they had left the beach.

CHAPTER SIXTEEN

They were back in Clearwater a short time later after managing just a few hours of sleep. The senior citizens were out walking the beach and the laughing gulls were gathering in the sand in front of the snack bar, waiting for breakfast scraps or the arrival of the careless tourists.

Nick went to the employees working the counter and then to the cooks preparing the food, describing MamaLu and asking them if they had any idea where she lived or how he could find her. Several of them recognized her and said she was a regular but didn't know anything more about her.

They moved across the street to the restaurants and shops that were open, catering to the early morning trade. Nick asked the questions while Reed as often as not waited outside, fighting down his lack of sleep.

A little over an hour into their search, Nick walked out of a corner diner that looked like it had been serving greasy breakfasts since before any of the chain hotels had been built across the street on the beach. "We've got something," Nick said as Reed fell into step beside him. "Guy inside says he knows her well, she's eaten breakfast there for years. Said she lives in the apartment building a block up this way. He said he would be surprised if she didn't show up for breakfast in an hour or two." Reed didn't answer; he wasn't sure what to say.

They walked up to the apartment building, what looked like a large two story gray house with painted white shutters and window trim. Outside of the front door were eight rusty black mail boxes hanging in two rows on nails driven into the wooden siding. A black plastic label said 'L. Bates" on the mail box third in on the bottom row. "This is it," Nick said.

There were eight worn and weathered doorbell buttons mounted vertically along the right side of the door frame. Standing behind Nick, Reed could see no way to match the proper buttons to the names on the mail boxes.

The door itself was a steel screen mesh with broken supports welded laterally a third of the way up from the bottom and a third of the way down from the top. The middle section was pushed in, partially broken off of the frame. It looked as if it had been kicked in a number of times. On the other side was a hallway leading back to the rear of the building.

"Push this in a little more, will you?" Nick indicated the broken mesh. Reed stepped up and applied pressure with both hands until Nick could reach in and turn the handle from the inside. As the door started to open, Nick said, "Hold it until I get my arm out."

Once inside, they walked down the hallway reading the little cards tacked to the front of the four apartment doors on the ground floor. At the last door on the left hand side, Reed stopped and said, "Here it is." The faded white paper had the name 'Bates' typed crookedly across its front.

Reed stepped to the side as Nick joined him. "Now what?" he whispered. "Do we knock?"

"Not if we don't have to. I don't want anybody else to hear." Nick grabbed the door knob and turned it lightly until it stopped. There was a dull click as the latch cleared the catch in the door frame. It was unlocked.

Nick let go of the knob and they stood in the hallway and watched as the door swung slowly open, carried inside to the wall by the force of its own weight. They had a view of half of the apartment, neatly decorated but without much style. Across from the door, on the other side of the living room, was the small kitchen. Nick could see something large on the floor. "Get inside," he told Reed. "Quickly."

They entered the apartment and Nick gently pushed the door closed with the top of his foot. "Don't touch anything."

"No problem," Reed said. He put his hands in his pockets and swiveled his head as he scanned the room. His eyes followed Nick as his friend moved toward the kitchen. Then he saw it, too. "Oh, shit," he said, whispering again.

MamaLu's immense body lay in a grotesque sprawl across the kitchen linoleum. Her eyes were wide open but there was no life there. Her throat was an ugly series of black and purple blotches.

"She's dead, isn't she?" Reed asked.

"Yes, she is."

Nick knelt down beside Lu Bates, careful to avoid the sticky puddle of half evaporated waste that framed the lower half of her body. He examined the marks he saw on her wrists and then studied the fingers on her left hand. Reed watched, simultaneously repulsed and fascinated, unable to turn away and unsure of why.

"She was handcuffed," Nick said. "And some of her fingers are broken, you can see by the knuckles." Reed didn't comment.

Her shirt had been cut open from the collar all the way down and one half lay across each breast, not meeting in the middle, leaving a gap of several inches. She looked as if she were wearing a vest. Nick gingerly lifted the edge of the fabric and slowly pulled it up and back. MamaLu's bra had been cut as well and it lay across the top of her breasts, one of which was now exposed to the still air of the tiny kitchen.

Nick counted twelve small but deep puncture wounds surrounding the nipple. He thought of the carving Fetterman had left on the picnic table in the park that Monday several weeks before, of the Swiss army knife he had used and how many corkscrews, blades, and scratch awls it contained.

He stood up and turned away from the body. Reed's face was ashen as Nick took him by the elbow and steered him toward the door. "You going to be all right?" he asked.

After a moment, Reed nodded his head. "I just need a minute."

"No time, buddy. We have to go now." He opened the front door and motioned for Reed to pass through, thankful that so far, at least, Reed hadn't bent over and emptied his stomach.

The hall was as quiet now as it was when they had entered. Without rushing, the two men walked out of the building and down the block the way they had come. When they were back at the car, Nick asked Reed how he was feeling. "A little better. The air helps."

"If you're going to lose it, now's the time."

"No, I'm alright. Just be thankful we didn't stop for an Egg McMuffin on the way over."

They got into the car and Nick pulled out onto the street. "Something I didn't tell you about Hill and Fetterman," Nick said. "One of them likes his pocket knife."

* * *

As they came to a stop in front of Nick's garage, another car pulled in behind them, blocking the mouth of the driveway. Nick recognized it in the rear view mirror while Reed swiveled in his seat. "What's going on?" he asked.

"Turn around and don't say anything."

They heard one of the doors open and slam shut. Nick opened his own door, said, "Stay here," and stepped out onto the concrete.

Through his window Reed heard him say, "'Morning, Hill. Nice of you to turn up."

The other man's footsteps stopped and a gruff voice said, "Is that so?"

"I've got something for you."

It was occurring to Reed that if these cops were doing the things Nick thought they were doing, both of their lives were probably in danger. For the first time, the reality of what they were involved with hit home. It was suddenly easier to sit in the car and stare at the glove compartment.

He heard Nick say to Hill, "What's wrong with Fetterman?"

"He's not feeling well. He's good where he is."

Nick considered that for a moment. "Okay," he said and began to walk toward the house.

Hill followed him for a few steps then stopped, turned, and bent forward. With his hands on his knees, he peered through the windshield at Reed. "What about him?"

Reed felt his insides tighten as, still staring at the glove box, he heard Nick say, "This has nothing to do with him. This is just us."

Hill stayed where he was for a moment, studying Reed's face before straightening and turning away. "If you say so," he said.

Nick hadn't stopped moving and was already at the front door. As the two men disappeared inside, Reed tried to force himself to relax. Images of MamaLu's pale white body lying gracelessly in a puddle of filth made him keenly aware of the second policeman sitting in the car behind him, not fifteen yards away.

He had a wild thought about getting out of the car and running madly down the street. Fight or flee. He didn't know what Nick was planning, if anything, and he had no idea what was going to happen inside that house.

* * *

"I haven't been completely honest with you," Nick said.

"You're kidding."

Nick ignored him. "I've been able to get information off of Lankford's computer system for the past week. I haven't seen any sign of illegal activity but I haven't had a chance to look for anything regarding those names you gave me. I want to give all the information to you now, see what you can do with it."

Nick moved to his computer and turned it on. Hill didn't say anything. He just stood where he was, hands in his pockets, watching Nick.

"I'm going to show you how to use a program I wrote that will let you look at what was happening on Lankford's computer. It's easy but you should probably take a couple of notes." He looked to Hill in the center of the room. Move, you bastard prick, Nick thought. Do something.

"Why all the bullshit, Nick? Why not let me know you were in there? I gotta tell you, I'm bothered by this attitude. This whole dishonesty thing."

Was he serious? This murdering son of a bitch? Cool it, Nick told himself. He had to sell his story right now or both he and Reed might not make it past this afternoon. "You know why I'm doing this. I want to find who killed Tim Clayton, and why. If I got you in there, at Lankford's, you wouldn't need me any more and I'd be out of it. I didn't want that to happen."

From his spot in the center of the room, Hill stared at Nick, who was fighting to keep his pulse from accelerating, keep from showing signs of the stress and nervousness he was feeling. He was tight beneath the skin, but he couldn't allow any of it to show. Not yet.

Slowly Hill said, "So why change your mind now?"

Forcing himself to speak at the same pace, Nick told him, "I don't know. I guess I'm older and wiser and I just don't want to put myself through it any more. I thought I did but I changed my mind. I'll do what I can to help you get them, but you get paid for the dirty work. You do it. It's just not worth it to me."

Hill grinned and looked at the floor, casually shaking his head back and forth. Nick knew this expression, the 'You never could make it as a cop' look he had seen from Hill before. "Okay." Hill reached inside his jacket pocket and pulled out a notebook and pen. He joined Nick behind the desk and said, "Show me how this thing of yours works."

It didn't take long. Hill knew how to use a computer and Nick walked him through the steps of restoring the program and captured files to the computer. He showed him how to start and use the reader program as well as how to exit it once he'd finished.

Hill took two pages of notes while Nick began to back up the appropriate files to a set of diskettes. "So you've got, what, a week's worth of info off of Lankford's system? You can see everything that guy did for the past week?"

"Yes."

"And you can get more." Meant as a question.

"Let me know when you're done with what I've given you and I'll get more."

Hill held out his hand and Nick gave him the box of diskettes. Without another word, they left the house and walked out to the cars parked in the driveway. The single occupants of each vehicle were as they were when Nick and Hill had gone inside. Nick stopped next to his car. Hill didn't seem to notice. "Let me know what you find," he called.

"Of course," Hill said as he opened his door and slid into the seat. He pulled the door shut and stuck his head through the window. "Just be sure you're somewhere I can find you."

Nick gave him a wave and watched as Hill started the car and backed it away. Don't worry, he thought.

After the two cops had disappeared down the block Nick turned and motioned for Reed to get out of the car. "How you doing?"

"Oh man oh man oh man."

"You okay?"

Reed looked down the block to make sure that the car was really gone. "I feel like I've been sitting in front of an ornery King Cobra, waiting for him to get hungry or pissed off enough to strike out at his dinner."

"Did he do anything?"

"You kidding? He didn't have to." He combed his hair back with his fingers. "How'd it go in there?"

Nick told him what had gone on inside the house. "Now we have to hurry."

"Why?" Reed asked. "It sounds like he bought it."

"He did. That's why he left. But he'll be back."

"Why is that?"

"Because I didn't give him Lankford's data. I gave him the junk I used for testing while I was writing the program."

"Oh boy." Reed followed Nick into the house, who led him back to the room with the computer. "So tell me this," he said. "Which is the one with the knife? The one that was with you, or the one that stayed with me?"

"The cobra."

"It figures."

Nick picked up the phone and dialed the number for his partner, John Sanders. He recognized the voice that answered and said, "John, this is Nick."

"Nick! I was just thinking about you. How are you doing?"

"Not too bad." His partner's voice reminded him there was another world out there, the one he tried so hard to find when he quit being a cop. No dead bodies, no lost friends, no dirty policemen. Katy.

"Seriously? I know you, buddy, and that's your stock answer."

"Things are kind of complicated right now, John. Look, I need you to do a couple of things."

"Sure, Nick. Anything you need."

"You've got to get to the office and make sure we have backups of everything and get them off site. Don't leave anything we can't afford to lose."

John said, "Okay," somewhat hesitantly, like somebody was speaking to him in a foreign language and he wasn't sure he was quite getting the meaning. "That's mostly done anyway. Are we expecting a hurricane I haven't heard about?"

"Something like that."

"Alright, then. I'll do it first thing Monday morning."

"No, John, you've got to do it now. As soon as we get off the phone. And I want you to make sure that nobody, even you, is alone in the office after hours. Especially you."

There was an uncomfortable silence on the line. Then, "What's going on?"

"Probably nothing, John. These are just precautions."

"Against what? Is something going on we should know about, Nick?"

Nick wasn't sure what he meant with that 'we.' "I don't think so."

"Are you all right?"

"John, I've got to go. Get over to the office, get the backups, then get out of there. If any police show up, don't tell them you've spoken to me."

"Oh, Jesus, Nick, the police?"

But he had hung up.

"What was all that about?" Reed asked.

"I don't want Hill trashing my office looking for the real data from Lankford's computer." Nick opened a desk drawer and withdrew a blank tape for the backup unit attached to the computer. "And we have to do the same thing I told John to do. We need to get this stuff off of this computer and get the hell out of Dodge." Nick inserted the tape into the drive and typed a command into the computer while a high speed whirring seeped out of the backup unit.

"Could you please just talk to me for a minute? I mean, I know we're in a hurry, but I don't like having this feeling that I don't understand what's going on. You can tell me to go to hell if you want but I would really like to know what's happening here, especially if we're in more danger now than before."

Nick forced himself to slow down and sit back in the chair. He was tense, like a sprinter in the blocks waiting for the starter's gun, but he didn't want to overlook Reed.

"I'm sorry," he told him. "I wasn't expecting anything like this to happen to you. Or to Lu Bates, either." He held his palms to his eyes and applied pressure. Tiny explosions of light rebounded from somewhere in his skull to the insides of his eyelids. Reed lowered himself into one of the chairs and waited.

"As of now, we know of three people killed because of this thing. Tim Clayton, my friend, someone named James Rooker whom I don't even know, and Lu Bates." Nick looked somewhere deep into the computer monitor. "I should have handled her differently. It's my fault she's dead."

Reed wanted to argue but didn't know what to say. After a minute he asked, "What was she doing at Lankford's?"

"I think she made a set of keys for herself and I think she was trying to get her hands on whatever it was she thought we were after. Or something like that. It doesn't really matter. Whatever she was doing, it crossed her with Hill and Fetterman and she didn't deserve that. She didn't know anything worth killing her for."

The same ugly images filled Reed's mind and imagination and he fought down another wave of nausea. He wondered how long it would take for him to be able to forget the details of what he had seen in the apartment.

"And now, we have to assume that Hill and Fetterman know everything she did, which means we have to assume they know about you." He caught and held Reed's eyes. Although Reed couldn't see it, he could hear the emotion behind his friend's words. "We have to be very careful about everything we do from here on."

"And what are we going to do?"

"Something's broken here and we're going to fix it. The first thing we do, we get our stuff together and get the hell out of here. I don't think we want to be here when Hill and Fetterman come back." Reed nodded emphatically. "Then we get your car out of the lot at my office and back to your apartment. From there we'll find a hotel in St. Pete or somewhere and set up shop."

"Which means what?"

"We find out who those four names belong to and why they're so important."

* * *

They wound up at an unlikely place called the Tropicana Resort on St. Pete Beach, southeast of Tampa on the Gulf of Mexico. Nestled between two hotels belonging to two different national chains, the Tropicana catered mostly to senior citizens and college students, guests with enough money to stay at the beach but not enough to complain about the quality of the facilities.

Nick took a first floor single room with a set of double beds and he and Reed unpacked their suitcases and the notebook-sized portable computer Nick had brought. "We need to find a phone," he told Reed when they had finished.

"What's wrong with this one?" Reed asked, pointing to the telephone that came with the room.

"It's not a pay phone," Nick said. "If anything else goes wrong, I don't want to leave a record pointing to someone else who could be hurt."

"You're getting awfully serious on me, Nick."

"It should have happened sooner."

Reed followed him out of the door and they walked two blocks up Gulf Boulevard to a phone booth where Nick paid in a quarter and dialed a number from a piece of paper he had tucked in his pocket. He let it ring until it was answered by a machine and then he hung up.

"No go?" Reed asked.

"We'll have to keep trying. In the meantime, let's go back and take another look at the data from Lankford's. Now that we have some specific names to look for, hopefully we can learn something about what's been going on."

CHAPTER SEVENTEEN

Nick finally reached Jody Ebberts just after eight o'clock that evening. Jody was a research consultant that Nick had worked with professionally. She told him that she was surprised to hear from him and was on her way out for dinner.

"Surprised?" Nick asked. "Why?"

"Just because it's been a while since I've talked to you. How're things at good old Kingman-Sanders, Inc.?"

"Same as always," Nick answered carefully.

"So what are you doing calling me on a Saturday night when I'm about to go out on a date? What's so critical?"

Nick told her that he had a job for her that he didn't think would be anything unusual. But it was very important and he needed it done as soon as possible.

"You're not going to ask me to cancel my plans for tonight, are you? I've really been looking forward to this date."

She offered her services on the following day, but she would have to charge him her weekend rates plus a rush fee.

Nick agreed easily. "That's fine, Jody," he told her. "Let me tell you what I need."

"Hang on one sec while I grab a pen." Nick heard a hollow clunk as she dropped the phone onto a table or counter. A few seconds later she picked it up again. "Go ahead."

Nick read her the four names that he had gotten from Hill from a piece of paper in his pocket, being careful to spell each one so there wouldn't be a mistake.

"Geez," she said. "A couple of these guys are familiar, I think. Who are they supposed to be?"

"I don't have any idea whatsoever. I need anything and everything you can get me on these guys. I assume they have something to do with the Tampa Bay area or Florida but I could be wrong. Other than that, I don't know a thing about them."

"Okay," Jody said, considering. "Are there any particular places you want me to check?" Jody performed her research by using her computer to query enormous collections of magazines, newspapers, databases, encyclopedias, and a number of other on-line sources.

"I don't want to tell you to look for anything in particular," Nick said. "I'd just be guessing and I wouldn't want to steer you in a wrong direction. I just need everything you can give me."

"That's pretty wide open, It could take me more time than you think."

"Time is critical, Jody. I won't tell you why, but it goes beyond business and I need your help."

Nick heard the sound of a sigh come over the phone. "Alright, Nick, you got me. But not until tomorrow, okay? Then I'll hit it hard until I get what you want. Deal?"

"Deal."

"Good," she said. "Now I've got to get moving or I'll be late. Give me your phone number so I don't have to look it up."

"You can't call me, Jody. I'll have to check in with you."

"Are you out of town or something?"

"Something like that. I'm staying away from the office for a bit and I'm a little hard to reach."

They said a quick good night and Nick returned the phone to its cradle.

At least I hope I'm a little hard to reach, he thought. He walked back to Reed and the hotel, looking up at the darkening sky, trying to remember when was the last time he had taken Katy out on a date on a Saturday night.

***

"You are one pale skinned white boy."

Reed looked at his reflection in the hotel room mirror. "You forgot to mention my bathing suit's ugly, too."

"I didn't want to come on too strong."

"I see." Reed puffed out his chest and turned sideways. "Nobody's going to believe I'm not tan because I spend all my time in the gym, are they?"

"'Fraid not." The lights were out in the hotel room and Nick was standing at the window, looking out between the edge of the curtain and the door. It was nine o'clock on Sunday morning and already the sun was hot and the sky a rich blue. "You know what the problem with Florida is?" he asked Reed.

"What's that?"

"You look out at a day like this, sunshine, blue skies, gentle breezes, waves beaching themselves at your feet, and it's just too damned hard to believe in all of the crime, violence, and drugs we live with after dark. We should probably just give it all back, the whole state, to the old people and the cattle. Pre-tourism days. Better yet, to the Indians. Let them handle it."

"What about the cow pies on the shuffleboard courts?"

"It's better than tortured bodies on the kitchen floor. Or broken ones pounding into the ocean."

Reed stepped away from the sink and sat on the edge of one of the beds. "Nick, you know I'm sorry about what happened to MamaLu."

"It's okay, Reed."

"I feel so disrespectful, like I need to apologize to somebody but I don't know who or why."

Nick turned around and cleared off the top of the lone table in the room. He took the portable computer out of its case and set it on the tabletop, along with a legal pad and a pen. He didn't answer Reed.

"Nick, I've got to ask you something."

Nick had powered on the computer and was waiting to begin the process of loading in the captured data from Lankford's. He looked up at Reed and waited.

"You're going to look for the presence of those four names in the data that we've got, I'm going to burn like a lobster killing time on the beach, and in the meantime we wait for your friend to do her work."

"Yeah?"

"Well, what then? What exactly are we going to do once we get to that point?"

Nick typed a command into the computer and fed it a disk. He pressed the return key and the sound of the spinning three and a half inch platter resonated through the dim silence of the room.

"We're going to stop this thing." Again he met Reed's eyes. "Whatever it is, we're going to see it end."

After a moment Reed nodded his head and mouthed the word, 'Okay.' Then he plucked a towel from the wire rack on the wall above the sink and left for the beach, momentarily flooding the room with morning brightness as he softly opened then closed the door.

Nick had been serious. He could see it in his face despite the dimness of the room. He trudged through the warming sand towards the salt water of the Gulf of Mexico and thought about what Nick told him. We're going to end this thing. Reed hadn't known what to answer. All he could think of were two questions that seemed stuck, spinning unanswered in his mind: What would they be able to do to stop Hill and Fetterman, and what would he have looked like if they had found him at Lankford's instead of MamaLu.

* * *

"I've got all four of them. It wasn't that hard, either. Actually, you'll probably recognize these guys yourself from reading the morning paper."

"I don't think so. I don't do that anymore."

Jody Ebberts laughed. "You're probably better off that way.

I'm kind of a news junkie myself, though. Comes in handy in this line of work."

"What kind of stuff did you get on these guys?"

"Let's see, mostly what I have are Florida newspaper accounts, along with some magazine things, a few of them national. It fills in who they are, where they're from, and what they got arrested for. I need to ask you how far back you want me to go."

"What did they get busted for?"

"The drug trade, Nick. You really don't know anything about these guys, do you?"

Nick told her no, that's why he called her. She laughed again.

"Well, here's a synopsis of what I've got."

He listened without interrupting for fifteen minutes until Jody stopped and asked, "Now do you need more than that? I mean, I can keep going, try to find out what their sixth grade teachers wrote on their little report cards, stuff like that, and that's assuming they have those things back in old Mexico. Or do you think you have what you need?"

What she had was probably perfect, he told her. "But I have one more favor to ask you," he said.

"Oh oh. And you've already used most of my Sunday. What is it now?"

Nick glanced at his watch. It was nearly six o'clock and he hadn't seen Reed since mid-afternoon. "Could I talk you into meeting me somewhere with everything that you've found? You can stay on the clock and I'll buy you dinner. I would really appreciate it, Jody. This is important."

She hesitated just a moment before answering. "You've got something going on here that involves more than just your business, don't you?"

"Yes," Nick answered. "It's something of a personal situation."

"Alright, Nick," she said with no more questions. "Tell me when and where."

He suggested a time and a restaurant in the area called Rocky Point, near the Tampa airport. Jody said she'd meet him there and they hung up. Nick stood for a moment, leaning against the pay phone kiosk, wondering if he had all the pieces now. And if he could make them fit.

He left the sidewalk and walked across the sand, angling toward the water in the direction of the hotel, looking for Reed. There was another piece that had to be figured out. He had to find something to do with Reed.

* * *

They met Jody at the restaurant and spent an hour going through most of the material she had brought. While Nick read the newspaper and magazine accounts, Jody spoke with Reed, whom she claimed looked like a raccoon because of the white image of sunglasses that seemed tattooed on the red skin of his sunburnt face.

After the dinner, Jody left for home with her fee and a generous bonus, and Nick and Reed drove into Tampa, contemplating what they had learned.

"Where are we going?" Reed asked.

"I want to check something."

The two men rode in silence, Nick driving while Reed watched the lights of the city flash and sparkle as they traveled by.

They left the highway at the exit they would take if they were going to Nick's house, but drove on past the normal street and turned two blocks further down. Before Reed could ask him if he had done that on purpose, they turned again and Reed decided to keep silent. Nick drove for another quarter mile before pulling the car over and parking at the curb.

He reached up and slid the lever for the car's dome light to the 'off' position so that it wouldn't come on when the doors were opened. "I know this sounds cloak-and-daggerish, but I want you to sit here in the driver's seat and keep the keys in the ignition. If anybody comes up to you or if I'm not back in twenty minutes, I want you to get out of here and get your ass back to the hotel."

"And do what?"

"I don't know, get a good night's sleep then work on your tan." He opened the door and got out of the car. Reed slid across the seat and took his place.

"What are you going to do?"

"I told you. I'm going to check on something." And then he was gone, heading across the street and away from the car.

Crickets filled the air with night sounds and the sulfurous smell of reclaimed water erupting from underground sprinklers assaulted his sense of smell. He walked quickly to the corner, and rather than turn and continue down the sidewalk, he moved into the front yard of the house that was there. He walked down the block this way, along the fronts of the houses, until he reached the next corner. There he paused, observing.

Nothing seemed out of place or looked any different than it should. Intellectually he knew that this didn't mean much, that if somebody were watching for him, they would have placed themselves in a position far harder for him to spot. Satisfied there was no obvious surveillance, Nick turned and ran past the first three houses to his left, away from the street he had been following.

Here he stopped again, hesitating just long enough to see that nothing save himself had moved. He sprinted silently across the lawn in front of him, crossing the street and pulling up in a crouch between two sleeping houses. His chest was heaving as he fought to control his breath and subdue the effects of the adrenaline rushing through his body.

He had no idea what Hill's next move would be. He was only just now beginning to figure out what had been going on. But he was reasonably sure that they would be coming after him. How desperately or how hard he had no idea. If they were as motivated as he suspected, they almost certainly would have made a stop at his house.

His breathing slowly caught up to him and he studied the back of the structure. The yard in front of him ended at a low cinder block wall that separated the two properties, the one he was on and his own. He crept across the St. Augustine grass to the row of cinder blocks where he stopped again, crouching behind it. His house looked normal. A layer of sweat, drawn out by the humid night air, blanketed his body as thick as a second skin..

Staying low, he slid over the two foot wall and used his hands to help him in an almost crab-like walk that took him to the back of the house. He stopped again, the only signs of movement his own. A cricket silenced its chirping as he leaned against the outside wall, apparently not comfortable with Nick's presence.

He had positioned himself beneath the windows that looked into the room that was his home office. From the back pocket of his black denim jeans he pulled out a slender miniature flashlight.

In one motion, Nick stood, turned, and clicked on the flashlight as he directed the beam through the glass and into the house. Immediately, it was clear that the room had been wrecked. Papers from his file cabinet were everywhere, his desk had been overturned and the chairs were on their sides against the far wall. His computer lay smashed and broken on the floor.

The violence of the sacking was apparent as the beam of the tiny light tracked across the numerous gaps and holes that cratered the interior walls. Violence that had been directed, Nick knew, at himself.

These bastards are for real, he thought. They are the ones that killed Tim.

He moved his thumb over the switch of the flashlight and swung the beam across the room once more, terminating its arc at the office entrance. Nick had seen what he had come to see and now it was time to go.

As he cut the power to the light, the door exploded inward, freeing itself from the top hinge and slamming hard into the wall. Without hesitating, Nick pushed away from the house and took off in a sprint, across the yard and angling away from the line of sight of the window.

He gave in to the adrenaline as he felt it drive his legs in a pounding rhythm, pushing him farther and faster than he thought he could go. Behind him lights appeared in the window he had just left as he rounded the corner of a neighbor's house. He didn't like the idea of running away but he knew that at this point he had no real choice.

They had wrecked his house, he thought, and they were still there, waiting for him to come home.

CHAPTER EIGHTEEN

Early Monday morning, two men riding in a brown four door sedan pulled into a parking space just outside of the Gulf Coast Memorial Hospital in northeast Tampa. In front of the space was a painted metal sign that read, 'EMERGENCY ROOM PARKING ONLY.'

The two men got out of their car and looked at the entrance to the building. One of them said to the other, "What time you got?"

The second man checked his watch. "'Bout eight thirty."

"When I called this morning, they said she'd be here by eight, eight fifteen. Jump in the back seat and wait for us." He started walking toward the entrance. Without turning his head or raising his voice he said, "This shouldn't take too long."

Inside the hospital, there was no sign of the frenetic energy and activities that would have taken place during the weekend. Instead there was a sterile quiet, made up of an empty pastel waiting room and a woman in a white sweater reading a newspaper behind the receptionist's window. "May I help you?" she asked as he approached.

"Yes, ma'am, I believe you could," he said, flashing his best southern gentleman smile. "I'm looking for a Ms. Katherine Kingman. I was told I could find her here this morning."

"Oh, Katy's in one of the doctor's offices," the woman said, returning the smile and reaching for her phone. "Who can I say is calling?"

"Just tell her a friend of her husband's is here to see her, if you would."

"I'd be happy to."

He waited at the window while she dialed an extension and

spoke a few words into the phone. When she replaced the handset in its cradle, the man said, "Thank you very much," and wandered back towards the waiting room, out of easy hearing of the courteous woman.

A minute later, a tall woman dressed in a nurse's uniform came out of a door further up the hall and stopped briefly at the window, exchanging some words. Then she turned and walked up to the man in the waiting room.

"I'm Katy Kingman," she said. She kept her hands in the pockets of her smock, unsure of how to take her early morning visitor. "You asked to see me?"

Dark hair, dark skin, nice figure. Old Nick's done alright for himself. "I'm Detective Randolph Hill of the Tampa P.D., Ms. Kingman. I'm here at your husband's request." As he spoke, he offered one of his business cards, which she accepted.

"Nick? Is he alright?"

This is good, Hill thought, relaxing. She doesn't know anything's wrong. "Ma'am, I'd like you to step outside for just a moment, if you would. There's a gentleman in my car and I'd like you to take a look at him."

"A gentleman?" An expression of concern wrinkled her forehead. "Should I get a doctor?"

Hill shook his head no. "That's not really necessary, ma'am. Your husband told us where to find you and suggested we come here."

With a quick glance back at the receptionist's window, Katy nodded and said, "After you."

Instead of turning and leading her out the door, Hill reached forward and took her elbow, intending to guide her to the car. After a moment's stiffness, she allowed it and they walked side by side down the short hallway, through the glass electric sliding doors and out of the building. The bright morning sunshine was already promising a hot and humid day, making itself felt as they walked away from the hospital air conditioning.

"He's in here," Hill said, bringing her to the sedan and opening one of the rear doors. The door he chose was the one across from where Fetterman sat, picking at the dirt under his fingernails with one of the small tools from his pocket knife. Katy climbed in and Hill quickly closed the door behind her.

"What do you want me to do?" she asked as Hill got into the front seat on the driver's side.

"Look at him," he told her indicating Fetterman, who turned his face past her toward the rear window so that she could see the red and purple bruise on the left side of his face.

Katy brought her hand up and gently felt the bones in his cheek and jaw, and then looked into both eyes one at a time. Then she did it again. "Well, this doesn't look like it's anything serious. Did you get in a fight?"

Hill made a snorting sound from the front seat. "Somebody hit him, all right. Didn't she, Fetterman?"

"Yeah, but you should see the other gal."

Katy sat back against the seat, away from Fetterman. "Where's my husband?" she asked.

"Actually, we were hoping you could tell us."

Katy looked at Hill for a moment, and then at Fetterman. Feeling uneasy, she turned and grabbed the door handle, pulling it towards her with both hands. The door was locked. Before she could do anything more, Fetterman grabbed her by the shoulder and pulled her into the back of the seat.

In a voice loud enough to make her stop squirming, Hill said, "We want to know where we can find you husband."

Katy, still pinned to the seat by Fetterman, said almost proudly, "I don't know. We've been living apart for a couple of weeks."

They looked at each other for a long moment, each taking the other's measure. Hill was impressed by the control in this woman's attitude. Finally he said, "Okay," and turned to start the car.

"Wait a minute," she said to his back, struggling to sit up. "You can't just take me away from here!"

"Sure we can." Hill backed the car out of the parking space and then put the car in drive and headed toward the street.

Behind him, Fetterman was attempting to lock a set of handcuffs to Katy's wrists. "No!" she screamed as loud as she could. "Somebody help me!"

Hill stomped on the brakes and inertia carried both Fetterman and Katy to the edge of the rear seat. "Somebody help me!" she screamed again as she lurched back. The windows were rolled up and there was little chance that anybody outside the car could hear her. There was nobody in sight.

"Silly girl," Hill said. "Don't you know you have the right to remain silent?" He brought his left hand up and over the edge of the front seat, already clenched into a fist, and sharply drove it into her chin. Katy slumped sideways into Fetterman.

"That's better," he said. "We have a long drive and I'd rather listen to the radio."

"Good morning," Reed managed through a yawn, contorting his body into a crooked stretch. He pinched the sleep from the inside corners of his eyes and pushed himself up into a sitting position. Nick was in the chair in front of their little round table, his face illuminated by the dull glow of the computer screen. Like the morning before, the heavy drawn curtains kept the hotel room dim, depriving them of the mid-morning sunshine.

"You haven't been sitting there all night, have you?"

Nick answered first with a yawn of his own then, "No. I went to sleep a little after you did. I just got up about a half hour ago."

Reed looked doubtfully at the other double bed. It did look as though it had been slept in. He threw the covers off his own bed and yawned again. "Well, I'm no good without my morning shower. I'll be out in a minute."

It was more like thirty. Reed eventually emerged from the bathroom wrapped in one towel and scrubbing the wetness out of his hair with another. He dug a set of clean clothes out of his gym bag, dressed quickly, then moved to look over Nick's shoulder. "So where are we at?"

Nick was slow to answer. He still had to decide what he was going to do with Reed. On the screen was an image from Lankford's captured data. It was a complex form and one of the four names Hill had given them was at the top. In the bottom right hand corner was a number with a dollar sign in front of it, something over fifteen million dollars.

"Whoah," Reed said. "That's some serious bucks." He watched as Nick picked up a pen and copied the amount to a sheet of paper. He wrote it below another number, one that was even greater.

"Follow the money," Nick said, laying his pen down on the pad.

"What do you mean?"

"It always leads back to the center of whatever is happening."

"Are we there? Do we know what the center is yet?"

"Not quite, no." Nick hit the escape key to exit the program then reached to the side of the computer and powered it off. "I have a good idea but I have to do some more digging before I can be sure."

Reed grew excited and stepped around the table into the center of the room. "Then that means we're almost through, doesn't it? It's almost over." Nick didn't say anything.

"We can take what we know, turn it over to the D. A., someone who won't try to kill us, watch the bad guys go to jail, and check the hell out of this vacation paradise." Reed felt the pressure they had been under flow out of his body as he spoke, making him feel lighter as he paced a circle on the floor. He was on the moon, disregarding the effects of gravity. He hadn't been aware of just how much tension he had been holding.

"Not quite."

"What's that?" Reed asked, a blanket falling over his euphoria.

"We don't have any hard evidence."

Reed looked at Nick with wide eyes, incredulous. "Boy, there's one in every crowd, isn't there? What do you call all this?" He gestured toward the computer. "And MamaLu, your friend, this Rooker guy. What about them?"

"We know they're behind all this, Reed. We know what they're doing. But they can come right out and tell us to our face and unless we can physically demonstrate it in a court of law it won't mean anything to anybody."

"Well, that's just great. That's fucking great. What about us then, goddamn it? Are we supposed to just slink around like rats or cockroaches digging for scraps while they go off killing anybody they choose? While they come after us?"

Reed's characteristic good humor was gone. Nick sat up in his chair slowly. Damn it, he thought. He should have seen this coming. Now he had to see if this thing would blow itself out or if his friend was truly going to lose it.

Reed spun in a circle in the center of the room, then stopped facing his unmade bed. He raised his arms high above his head, hands clenched into fists, and pounded his upper body hard into the mattress, bending at the waist, folding his knees and letting himself sink to the floor. He lay there for a moment, his face in the sheets, while Nick remained in his chair, poised to stand. Half ready to help, half ready to thump the bed himself.

After a minute, Reed rolled over with his back propped against the bed, and pulled a sheet down over his head. "That really sucks, Nick, you know that?"

"Yes, it does."

"No, I mean this sheet stinks." He pulled it off his face and cast it back on the bed. "What the hell are we paying for, anyway? No HBO and smelly sheets. I knew we should have packed our own linens." He pushed himself to his feet and smoothed his hair back with his fingers, then managed a shy grin. "Sorry for venting there."

"That's all right," Nick said, relaxing himself. "I would have done the same thing last night but I didn't want to wake you."

Reed bent down and shoveled the remainder of the sheets and bed spread back onto the mattress. "So take a shower and let's go get breakfast or lunch or whatever's appropriate. I don't even know what time it is."

He moved to the sink and picked his watch up off the

counter top. It read half past eleven in the morning. "Then you can tell me about all this circumstantial evidence we've got and what it all means."

Nick pushed back from the table and got to his feet. He's better now, he thought. At least for a while.

* * *

The car stopped again. It had stopped before, but she couldn't remember how many times. Two, she thought, but it may have been more.

Katy lifted her chin and watched the clouds of dust roll and swirl outside the car windows as it settled. She tried to sit up but her back ached from the bumping and jarring of the last part of the drive. They had turned off the highway a while ago; she couldn't remember when. She hoped it wasn't important.

The two men who were with her were talking but it was too hard to listen. They weren't looking at her anyway.

Dusty heat pushed its way into the car as two of the doors were opened and the men got out. She watched through the windows as they walked away into a small stand of trees and disappeared. She was alone. This should be significant somehow, she knew. She should get away.

Using her hands, she grabbed hold of the back of the front seat and pulled herself into a sitting position. That was better, but she didn't like having to move both hands at once. Why were they chained together?

It was hard, forcing her body to move sideways across the car seat toward the open door. It was difficult to move at all, with the dull pain in her jaw and the murky cloudiness in her brain. The fog was telling her to lay back, to close her eyes, give in to the dull sleep she had been fighting for a lifetime.

She wouldn't do it, though. She knew what was wrong with herself, the word for it was in her mind somewhere though she couldn't come up with it, couldn't separate it and pull it down from the clouds. You've got to move, you've got to get away from these men, she told herself.

She swung her feet out of the car and tried to lean forward, to move her weight over her legs so she could stand. Instead she had to half turn and use both her hands to push off the metal frame, eventually getting to an upright position, surprising herself with how steady her legs felt.

Go, she commanded herself. Start walking. Don't be here when they come back.

Dust was in her eyes and nostrils and she was squinting against the midday glare. She had no idea where she was and no idea how far they'd come from Tampa. Tall grasses, clumps of trees, and a pair of worn tire ruts that disappeared off to her right were all that she could see.

She focused on the trees where the two men had gone. What were they doing? They didn't abandon her here, did they? But that would be good, she thought, suppressing a momentary panic. Then she could go and find her husband, Nick. He'd help her get home. He'd deal with these two men.

Something about the tire ruts called out in her mind, something about a road, and she began to think that she should walk that way. That makes sense, doesn't it? Follow the road around the trees. Roads lead to places. Places away from here.

She was going to move, going to start, when they walked out from the trees. She felt another rise of panic as they dropped the boat they were dragging and began to walk towards her.

"No!" she yelled and took two steps backward, away from the men. There was a new feeling, a falling sensation, and somewhere inside she tensed for the impact she knew would come. Instead, there was a scratching and scraping as her body dropped backwards into a young mangrove tree. Twigs and branches pulled at her hair and clothes and a feeling of helplessness rose out of her stomach as she watched her feet rise higher than her head and she sank past the ground.

And then she was through, splashing backwards head first into brown, shallow water she hadn't known was there.

* * *

"Leave her in the car, she's not going anywhere. She's still loopy from when I hit her."

Fetterman shrugged okay and both men opened their car doors and stepped out of the air conditioning and into the heat of Florida's spring sun. They had left their jackets in the car and Hill undid the buttons at his wrists and rolled his sleeves up to his elbows as the disturbed dust from the road settled around them. A last look into the car showed the woman still slumped in a corner of the back seat.

"You think it's serious?" Fetterman asked.

"No. Mild concussion, at most. I tagged her pretty good, though." Hill began walking toward a stand of low trees. "Let's get the boat."

They walked a few yards to the trees and disappeared into the clinging branches, both men protecting their eyes from little branches and twigs. They stopped at a regularly shaped mound covered by a camouflage net. "Let's drag it out first and then get the motor."

They pulled the net off the flats boat and left it to one side. There was enough room here to flip the shallow water boat onto its bottom so they could drag it to the river. Hill took hold of it by the bow on one side, and Fetterman took the other. They cleared the trees with the boat between them and angled towards the car.

"Look who's up," Hill said. He motioned forward with his head and dropped his side.

Fetterman looked ahead and saw the woman watching them over the roof of their car. He lowered his side of the boat to the ground and began to walk toward the rear of the car while Hill walked toward the front. They weren't too worried about her at this point. There really wasn't anywhere for her to go. Besides that, she was half out of it and still handcuffed.

Before they had taken half a dozen steps toward her, she screamed the word "No!" then disappeared suddenly behind the car.

"Shit," Hill swore and broke into a run, quickly covering the remaining twenty yards between them and the woman. His partner was just behind him as they came around the car in time to see a single white clad foot disappear through the edge of a mangrove tree.

"The crazy bitch fell in the river," Hill said. They stood for half a minute trying to see signs of Katy through the leaves and branches but the foliage was too thick. Hill moved off to his right about forty feet where they had planned to put the boat in the water. There was a break in the mangroves and the land sloped gently into the water. Standing at the edge of the mud on the river bank, Hill leaned forward but all he could see was part of a single white smocked arm.

"I don't know what she's doing," he called to Fetterman. He began to draw his gun out of the holster on his belt but turned and scrambled up the bank instead. "She looks like she's just sitting there. Let's hurry and get the damned boat. Mating season for gators should be over but I don't want her in the water with those dinosaur sons of bitches.'

"Did you see one?"

"No, but there could be a gator hole anywhere in here."

Both men jogged back to the boat and quickly slid it down to the bank of the narrow river, where they left it with the bow just in the water. The white arm was no longer visible but they could hear Katy moving around in the water. Hill thought about wading in after her but knew that with the soft mud on the river's bottom he wouldn't get there faster than the boat.

They turned and ran back to the trees and their camo netting. A five horsepower motor had been wrapped in a piece of tarp and stored underneath the boat itself. Leaving the blue plastic behind, they carried the motor to the river and hung it off the boat's stern. Hill climbed aboard and Fetterman pushed off, jumping into the back as they drifted away from the shore. He began to work at starting the motor.

As they floated into the middle of the river they could see Katy as she stood bent over in the water, swinging her arms below the surface. "What the hell's she doing now?" Hill asked of no one. After a minute or two the motor caught and sputtered into a steady purr. Fetterman guided the boat upriver and Hill climbed over the side of the boat into the river muck and scooped the woman into his arms.

She tried to struggle but his hold on her was too tight. "Bring it in closer," he said to Fetterman. "I can't walk with her in this crap." Fetterman eased the craft in front of his partner who dropped the exhausted woman onto the bottom of the boat.

"My shoe," she moaned. "I lost my shoe."

"I know the feeling," Hill said, easing his way over the bow. "But don't worry. You're not going to need it."

Katy never heard him. She stopped trying to sit up and let her eyes close against the sun. In a moment, she was asleep where she lay.

"Let's get back to the car and load the supplies, then get the hell out of here."

* * *

She woke up later to a gentle rocking and constant vibration, something different than the car had been. She had no idea how long she'd been out but the thoughts in her head seemed clearer.

Her body was stiff and sore and the longer she was awake the more aware she grew of how uncomfortable she was and how much she needed to move. She struggled to get into a sitting position and as the small boat rocked back and forth from her movements she remembered what had been happening to her. The realization froze her body and she turned her head to look at the men who were with her.

"Don't worry, little darlin'," the one in front said. "We're almost there."

She sat still for a moment, her shackled hands grasping the edge of the boat. She turned to her right to look at the other man, the one who had been in the back seat of the car with her, but he just looked back with a blank expression on his face.

Gradually, she settled into a seat on the floor of the boat, oblivious to the thin layer of water there. She noticed she was only wearing one shoe. She tried to swallow but her tongue was thick and her throat was dry, making her gag.

"Here, drink some of this." The man in the front held out a clear plastic water bottle and she took it from him. Hill, she thought. His name was Hill.

She coughed up the first swallow but then was able to keep some down. She cleared her throat and knew she could speak if she wanted, but she had nothing to say. Instead she looked out at the acres of empty scenery as they drifted steadily by.

The river was much wider here than it had been by the car. On all sides, except for the path of the river stretching out in front of them and the trail of it behind, the landscape looked the same. Bushy Red mangroves lined the shore, sawgrass and clumps of pine and cypress trees punctuated the land behind. Except for the sounds of the motor and the boat moving through the water, the air was still and quiet. Long, tall American egrets, white ibises, brown pelicans and other birds punctuated the isolated landscape. Wherever they were, it was not close to civilization.

She thought about jumping off the boat, maybe try to capsize it and then swim for shore, but she had nowhere to go. Her hands were still chained together, she had only one shoe, and she had no earthly idea where she was. In a swamp somewhere in a small boat with two armed men, who said they were policemen, who were kidnaping her.

The man in the front of the boat pointed a little ahead and to his left. The other one said, "Got it," and turned the boat in that direction. Katy turned her head to see where they were headed.

At first she couldn't make out anything more than just unbroken shore, but as they moved closer she could see a break, an opening into another branch of the slow moving river. It was partially obscured by a clump of mangroves which made the opening only visible from one direction, but there was enough room for them to go through it easily.

This part of the river wasn't as wide across, maybe thirty or forty feet, and the water appeared slightly darker, a deeper shade of brown. A horsefly buzzed around her head, lighting several times as she tried to shoo it away. She saw bright spots if she moved her head too quickly.

Why were they doing this to her? They had mentioned her husband and she wondered if something could have happened to Nick. She looked at Hill sitting in the bow of the boat and decided not to say anything. They weren't going to tell her what was really happening.

They followed the river around another bend and stayed closer to the shore. They moved along the inner bank to a small break in the vegetation where there was a low wooden dock that was little more than some boards laid in the mud and dirt at the water's edge.

Hill clambered out over the bow and tied the boat to a mangrove branch as the other man silenced the motor. The rear of the boat drifted lazily back toward the direction they had come.

"Come on out, missy. The ride's over." Hill stood with one foot on the planks and the other in the boat where he had been sitting. He held his right hand out toward Katy where she would have to stand to be able to reach it. She sat there, staring at it, unable to decide what to do.

"Come on, let's go. You know the line, lady. There's two ways we can do this. Hard or easy, but we're doing it now."

Katy remembered this same man offering one of these hands to her as a fist in her face earlier in the day. Slowly, she brought her stiff legs underneath her and with her hands on the seat ahead of her for balance she forced herself to stand. Hill reached forward and grabbed the chain linking her wrists and pulled her all the way up and out of the boat.

Her legs didn't work quite like they were supposed to and she couldn't make them keep up with the strength and speed of Hill's pull. She scraped one of her shins along the side of the boat and would have collapsed on the shore if Hill hadn't grabbed her around the waist. He started half walking, half dragging her along the wooden dock toward a weathered shack, an ancient hunting cabin made of wood.

There was a hasp and a padlock on the door which Hill opened with a key from his pocket. The one room cabin was dark, the only light coming from the opened doorway.

"Get in," said Hill.

Numbly, Katy stood her ground on the muddy sheet of plywood that terminated this end of the makeshift dock. She didn't want to go in there. In desperation, she looked around her and saw Fetterman walking up the dock with his arms full of grocery bags. To her left and to her right were fields of sharp edged sawgrass, capable of tearing at her thin cotton clothing and slicing into unprotected skin. She knew she was in a swamp, probably far south of Tampa, though she couldn't be sure. And she knew she had no place to go.

Roughly, Hill grabbed her hair and drew it tight around his fingers as he clenched it in his fist. He pulled her face close to his and said in a low voice, "Don't make me tell you twice."

A beat. Then he released her hair, surprisingly gentle, as if to give her a real choice about whether or not she actually wanted to go inside.

Fetterman came up behind them and stopped. Hill moved back from the doorway, leaving her room to pass. Slowly, her eyes down, she walked inside and stood, waiting, while the men came in behind her and closed the door.

CHAPTER NINETEEN

"I think we need to send you on a little vacation."

"What?" Reed lifted his arms, palms up, and turned a slow 360 in the center of the hotel room. "Away from all this?"

Nick ignored him. "Do you have a passport?"

"Sure, back at my apartment. I spent a few weeks in Europe back in high school. Where do you want me to go?"

Nick took the local yellow pages off the top of the dresser and brought it to the table next to the computer. He opened it and found the listings for travel agents, then copied several numbers onto his legal pad. "The Cayman Islands. I think it's the best way to short circuit Hill and Fetterman's plans without anyone else getting hurt." Including you, he thought.

Reed plopped down on the corner of the bed nearest Nick and the table. He was excited at the sudden prospect of going somewhere, doing something positive. "I've always wanted to go to a place like that. What do you want me to do there?"

Nick closed the book and folded the sheet of paper. "Find a really big piggy bank." He put the paper in his shirt pocket and sat back in his chair. His watch showed a time a few minutes past five o'clock in the afternoon. Too late to call an agent today.

"We don't have any hard evidence against Hill and Fetterman, at least not yet, and without it we can't make them stop playing at whatever game this is. But I think we can take away their little prize. With no carrot at the end of their stick, maybe they won't follow it so far."

"Okay," said Reed. "So what exactly do I do in the Cayman Islands?"

The air conditioner kicked to life and Nick had to raise his voice.

"You're going to become a very rich man. I need you to get down there and find the biggest bank you can and open an account. Call me with the details and get a good night's sleep in a nice hotel. If everything goes all right, a day or so later and you can walk in there and collect the object of Hill and Fetterman's wet dreams."

Reed gave a low whistle through the space between his two front teeth. "You can do that from here? You can make that happen?"

Nick nodded at his friend. "I think so. We have the passwords for the four accounts they're interested in from our original keyboard bugging program. Lankford actually accessed all of them on the day we had that thing installed. And after watching a week's worth of business replayed on our own computer, I think I can arrange to transfer most of the money."

Reed lay back on the bed, staring at the mold-accented relief of the textured ceiling paint. It looked like a giant piece of white bread that had been left in the refrigerator too long. "Then what?"

"I don't know yet," Nick said after a minute. "I call Hill, tell him the game's over, we've got the prize. Then find a way to pin what they've done on them somehow. This thing won't really be over until they've answered for what they've done. I won't let it."

Reed thought about it, then said, "You know they're going to be royally pissed." Still staring at the ceiling.

"Good," said Nick. "We'll have that in common."

They drove to Tampa to Reed's apartment building. They had no idea whether or not Hill and Fetterman knew enough about Reed to find out where the young man lived, but Nick wanted to be sure. From a pay phone on the same block he dialed the number for the Tampa police headquarters on Florida Avenue and asked for Detective Hill.

"Just a moment," the voice on the other end said.

"Whoa, hold on there a second," Nick said before she could put him on hold. "I don't want to leave a message on that damn voice mail thing of his, I want to speak to him directly. This is important." He pronounced the word 'important' as three long syllables without the letter 'r.'

In the same practiced monotone, the voice answered with, "You won't have to, sir. He came in a few minutes ago. Please hold and I'll put you through."

"Damn!" Nick said loudly into the phone, holding the voice again. "I can't speak to him now. My pen ran out of ink."

"I'm sorry, sir."

"I'll have to call back," Nick said and hung up. In his normal voice he told Reed, "Let's go inside. We should be okay."

Nick waited near the front door of Reed's second floor apartment after checking for signs of a possible visit from Hill and Fetterman. The apartment was a mess although not in the same way as Nick's house had been. "It always looks this way," Reed offered.

"You need to hire a cleaning service."

Reed dug through some drawers in a bureau until he found his passport, which he dropped into a plastic grocery bag along with some extra clothes. He filled another and said, "All set."

They drove back to St. Petersburg, admiring the silver blue color of the rolling water as they drove over the long bridge that crossed the bay. It had been a long time since either of them felt like they could notice things like that. The color of the water, the shape of the clouds, the beauty of Florida.

They weren't going to hide, they weren't going to run, they were about to mount an attack. It felt good, a measure of control restored to Nick's life. He let his mind wander with the pleasant feelings, drifting to a place where this was all over and he could go back to the life he knew. Back to the life he shared with his beautiful wife. Back to Katy.

God, how he missed her.

* * *

The euphoric feeling from the evening before carried over into the next morning. Reed whistled and sang as he showered and went through his daily ritual, and Nick could see that the earlier tension had all but evaporated. The stress of being sought by men like

Hill and Fetterman had given way to a mild sense of adventure, courted by the anticipation of an unexpected trip to an exotic island.

The only problem with that, Nick knew, was that the feeling wasn't deep. A light in a child's room to give comfort in the dark. But in this case there were real monsters under the bed.

After a sit down breakfast at a local diner, they drove to the offices of one of the travel agencies on Nick's list. There, they reserved a seat on a flight from Miami to Owen Roberts International Airport in George Town on Grand Cayman island. Though the travel agent assured them in her best promotional manner that the tourist season lasted all year round, there was no problem buying a ticket on the 4:30 p.m. flight. There was also space at all of the hotels and they ended up selecting a place called the Clarion.

From there they went to a branch of Nick's bank where he made a withdrawal and gave the cash to Reed for spending money. The final stop was at the Tampa airport where they waited for a shuttle to carry Reed to Miami.

"They do speak English there, don't they?" Reed asked Nick as they sat in one of the airport bars. A waitress appeared at their table and they both ordered a coke.

"Yes, they speak English but they drive on the wrong side of the road."

"That's okay. I'll look both ways before I cross the street."

"Just look the other way first."

There were no windows in the bar, no distractions except for a pair of big screen TVS that were both tuned to the same daytime talk show. The waitress came back with their drinks and Reed paid her with money that had come from Nick. "Thanks," Nick told him.

Reed smiled back. "It's the least I can do for the man who's going to make me a millionaire." He tipped his drink to Nick in a mock toast. "Seriously," Reed said after draining half of his drink. "I arrive in George Town this evening and take a cab or a shuttle to the hotel. Tomorrow morning, I choose a bank, open an account, and get instructions for wiring money to it. Then I call you in St. Pete, give you the info, go back to my hotel and slurp strawberry daiquiris with the tourists."

"That's all there is to it," Nick told him. And there won't be anybody there trying to hunt you down. "Tomorrow night I'll go into Lankford's and arrange to convert as much of the four accounts' holdings as I can and have it all wired to your bank. If everything works out, in a few days you'll be loaded."

"But then what? I buy a yacht and skip out on you with the cash?"

Nick finished his coke and shrugged. "There are worse ways for this to turn out." On the television screens a skinny man and an overweight woman dressed in leather biker clothing were performing a strip tease. Even with the sound turned down they could hear the hooting and cat-calling from the studio audience. The more leather the wannabe bikers peeled, the more tattoos became visible. I'd pay not to see this, Nick thought.

"Seriously," Reed said. "What do you want me to do after I get the money?"

"Seriously, I don't know yet. After we get the money, I need to talk to Hill. And then we'll have to see."

"But he still knows you know about the people they've killed. You don't think he'll come after you?"

From the TVS came a burst of applause as the people on the talk show were down to exactly three pieces of clothing between them. Together they made up approximately one half yard of fabric. Their tattoos did a more thorough job of covering their pale bodies.

"Like I said, we'll have to see."

* * *

With Reed on his way to the Caribbean, Nick returned to the hotel on St. Pete Beach. He spent the following day reviewing Lankford's data and adding to the notes he had been taking. A large percentage of the four accounts' holdings were in cash and they would be easy to transfer. He would simply do his best with the rest of it.

Reed had called that morning at close to ten o'clock. There hadn't been any problems with the bank and everything was ready to go on that end.

The last concern was that Hill or Fetterman could be watching Lankford's, although Nick thought that unlikely. There was no longer the ruse of uncovering murderous money launderers to entice Nick to ferret out information from Lankford's system. Since they didn't know Nick was aware of what was really going on, they would have no reason to expect him to go back there.

* * *

"Nick!" Hill boomed into the phone. "How the hell are you? Is this a social call or are you calling to report a crime?"

Nick didn't answer for a minute. After his long night at Lankford's, he had come back to the hotel and taken a long, steamy shower before passing out on top of one of the room's stiff double beds. When he had finally awakened, he had gone down to the beach and plunged into the warm Gulf water for a slow, easy, methodical swim. After an hour or so, he left the relaxing water, took another shower, then slowly drove in to Tampa and yet another anonymous pay phone. The policeman had been at his desk when Nick finally placed the call. "It's not social, Hill," he said.

The other man chuckled. "So you have knowledge of a crime, do you?"

Nick was feeling at ease, no longer harried and desperate like he had been a few days ago. He was actually looking forward to tearing apart Hill's bravado and listening to the man as his cocky composure inevitably fell away. "Just yours, you cheap bastard."

"Really."

"Yes, really. Four convicts, pushers and smugglers, all investigated by you and your partner. They went to jail, their money went to the Walter A. Lankford Company. While they do their time, Lankford manages their portfolios. Presumably they get out of prison one day and their fortunes are there, intact and waiting for them. The money got by the Feds but it didn't get by you."

"Not much does."

"Save it, Hill. You don't have to act tough anymore. You got Tim Clayton involved somehow and when he found out what you were after, you pitched him out of an airplane. What did this James Rooker do, Hill? Who was he? Was he part of your master plan or did you just pick him up along the way?"

For the first time, there was a change in Hill's voice, but it wasn't a softening. Although he lowered his volume, it wasn't a break in the macho facade. "Him and that fat friend of yours, the pig from the beach. She died poorly, that one. She was a fighter, though. She got her licks in on poor Fetterman. Of course," Hill said quietly, unashamedly. "She paid for it in the end."

Nick would have hit him if he could. "It's over, Hill."

"Is it, Kingman? You know about Rooker. I'm surprised. And I'm curious to know just how quickly you found our Ms. Bates. I wasn't sure how much I trusted you that morning at your house but you must have known about her by then, I think. Obviously you knew about us." He paused for a moment, trying to prompt a response from Nick. "Can you prove any of it?"

I'm going to enjoy this, Hill. "Not yet. But I will. That's not the important thing right now."

"No, I'm sure it's not. You're absolutely right." Unflappable.

"Listen to me, you pompous asshole. You have no idea how happy I am to give you this piece of news. As of now, this game is over. There is no more money. There may be a little real estate left over, your standard pot to piss in, but the rest of it is gone, pal. You played this game, you son of a bitch, and you lost."

"What are you trying to say, Kingman?"

Nick thought there was a slight edge to his voice. If there was, good. Fall hard, you prick. "I transferred the money, Hill. I took away the pot at the end of your sick, twisted rainbow."

Hill didn't say anything.

"You've done all this for nothing."

Still silence. Have a heart attack, you fucker. Save me some work.

In the same jaunty voice, Hill said, "Well, I think that just may be your problem, old son. You'll just have to get the money back."

Nick didn't believe what he was hearing. "I don't think so, Hill. What I think is you're going down."

Again, Hill chuckled into the phone. "Before you get back up on that high horse of yours, Nicky boy, let me ask you one question. Listen well."

"What is it?" Nick was losing his patience.

"Have you talked to your wife lately?"

An icy fist grabbed Nick's heart and squeezed. The world in front of him shattered like a pane of glass, shards filling the air around him, closing up his nose, his mouth. Choking him. Oh my God. Katy.

In a painful movement, he forced air into his lungs, back up through his throat, then out of his lips. A slow, hoarse whisper cracked his awareness. "What did you do?"

Hill's maddening laugh again. "Go home, Nick. Check out your mail box. There's a little piece of something in there. A piece of her soul."

Before Nick could produce another sound, the phone went dead in his hand.

CHAPTER TWENTY

Gene McFarlane was a Florida cracker, so called because of the place where he was born, the family he was born to, and the way he lived his life.

Gene's older brother Roger had a lot to do with that life, given that he assumed responsibility for raising Gene after their parents had been killed in a boating accident. Roger McFarlane spent his time growing up as both a mother and a father, trying his best to be something he wasn't. Gene spent his time growing up trying his best to be like Roger.

It was hard for Roger, as it would be for any boy. Barely eighteen and taking care of his ten year old brother, he had to be creative in order to survive. There wasn't a whole lot of industry coming out of the tiny man-made piece of ground known as Everglades City, but he worked at what there was, usually scraping enough to get by.

He built docks and cleaned boats on the Barron River for the rich Northerners that came down and lived in the quarter million dollar homes in the otherwise poor city. Maybe six hundred people lived here year round and most now lived off what they made during the winter, in tourist season when the Yankees came down.

Other times of the year, when money was harder to come by, Roger would pack supplies and his little brother into their small shallow water boat and head into the Ten Thousand Islands to do a little gator poaching. From his father, Roger had learned that country well, better than most of the rangers that worked the Everglades National Park. Roger had never been caught.

It was hard work though, and there was no way they could ever kill enough Gators to really get ahead. They just took what they needed to hold them over until the next building or cleaning job came through. The odds of staying out of prison were better that way.

As the years went on and Gene grew bigger and more able to take care of himself, Roger began to disappear overnight. He told Gene he had some special work that he and some of his local buddies had agreed to perform, and that the late hours meant it paid better.

Uh huh. Gene knew what that meant. He may not have been book smart like the tourists he met but he knew what was going on. But life did get better over the next couple of years. The two men moved into a newer double-wide trailer closer to the water and burned the old one, the single that had belonged to their parents. Gene regretted it a little after it was done but he had been too drunk to really remember the circumstances. "The evils of the drink," Roger told him as he drained the last of another six pack. "I don't recall it much, neither."

It was a little ironic when Gene got himself a job giving boat tours out of the Everglades Ranger Station into the park itself. He thought it was funny that he was making money off his knowledge of the area, same as his brother but in a different line of work.

Roger was spending a lot more time away from the trailer than he had in the past. Gene suspected that he was out of the country a lot having graduated from the job of running shallow water boats through the maze of mangrove islands and sand flats between the mainland and the Gulf. There seemed to be a lot more money, too. Boxes of it, sometimes, that Roger couldn't always hide.

"One day soon," Roger would tell him. "Maybe next year, we're gonna move ourselves outta here, get us a nice house like those Yankee tourists got. Some place away from here."

Gene didn't feel too comfortable with the idea of moving away, leaving the only place he had ever really known. Sure, he'd gone into Miami a few times, and Naples, but he couldn't imagine actually living in places like that. Too many people moving somewhere way too fast. "Why don't we buy us one of these houses here, on the river? We can stay home and have some Yankee build us a dock."

"Can't get us one of these big houses down here," he said. "Wouldn't look good." That was as close to talking about Roger's line of business as they ever got.

Things changed for Gene when his brother failed to come home one day. It had happened before, Roger staying away later than he had said he would, but he had never been gone this long before. The days stretched to weeks and Gene finally began to realize that after all these years of feeling lonely, ever since their parents had died, for the first time he would be facing life by himself. All alone.

The men around, all the local swamp rats and smugglers that had known Roger, weren't any help. None of them would admit to knowing anything about the affairs of the man, their one time confederate. "The trouble with this business," one of them told Gene, "is that everybody you deal with is a criminal. You cain't trust nobody."

There was some money in a shoe box under Roger's old bed but not enough to last. Gene had no idea what Roger had done with all the money he had made. Gene tried the one bank in town but they wouldn't talk to him either. For all Gene knew, the money could have been buried in the swamp somewhere, or stored in a locker on some boat. Wherever it was, Gene knew, it wouldn't help him now. He'd have to help himself.

Doing what, he had no idea.

Gene began to realize that all his life he had been taken care of. The money in his pocket came from the tips and wages he made giving the tours but it had been Roger who paid all the bills each month. It had been Roger who put the food on the table and the beer in the fridge. Now there was no more Roger and Gene had to decide what to do.

There really wasn't much of a choice. He could move to Miami, compete with all the Cubans and Haitians for some low paying unskilled laborer's job but being a cracker he knew he couldn't exist in the city. Wouldn't matter if he could get a job. He knew the city would get him somehow. Suck away his mind.

He wasn't much of a carpenter, like his brother had been, and he didn't really care for the idea of scraping the hulls of rich men's boats. Poaching might be something if it paid more but there were too many gator farms out there now, raising the animals in concrete block houses and butchering them when they got to be eighteen inches across the belly.

Gene came to the conclusion that if he was going to have to provide for himself he was going to try to do it like his brother. Who knows, he thought, maybe a knack or something ran in the family.

Gene himself had no connections and no real idea of how to get any. He didn't even have a boat big enough to haul anything worthwhile. It wasn't as though business was likely to find him. He decided to have another talk with his brother's friends.

The first time he tried, he got lucky. There was a man they called Midge, Gene never knew why, that used to go off with Roger on some of his earlier overnight trips. Midge clapped Gene on the back with a powerful hand and said he could probably help him out.

Midge was an enormous bearded man who wore a string around his neck with dozens of shark, bear, and alligator teeth hanging down, making clattering noises in his long, tangled chest hair as he walked. His 'Florida pearls,' he liked to call them. He led Gene out to the back of the bar and asked him if he knew what a mule was. Gene shook his head.

When Midge told him, Gene smiled. He'd heard of people doing that, he just hadn't known it by that name. He said he thought he could do it. Swallow and shit. He'd been doing that all his life. Shouldn't be a problem.

Midge took the string from around his neck and held it draped over a massive palm. With his other hand he unsheathed a highly polished Bowie knife and used it to separate some of his bony charms. After a few seconds of work, four small yellowish objects were centered in his hand. Midge pointed at them with the tip of the knife and said, "Don't fail on me, boy. I won't be happy."

Gene assured him he wouldn't and Midge closed his fingers over the human canines then put his knife away. The next night he handed Gene a plane ticket and a list of instructions as he again advised Gene against the circumstances of failure. Gene told him he'd handle it and took the ticket.

A week later, after obtaining a passport over in Naples, he left for Colombia. It was the first time Gene had been on an airplane and the first time he had been to another country. Both were unsettling to him.

He began to wonder about what it was he was planning on doing. The plan was to meet a man in a hotel room who would hand him up to eight sealed condoms filled with cocaine. He would take them back to his own room, roll them in some oil, and swallow them whole, one at a time. After that, it was board the plane for home, induce vomiting or diarrhea, whatever it took, and get the damned things out of his system. Once he delivered them to Midge, he would collect his money and appreciate the retention of his dental work.

But what if they broke? All it would take was one, the latex condom rupturing in his stomach or his intestine, releasing who knew how many ounces or grams of that snow white shit directly into his body. He'd die, he knew. He'd never taken drugs before in his life, but he knew he'd burn up fast, overdosing in the heat as his body temperature approached 110 degrees. He didn't want to die like that. When the man in the hotel had given him the condoms, he had slapped him on the shoulder and said in heavily accented English, "Get home quick." Gene could still hear his wicked little chuckle.

The plane ride back to Miami had been sheer hell. Before they had even taken off from the airport in Bogota they had been delayed on the tarmac for almost three and a half hours. A mechanical failure of some sort. Before they left the ground, Gene's shirt was soaked through with perspiration. He could almost feel the acids in his stomach dissolving the thin latex tubes he had swallowed.

Once in the air, he wondered if the change in air pressure of the altitude would make his digestive system work harder.

This was a mistake, he thought, mopping his forehead repeatedly, trying consciously to slow his breathing. Ferrying drugs aboard a boat, eluding authorities in the islands where he had grown up, that was something he could do. But this, this was something else entirely. He was smuggling the drugs inside his own body, for Christ's sake. This wasn't normal.

Aside from the vision of his veins and arteries choking themselves on the sudden influx of narcotic powder, his heart bursting and exploding inside his chest, Gene vividly recalled the polished knife lovingly caressing the human teeth on Midge's pearl necklace. He had no doubt that Midge had shown him the knife for a reason, and the least Gene had to fear was the loss of hiss teeth. In a constant state of near panic, Gene kept himself rooted to his seat for the entire length of the three hour flight. He was afraid to move, afraid to add any ingredient to the possible disaster he carried inside himself.

When they touched down in Miami, Gene could have passed out in relief. In a superhuman test of will, he forced himself through the cattle call of customs without drawing attention to himself. From there he almost ran to the nearest rest room and claimed the first open toilet as his own. He had pains in his gut now, his lower abdomen, and he swallowed two Ex-Lax tablets as he lowered himself onto the toilet.

It was a very unpleasant feeling when the first one came out, goose bumps breaking out across his thighs and arms, but Gene almost cried he was so thankful. He counted carefully, not wanting to get up until every last one of those damned things was pushed through his body, never relaxing, always afraid that anyone of them might rupture, get caught on something on the way out, just before it cleared his asshole. Never again, he thought. His days as a mule were over.

Finally, the last condom exited his spent body and Gene slumped forward, exhausted. He had to spend some more time waiting for the effects of the laxatives to subside, but he didn't mind. It was over and he had made it. He was tired and stinking of dried sweat and public bathroom, but he had brought the drugs in. All he had to do now was pick those little white torpedoes out of the toilet and get on back to Everglades City. To Midge and his knife and that damned spooky necklace.

Gene finally stood up and looked over his shoulder. It was hard to imagine how much money that ugly mess was worth. He took a half step forward and bent over to pull up his pants then stumbled and fell into the door of the tiny cubicle. The whoosh of water from the flushing toilet sent a bolt of electrified panic down his spine.

On his knees he turned and dove towards the toilet bowl in time to see the last wad of crumpled tissue get sucked into the hole at the bottom. In a futile gesture he grabbed for it, grabbed for anything, jamming his hand up to the wrist into the small opening.

Oh my fucking lord, Gene thought as he looked up at the piping coming out of the wall. What the fuck happened? There was no way to flush the damned thing, no goddamned lever to pull. Christ! he swore again. He hadn't done anything!

He pulled his hand out of the toilet and wiped it in his shirt as he got to his feet. Staring in disbelief, he finished fastening his pants as he took a step back toward the door. Again the toilet flushed itself.

The damned thing was like the automatic doors to the terminal! It flushed itself when he moved away from it! How the hell was he supposed to know, God damn it? Nobody ever told him anything about fucking automatic toilets.

The coke was gone because Gene didn't know how to take a shit in the city. What the fuck was he supposed to do now?

He stood in the stall for another half hour, trying to comprehend what had just happened to his life. Things had looked so good just a few minutes ago, and now . . .

Numbly, Gene made his way out of the airport and bailed his truck out of the long term parking lot. He tried to guess at what exactly Midge's reaction would be when Gene told him that his entire shipment was gone, lost to the sewers in automatic toilet land somewhere south of Miami. Gene's thoughts weren't pleasant.

He decided he couldn't go home, at least not to stay. To go at all would be a risk since Midge knew when he was due back but Gene couldn't think of anything else to do. He began the long drive north and west down highway 41 toward home.

Hours later, he arrived at his trailer, packed some more clothes into his bag, and jogged down to the beach. No sign of Midge.

The bass boat with the 9.9 horse was tied to the dock, exactly like it should have been. Gene untied her and climbed aboard, never looking back at Everglades City, his home, afraid of what he might see.

He headed north, away from the national park, eventually arriving at the mouth of a river almost at the very top of the Ten Thousand Islands. The river had been straightened by the Army corps of Engineers and it looked more like a man made channel or canal than anything that was created by nature. Gene followed it upstream for several miles, heading inland, before turning into one of the many small tributaries that took him even deeper into the swamp.

He knew this area almost as well as he knew the flats and islands near Everglades City. His father and older brother had built a primitive cabin deep in the swamp, a secret place to store their gator skins after a hunt. Gene didn't think anybody else knew it existed. He could hole up there until he figured out what to do about Midge.

It was remote country, similar in that regard to the Everglades. It was a few feet higher above sea level so the collection of plants and animals was quite different, but there were no roads back here, no tourists, and no federal park rangers. This made it all the more shocking for Gene when a screaming woman in dirty white clothes burst through the brush and plunged into the water alongside his boat, crying desperately for help. Could this day get any weirder, he thought.

* * *

Nick drove past the edge of recklessness as he wove through the four land traffic across the Howard Frankland Bridge into Tampa. Traffic was thick, there was probably a concert or something at the stadium, and Nick pounded his steering wheel with an open hand.

Cursing, he pulled onto the right shoulder and drove past the long line of cars to the next exit. He didn't care what was causing the traffic. He'd make it home on the back streets even if it took slightly longer than sticking it out on the freeway. He needed to be moving, going forward. He couldn't take sitting still.

Long minutes later he whipped onto his driveway, no longer wary of anybody watching or waiting for him. Why should they be, he thought. They had him in their back pockets now. Slamming the transmission into park, Nick was out the door before the car stopped rocking. Then he was at the front door, pulling handfuls of junk mail out of the box, throwing them onto the cement around him.

Nick feared to inhale, not wanting to validate the passage of time with his own breathing, afraid with all his soul to acknowledge what Hill had done. What Nick had allowed to happen. Now he had to discover what Hill had meant by "a little piece" of Katy.

At the bottom of the box was an object, very flat and wrapped in a man's handkerchief.

Nick, moving in slow motion, was puzzled as he gingerly reached in and picked it out of the box. It was a photograph, he could tell that before he pulled away the edges of the fabric. An instant Polaroid of Katy, a close up of her face, an ugly purple bruise around her chin. Her eyes were open and the whites were showing as she strained to look to her right. A man's hand was holding the top of her head immobile against a wall or a floor, and a pair of pursed lips were making contact with her cheek. Fetterman's lips.

Nick let out a vicious wail as he slumped to his knees and pounded the side of his hand into the sturdy oak of the front door. The sudden rage gave way to frustration and for an instant he stopped breathing. He tried to keep his heart from beating, alter reality, change the world with the force of his will. God, I am so sorry, he shrieked inside his mind. What have I done?

He held the photograph at arms length, tears blurring the image of his wife as he struggled to blink them away. This was the piece, a piece of her soul, that Hill had hinted at.

I am going to kill you, you son of a bitch. I'll see you and your bastard partner choke on each other's fumes as you fry in Hell.

The anger cut through the grief and Nick stood, focusing on his plans, on what he had to do to get his wife back. In a trance, he unlocked the front door and went inside.

The place had been casually searched, the brunt of it having occurred in his office. There were no holes in the walls and nothing was broken out here. Nick moved to the answering machine and pushed the play button.

After the third consecutive message from Rachel that opened with a string of profanities demanding to know what Nick had done to her sister, he stabbed the rewind button and silenced the machine. He'd call her in a while, after he figured out what he could tell her that would keep her out of the way.

He had to think of this whole situation as dispassionately as he could. He had to be logical, in control of himself as if he were still a cop and this was just a routine investigation. Somebody else's wife that had been kidnaped. If he responded to Hill with his emotions, he knew he'd lose everything.

Hill has Katy but what he really wants is the fifty eight million dollars Nick transferred to the Cayman Islands. Katy wouldn't be hurt as long as Hill thought he could get the money. The important thing was to not let him get his hands on both Katy and the money at the same time.

Nick walked across the room and began trudging up the stairs, shedding his clothes as he climbed. He needed a shower; a hot, steaming, cleansing waterfall coursing over his body as he tried to wrestle his mass of guilt into a different corner of his mind. Perhaps in the shower his tears wouldn't burn as badly. He didn't think so but he had to try.

CHAPTER TWENTY ONE

A long while later Nick picked up the phone and dialed Hill's office. He knew the man would still be there and he was.

"What's next, Hill? You seem to be calling the shots now."

"I take it then you found the picture. Sorry about her face but the girl didn't want to behave. That reminds me, you know the one about what fifty thousand abused women have in common?"

"I'm not playing your games, Hill."

"Sure you are, Nick. You just haven't admitted it yet. Come on, what do all those women have in common?"

"I don't know."

"They just wouldn't listen. Get it?" Hill barked a short laugh across the line. "I love that one. Used to tell my wife that joke all the time."

"Right up until she left you."

Hill hooted with laughter. "See, Nick? I knew you could play." The humor drained out of his voice. Now I want my money."

"I want my wife."

"And thus we have the basis for our new relationship."

"You can have it, Hill. Just give my wife back. Now."

"Not so fast, Nicky boy. It's not quite that easy."

Nick's stomach felt like it had been squeezed and compressed into a small brick, settling into the bottom of his gut. The longer they talked, the more painful it was for him to breathe. "Why the hell not, you bastard?"

"Mind your temper, Kingman. Strong emotions can get in the way of accomplishing your goals. Remember that."

The dictum of the lizard. Nick didn't reply.

"Once my partner and I receive the money, we will be requiring new identities to go along with our new fortunes. Needless to say we'll be moving out of the neighborhood, as well. This takes time to set up, Nick, you know that. I didn't expect you to find out the truth let alone do what you did, but I need a few more days to complete the arrangements."

Days? For an instant Nick's vision went black. He squeezed his eyes shut.

"If I give her back to you now I'm still vulnerable, aren't I? That wouldn't be a smart thing to do."

"How much time?" Nick stammered.

"I believe I can get everything done in four days."

"Four days? No fucking way. Damn it, Hill, you've won. Take your goddamned money and give her back!"

"Touching, Nick, but—" he drew out the words as if he were actually considering it, putting on a show. "I think not."

Alright, Nick told himself. Take a breath. Sit on your emotions. The goal is to get Katy back. Take some control. "Four days, Hill. Concourse G at the airport in Miami, four o'clock in the afternoon. There's a deli kiosk with a lunch counter about a third of the way down, in the north end. I want the three of you sitting there, including Fetterman. When I see my wife, unharmed and healthy, I'll bring you the money."

"Miami, Nick? For Christ's sake—"

"That's where it has to be, Hill."

There was silence on the other end as Hill considered it. "You know that once I have the money my interest in the Kingman family simply ceases to be?"

"As long as you don't have both at the same time."

Hill chuckled. "Alright, Kingman. We'll do it your way. Miami actually works out well. Will there be any trouble from Lankford? I don't like loose ends."

"Is that what Tim Clayton was? And James Rooker and Lu Bates? Were they 'loose ends' that you didn't like?"

"Don't push too hard, Nick. We made the mistake of offering your boyfriend a cut of the proceeds in return for his help. In the end,

I didn't trust him. Rooker was just a sleazebag shakedown artist and the fat lady was your fault. Let it alone, it's all history."

Nick slammed his palm into the table holding the phone. "Tim was never working for you! He wouldn't have done that!"

"You may be right, Nicky. I don't know what his real intentions were. I'd say we could ask him about it, but you know . . . " Hill trailed off.

In a cold voice, Nick said, "You are a true son of a bitch."

"Like I care. Now what about Lankford?"

Nick forced an answer. "He has his own problems, I think. He doesn't know about me and now the money is gone. Who's he going to complain to? He'll probably be standing right behind you in the line for a fake moustache and dark glasses."

"That's funny, Nick. But let me tell you one more thing. I can see why you picked the airport at Miami. It makes sense. But don't you fuck with me on this. There are other things we can do to your wife, you know, things that won't kill her. Do you understand me?"

Nick felt the brick convulse once then shatter into a million pieces, sending thousands of ceramic shards through his insides and into his heart. "You keep that sick motherfucking partner of yours away from her."

Hill gave a soft laugh as he hung up the phone.

* * *

Gene's first thought was to gun the engine and get the hell away from this woman. Out here in the swamps there was no sense of community, no love thy neighbor sentiment among the few misanthropic individuals that occasionally crossed each other's paths. Out here it was strictly mind your own business and don't look too hard at anybody who might pass by. Law in the swamp was something you made up as you went along.

But this woman moved quickly, and she was a looker, he could tell that even through the mess of her hair and the wild look on her face. Before he could decide what to do she had reached the side of the boat and was pulling herself in. Gene had to throw his weight to the opposite side to keep her from capsizing the boat.

He studied the place on the shore where the woman had come from. There wasn't a lot of solid ground around here but there was a good sized piece back in that direction. He couldn't see or hear anyone coming after the woman and there weren't any other boats on the river, so that was something. Still, her presence made him nervous and he had enough to worry about. "Woman, get the hell out of my boat."

She looked at him, wild eyed and exhausted, and Gene could see the shape of the bruise along her jaw line. No sir, he didn't want no piece of this.

The woman pushed against the side, forcing herself into a sitting position, again threatening to tip the boat. For the first time, Gene noticed the handcuffs connecting the woman's wrists. Jee-zus Christ, he thought. This one's in trouble. "Go on," he said. "Get out of my boat."

"No," the woman croaked at him, gasping for breath. "You've got to help me!"

She tried to pull herself towards the stern and the engine, but Gene reached across the boat and put a hand on her shoulder, holding her back. "We've got to get out of here," she shrieked. "Before they come back!"

Gene let her go as she ran out of energy and stopped trying to get past him. Nervously, Gene scanned the bank behind her. Still no sign of anybody else. From somewhere above came the whine of a small airplane.

The woman reached out and grabbed one of Gene's hands, who instinctively tried to pull it away. He wasn't comfortable with intimate gestures from anybody, let alone a stranger, but she was desperate and she held on. "I'm going to put you off my boat," he told her.

"No, you can't. You don't understand," she pleaded. "Two men forced me down here. They left me chained up in a shack but I got loose. You have to help me get away!"

"Lady, I got my own troubles and I don't have to do nothing you say." Gene snapped his wrist suddenly and his hand popped out of her grasp. He shifted closer to the throttle and said, "Soon's I find a break in them mangroves, you're getting out."

"How can you just say that? I was kidnapped! They hit me!" She moved toward him again but he half rose and put a hand on the top of her head, pushing her back down. "Please, you've got to get me to a town or some people. A phone, anything!"

"No, I don't. Now sit still and stop moving." Gene guided the boat closer to the shore line, looking for a place to unload this woman. He couldn't see where she had come out, but it couldn't have been big enough to beach the boat. He'd throw her overboard right now if she didn't look like such a fighter. He didn't want to risk capsizing, sending everything he had left in the world to the bottom of the river.

"Don't you want anything?" Katy asked him. She was trying to think of a way to get through to this man. She couldn't let him just leave her. She had to reach him somehow.

Gene tried to ignore her. He knew what he had to do.

"Money? Do you need money? A new boat, a truck, anything?"

For a minute she didn't think he was even going to answer her. But then, in his low guarded monotone he said, "How much money?"

Katy felt herself flush with relief. "Whatever you need. My husband and I aren't rich but we make a good living. We can get money against our house, we have our savings."

"A half million dollars?" Gene had no idea how much it would cost to replace the cocaine he had lost but that sounded like a big enough number. If this woman could get him out of trouble with Midge, he had a reason to help her out. He heard the whine of the small airplane again, this time louder, but when he looked up he couldn't see it.

Katy was thinking, how in the hell can we come up with half a million dollars? She and Nick couldn't possibly raise that much. Maybe half to three quarters of it if they sold everything and borrowed from all of their friends. It didn't matter whether they could or not, though. She had to stay away from that shack. "Yes," she said. "Half a million dollars."

Gene throttled the boat back, keeping just enough power to keep from drifting down river with the current. "What I will do is this," he told her. "I can put you off at a spot up ahead a ways, then head back down 'til I get to a phone. If somebody brings me the money, I'll come and take you out of there. Otherwise, I'll leave you. That's the deal."

Katy wasn't sure what to say. She couldn't bear the thought of being left out in the swamp for a minute longer than she had to be, but she was afraid that if she tried to dicker with him he'd just dump her out now and be gone. Her mind flashed back a picture of the inside of the shack where she had spent the previous night chained to a metal ring mounted in the ceiling. She was ready to agree to anything.

"Alright," she said. "Give me something to write with."

Gene slid his small tackle box out from under his seat and opened the topmost section. He dug his fingers through a compartment in the upper tray until he came up with the small stub of a wax pencil and handed it to Katy. She looked around her for something to write on then felt her own pockets when she didn't see anything. From her smock she pulled out the business card Detective Hill had given her back at the hospital. She felt sick when she recognized it for what it was.

She turned the card over on her knee and very carefully, so she wouldn't destroy the damp paper, wrote Nick's name and their phone number on the back. Satisfied that it was legible, she handed the card and the pencil to Gene. "Maybe it would be better if you took me with you," Katy tried, gently.

There wasn't any way in hell Gene was going to risk being seen anywhere along the river carrying this woman. "That ain't gonna happen," he said.

Somewhere upriver the airplane noise had been replaced by the sound of an air boat.

"Shit," Gene swore as he took the card and the pencil and put them away in his shirt pocket. He scanned both banks of the river but there wasn't any place to hide. "Who was it that took you, anyway? That's not them, is it?"

Katy turned her head toward the approaching sound, whose source was hidden behind a bend in the river.

"I don't think so," she said. "They had a boat like this one, and when they brought me I think it was against the current."

Gene didn't answer. He knew they weren't fast enough to outrun an airboat on the open river. Reluctantly, he kept them where they were, waiting for the craft to appear. He didn't know what kind of trouble this woman represented but he knew he didn't want any part of it. Except for that half million dollars.

It was an airplane, not an airboat, that emerged from around the point, a blue and white high winged Cessna on floats. Gene and Katy were close enough to the shore so they wouldn't have to move to be out of its way. Unable to do much else, they watched the plane slowly make its way down river towards them.

They could see two men behind the windshield, both were wearing sunglasses and green headsets that bulged over their ears.

Katy made a decision. She raised her arms above her head and waved them at the pilot. "Put your arms down, woman!" Gene hissed, but the plane was already angling towards them.

Twenty yards in front of them the noise grew louder as the pilot applied more power and swung the plane around 180 degrees, then quickly dropped to nothing as he killed the engine and the propeller stopped turning. Gene was reaching for the throttle of the boat when the man in the co-pilot's seat opened the door. In his hand was an automatic pistol and he was pointing it at Gene.

"I don't know you, mister," Gene said, raising his hands slowly. The man began was as he reached up and peeled the large green headset away from his face and replied, "But she does. Bring her here. Now."

Katy let out a short, involuntary scream. She would have jumped overboard if Gene hadn't reached forward and locked his forearm around her throat from behind, pulling her close to him as he settled back into his seat. With his free arm he guided the boat to a spot underneath the wing of the plane, his eyes never moving off the gun.

"Hand her over," Fetterman said when they were close enough to bump against the step of the plane. Katy tried to struggle but she could barely breathe from the grip on her throat. Somebody she couldn't see grabbed the chain between her wrists and began to drag her body up and into the plane, back first. Gene let her go and held onto the wing strut, keeping the boat close. As the pilot reached across his partner and pulled the woman into the plane. The man with the gun turned and stood completely on the step to make enough room for her to get by.

Gene had had guns pointed at him before but he realized perversely that those had all been held by people he knew. This was different. He could die in the swamp at the hand of a stranger.

He pushed off from the strut and reached for the throttle lever. The gun followed him around and was aimed into his face. Gene was aware of it as he slammed the throttle all the way forward, anticipating the bullet that would end his life.

A shrill "No!" came from the woman inside the plane and both of her legs shot out the door, catching the gunman in the back and toppling him face first into the water. Gene stayed low and ran the little boat for all it was worth. He barely heard the single gunshot that sent a bullet tearing into the water behind him.

When he finally turned around to see, there was no pursuit. The strut for the high wing and the propeller made it difficult for the stranger to get a good shot off and Gene rounded the bend the plane had come from feeling relieved. He had survived.

He knew where they were going. He'd seen that damn plane tied up outside an old hunting shack about a half mile from where they were now, well hidden up a branch of the river going east. The bastards.

He eased back on the throttle a little to conserve his fuel.

What a bitch of a day this had been. Two things he'd be reminding himself of every day for the rest of his life: Stay out of the goddamned city, and, especially in the swamp, it don't pay to mix in other people's business.

CHAPTER TWENTY TWO

Some time later, after dark, Nick dialed the number for Reed Larson's hotel in the Cayman Islands. In an unexpected way, Reed's voice helped to soften the acid darkness that had slowly been eroding the edges of Nick's stomach.

"Hey, man, what's up? You know what, being a millionaire isn't anywhere near as hard as you may have thought. Are you coming down here? How's it going back home?"

"They took my wife, Reed," Nick said in a low voice. "Those bastards kidnapped Katy."

A cold silence clamped onto the line, Reed feeling like all the breath had just been sucked out of him. Oh my God, he thought but didn't say. MamaLu Bates on her kitchen floor.

"I hate to keep asking you to put yourself in these situations, but I could really use some more of your help." Nick's voice cracked and he sounded tired. Tired and worn.

"Don't even ask, Nick. Just tell me what you need and I'm there."

Nick inhaled deeply and told Reed about his recent conversations with Hill, including the arrangements they had made for the meeting in Miami. When he was through, he said, "I need you to book a flight from George Town to Miami in time for the meeting. Keep a couple of grand for spending money but withdraw the rest of the money as two cashier's checks."

"Two?"

"I think that way we have a better chance of getting Katy away from Hill and then working some distance between us. I want to be able to control the situation as much as I can."

"Do you think you can trust him to do what he says?"

"Not really. But his main motivation is greed and that's what we have to use against him." Nick explained what he wanted Reed to do with the two checks. Reed repeated the steps and when he was done there was another pause, an awkward period of electronic silence. It was broken when Reed said, "We'll get her back, man. You know we will."

A moment later, Nick said, "We have to."

"What will you do between now and the meeting?"

"I don't know. Tomorrow I'm going to visit the state prison up in Starke, try something else. After that, I just don't know."

They talked about the money for a few more minutes before Nick finally ended the conversation. After they hung up, Nick lowered himself gently to a sitting position on the floor and stared at the faint shadowy patterns of the furniture in the living room. He and Katy had bought it together after he quit the police department and they had bought this house. As much as anything, this house and the things in it had been symbols of their new life together, an exorcizing of the demons that had pulled them apart.

He closed his eyes and held them shut until the next day's sun chased the dark away and the morning birds began singing in the front yard. The new life wouldn't help them now, he thought. But the old one might.

* * *

"Will you relax, God damn it!" Hill snapped at Katy. For the second time in two days he was half dragging her struggling body along the planks that made up the makeshift dock leading to the shack. Fetterman was behind them at the plane, extracting the additional supplies they had brought.

"Your husband isn't going to like seeing you looking like a porcupine from the splinters you're going to get when I drag you on your fricking face. Now cut it out!"

Katy stopped struggling. There wan't much of a point to it, anyway. There was no place she could go and the unpleasant emotional aftereffects of having almost gotten away, having come so close, were weighing her down like a suit of lead. It was a deeper despair than she had felt the yesterday, before she had had the time to fully comprehend her situation. Now she just wanted to close her eyes, squeeze them shut until everything changed back to how it should be, the smells and the sounds, the people around her. It was time to wake up and go home.

"That's better," said Hill. With a mild shove in her lower back, he started her moving again. She continued walking under her own power.

The inside of the cabin was as she had left it. A single room containing a small wooden table that was almost as worn and weathered as the planks that lined the uneven floor. Two old, crooked seats were nearly touching under the tabletop. A metal bucket hung on a hook in one corner and a filth covered air conditioner lay on the floor next to an old Honda generator.

The walls were simply the rough unfinished insides of the twelve inch boards nailed to the cabin's frame. A few pages of yellowed newspaper were scattered here and there across the floor.

A fitting place for pigs like these, Katy thought.

The air inside the cabin was hot, humid, and carried a musty stink that came from years of rot and uncirculating air. There was plywood covering the structure's two windows.

Sixty seconds after entering the cabin Katy's shirt was soaked through with sweat. Flies buzzed their way through the door and danced around her upper body.

There was a burning oil lamp propped on a shelf that jutted out of the wall to her left. Most of its light was lost in the glare of mid-morning that washed through the open doorway.

"Shame on you, girl, you left the lights on last night. I'd tell you to be more careful in the future but I don't think you'll have to worry about it." He turned a brass knob at the side of the lamp, lowering the burning wick and smothering it.

"Why?" Katy asked. "Don't I have one?"

Hill looked at her. "A future?"

Katy stood mute.

"Honey, we've all got one. For some of us it includes breathing, for others it involves feeding the maggots that live in the dirt." Hill laughed explosively, a short, unbecoming bark. "You got a few good days left, don't fret it. You're just forcing me to leave you a babysitter this time. I just can't trust you enough to leave you home by yourself, can I?"

Hill moved to the corner where they had left Katy the day before and picked up the slender length of chain that lay heaped on the floor. He passed it through his hands, examining each link until he got to the broken one. "Now how in the hell did you manage this?"

Katy didn't answer and Hill reached up and hooked his index finger through the iron ring that was bolted into the ceiling. He bent his knees, allowing the ring to hold most of his weight. There was no give at all.

Fetterman entered the shack and dropped two grocery bags onto the table. Katy started as he walked in. She hadn't heard him come up the dock. She looked back at Hill, half hanging on the ring, who hadn't moved his eyes from her.

"You know what, partner?" Hill asked, staring at Katy, perspiration beading on his forehead and upper lip. "She won't tell me how she did this." He held the broken link out toward Fetterman with his free hand. "And I think that's something that I would like to know."

Fetterman grinned in response but Katy didn't see it. Her eyes were locked on Hill's and she shivered involuntarily. The temperature in the little building seemed to drop a hundred degrees.

She took a step backwards, toward the door, but a body was there, making her stop.

"We're good partners, he and I," said Hill referring to Fetterman. "We both know what the other wants, what the other needs. Generally speaking, we do a good job of helping each other get it."

Fetterman put both hands on her shoulders and spun her around.

He held her in front of him for a moment, digging his fingertips into the muscles of her upper arms. Katy looked up and saw a dead look in his eyes, tiny panes of shatterproof glass on top of his lenses. The man wasn't sweating, either. He was as dry as a soda cracker.

He threw his hands forward, lifting her off her feet, driving her backwards into the wall. The air left her lungs and wouldn't come back. She lay against the wall, gasping through her mouth as Fetterman stepped toward her.

No, goddamn it! she thought, forcing herself to her feet. I will not let you do this to me, you bastard.

Katy swung toward Fetterman's face with both of her hands but the man sidestepped her blow easily. Still with no expression, he whipped a backhanded slap across her face, spinning her around and back to the floor.

She lay there, the dull ache seeping slowly back into her skull, not wanting to move. Barely able to keep her eyes open. Words, noises, lights.

You win, you creep. I can't fight you.

When she turned her head to look at the man, prepared for another attack, there was a dark trickle of blood running down her chin from the corner of her mouth.

Hill saw her face and stood up straight, releasing the ring. "She's bleeding," he said. "You know I like that." He looked at Fetterman.

Even in Katy's painful condition she could sense that the atmosphere in the room had changed again. An electric energy had formed between the two men and she found it hard to look away from either one. Fetterman never took his eyes off her face.

Hill moved behind him and put his hand on his partner's shoulder. Together they walked slowly to the door.

"The best thing you can do right now, little lady, is lay right there and not make a sound."

Fetterman went outside and Hill stopped at the threshold, one hand on the door handle. "I'm serious as a heart attack, girlie. We'll be just outside."

He turned and was gone, pulling the door closed after him. Katy let her body slump all the way onto the floor. She tried not to listen to the sounds that came from outside the cabin a few minutes later but in the dark and all alone, they were all she had.

CHAPTER TWENTY THREE

Gene McFarlane ran his little boat as hard as he could all the way up to the family hunting shack. Those motherfuckers had been set to shoot him, he knew, and if that woman hadn't kicked out they would have. "Shit!" he swore aloud to the swamp. Gene admitted to himself that without someone to look after him, he was failing. With his luck, the next new thing he tried would probably kill him for sure.

He tied the boat to a bush and waded ashore through half a foot of muck. The cabin door was unlocked and Gene kicked it open wide, hearing the sharp crack of splintering wood as the door rebounded off the interior wall. Gene stopped it with the same muddy boot that kicked it and stood in the doorway looking in.

This is a pathetic mess, he thought. A wooden table, faced by two homemade chairs on one side and a faded, cloth-covered couch on the other, stood in the middle of the single room. A few tin dishes dotted its surface, blanketed by heavy layers of dust and dirt. There were two windows, both broken, with pieces of screen mesh duct taped over most of the holes. Mismatching remnants of shag and pile carpeting, laced with mildew, covered most of the floor.

It's about as filthy and repulsive as the rest of my life, he thought.

He kicked over the table and smashed one of the chairs into the wall before slumping onto the damp and reeking couch. Loose springs jabbed sharply into his back but he didn't move. After a minute, he began to itch all over but he didn't get up.

Damned couch, he thought. I'd burn you now, you old pig, but I can't spare the gasoline.

Instead he scratched dirty patches of dead skin into the oily spaces behind his fingernails and felt the perspiration slide across his body, under and through his clothes.

This was as low a time as he had ever gone through in his life. It's not that there had been a lot of high times, either, living the life he had, but there hadn't been anybody trying to kill him before. Makes a difference, he thought. Makes a big difference.

He had to decide now what he was going to do about things. So far he'd been running but how long could he keep that up? Gene didn't hold a lot of lofty goals or ambitions but he couldn't see living the rest of his life out here, away from the only town he had ever known. Away from the Gulf of Mexico, the ocean. Even if he could survive in the swamp on a long term basis, the prospect didn't excite him.

Maybe he could try to kill Midge, or wait for him to disappear the way Roger had. That could happen.

Sure it could. And alligators will one day fly to Georgia.

Gene scratched at his neck, leaving a trail of thin red streaks etched into the surface of his skin. He thought about the woman that had jumped into his boat. Earlier that day there had been a moment, just before the plane had shown up, he had thought he might have found an answer to his problems.

A gun in his face changed all that. But maybe there was still something there. Maybe the woman had been telling the truth and Gene could score some cash from this lady's old man.

He found the worn business card in his breast pocket and read the name and number the woman had meticulously printed on its back. What could it hurt, he thought. He already had people trying to kill him but at least in this situation he could exert some control over things.

He stood up, walked outside, and slogged his way out to the boat. When this was all over, he told himself, there were three things that he promised himself he would never do again. He would never get involved with drugs, he would steer very clear of all strangers in the swamp, and never, ever would he take a shit on a goddamned toilet that knew how to flush itself.

* * *

The drive down from the small north Florida town of Starke was long and boring. More than three hours on long flat roads coming out of the rural north part of the state. There weren't many people around to complain so it was probably as good a place for a maximum security prison as any other.

Nick had been there twice before, when he had been a cop, and it had never occurred to him that he would ever have a reason to go back. It was frightening how little of what was happening in his life would have occurred to him as being remotely possible. It was like the kind of nightmare that was so scary and repugnant that you woke yourself up as soon as your subconscious realized what was happening. Before it took you all the way to the places true nightmares wanted to go.

Nick felt the now familiar liquid nitrogen freeze attack his internal organs, making them stiff and brittle, fragile, as he thought about Katy. He thumbed the button that lowered his window and stuck his head into the onrushing heat and humidity. There was an acid burning at the edges of his stomach.

He tried to imagine how she was, what she could have been feeling and going through, what she could have been thinking at that moment. He had no idea and it made him ashamed. I've made you a victim, he thought, and I don't even know what that means. One day I hope you'll have the chance to forgive me.

It was long past dark when he finally turned into his Tampa driveway. He had checked out of the hotel in St. Petersburg earlier that morning since there was no reason to hide anymore. Hill wouldn't care where Nick was or what he was doing as long as he made it to the meeting in Miami in three more days. And as long as he brought with him a very large amount of money.

The light on the answering machine was blinking when he walked into the living room. There was a single message.

He didn't want to acknowledge it, didn't want to listen to Rachel or a salesman or a business colleague or a friend. What he wanted to do was slip into a coma until Saturday night when he could magically awake with Katy at his side, safe and healthy. Hill and Fetterman could be on a fast train to a festering hell, money and justice be damned for all he would care. Revenge was best suited for people who had nothing to lose and didn't care what it cost.

He pushed the appropriate button and waited while the small cassette tape in the machine rewound to the beginning, then reversed itself and began to play. At first there was nothing, then the sound of recorded silence, and finally a slow, heavy drawl. The thick, almost slurred cracker speech of a deep south native. The message was simple and to the point.

"I met a woman today who said she was your wife. I'll call back tonight."

Nick sat down on the floor in front of the phone and hugged his knees to his chest. He did not move until it rang again, three hours later.

* * *

"Are you Nick Kingman?"

"Yes, I am. Where is my wife?"

There was silence on the other end. Nick bit the inside of his lower lip, not wanting to take control of the conversation. He needed to find o ut who this person was and what he knew about Katy. Let him talk.

"Take it easy, man."

Nick inhaled slowly and evenly. "Okay," he said. "What do you want to tell me?"

There was another pause but it was shorter than the first. "Can you find where I am from this call?"

"No," Nick told him. "I can't trace you."

"That's good. Though I guess it wouldn't make any difference. I know where your wife is."

Nick let out the breath he hadn't known he was holding. He squeezed the phone in his hand and said, "Go on."

"Pretty lady, beat up a bit. Someone had handcuffs on her, too. It was two guys in a float plane."

Was she at an airport? A private strip?

"When was this? What happened?"

Gene didn't know how much talking he should be doing. It sounded like the woman had steered him right, though. He just didn't want to screw things up before they talked about the money.

"Happened today. Woman jumped in my boat 'fore I could get her off. Wanted me to get her out of—" he stopped himself. "Where she was. She gave me this number and said you'd pay me."

She was somewhere near water. In the state of Florida that didn't narrow things down too much. "What happened? Why did you let her go?"

"They took her back. Nothing I could do about it except get killed but that wouldn't have helped you any. Your wife helped me get away."

"How do I get to her?"

"Bring me some money and I'll make you a map."

"How much money?"

"Your wife said half a million dollars." Gene waited to see if he would balk at the amount.

"That's a lot of money," Nick said drawing out the words and sounding as if he had difficulty with the concept. He waited for some kind of response from the caller.

There wasn't one.

The man was in no hurry to negotiate a lower amount, which was good. It meant that he could be telling the truth.

"If I can raise that much money," Nick said, "a map is no good. I need you to take me to her in person." Nick wiped his perspiring palms against his thighs.

"Who are you, man?"

"I used to be a cop. These men you're talking about killed my best friend and they're trying to get to me. I'll pay you the money, in fact I can pay you half again what you want, but you have to take me to her. We both go get her, then you get the money. That's the deal. I can't afford to fuck around with this."

Gene didn't know if he should just hang up the phone and get away from all this or what. Now this guy was telling him what to do. It wasn't supposed to work that way. "Man, what are you trying to pull on me?"

"Nothing," Nick told him. "But they've got her and they want the money, too. We have a meet set for Saturday but if you know where she is, and we move now, the money is yours. Seven hundred and fifty thousand dollars."

Jesus Christ. This was supposed to be a simple deal. Give me money, here's a map, go get your damned wife. But now he had to go back there and maybe face those two guys if he was going to get anything out of this at all.

Shit. After this, he'd pay off Midge and get a job cleaning fucking sidewalks or something. These past few days had been too much for him. How had his brother dealt with these people?

"You got a gun?" Gene asked Nick. "'Cause I think we're going to need it."

* * *

When Nick and the mysterious caller had finished making their arrangements, he immediately hung up and dialed Reed's hotel room on Grand Cayman. "We've got to make a new plan," Nick told him. "I'm going to get my wife."

"Slow down, partner." Both men could hear the excitement powering Nick's speech. "Slow down and tell me what's up."

Nick related the story of the man who had called earlier and what they had planned to do.

"Can you trust this guy?" Reed asked.

"I'm not sure."

"But you're going with him."

"There's no motive for him to do this other than the money he asked for. If he was working with or for Hill, you'd have to figure he'd know the stakes and be asking for a lot more. He described Katy, what her work uniform looks like. At the very least, I think he's seen her."

"Okay," Reed said. "What can I do?"

"Get to the bank and FedEx a cashier's check for seven hundred and fifty thousand dollars to me. I need it first thing in the morning. I'm going to meet this guy as soon as it comes."

"I'll go as soon as we hang up. What else?"

"I want you to set things up for the meeting on Saturday in case I don't get to Katy. Did you get a ticket to Miami yet?"

"Yesterday."

"Good. After the seven hundred and fifty thousand, get another cashier's check for half of what's left."

"Twenty eight million bucks, give or take."

"That's fine," Nick said, not caring about the actual amount. With Katy kidnaped it was just so much Monopoly money anyway. "Get the rest in smaller checks, say two million dollars each. You need to get to Miami early enough to get a locker in a particular place. Write this down somewhere."

"Hang on, there's a pad by the phone here," Reed said. "Okay, shoot."

"Across from concourse G there's a bank of silver lockers next to an elevator. You have to get one of those. There are some green lockers across the hall, but those are wrong."

"Silver lockers, next to elevator, across from concourse G." Reed read the words back. "What do I want with a locker there?"

When Nick told him, Reed blew a long, tuneless whistle into the phone. "Man," he said. "You don't fool around, do you? I hope you know what you're doing."

CHAPTER TWENTY FOUR

Nick had compared the directions he had been given to a map of Florida but it didn't tell him anything he didn't already know. He was headed toward swampland, either part of or quite near the Everglades.

He followed I-75 south past Ft. Myers to the last exit before the toll stretch known as "Alligator Alley," then went south to highway 41 heading east. It was close to a three hour drive from his home in Tampa and he had to stop once for gas and a cup of coffee.

The two lane highway cut a path through the swamp out of Naples then continued eastward away from one expanding Florida population toward another. For a time, garish billboards advertised gator wrestling and air boat rides, Indian souvenirs and boat tours; tourist related activities that a few long time local families had turned to for economic survival.

As he passed by the last manufactured home communities and into the Collier-Seminole State Park, the signs and billboards disappeared, giving up on the people who had found a way to resist the temptations and make it that far.

Man-made canals paralleled each side of the road, an additional buffer between the traffic and the swamp. Without mountains or deserts, Florida has only its beaches and its swamps, flat land barely above sea level, to fill its space on the map. Numerous stands of trees obscured his view to the south, but through the breaks, as well as to the north, Nick could see acres and acres of sawgrass and palmetto expanding outward toward the line where the land stopped and the sky began.

Eventually, he made it through the park territory and into the

Grand Cypress area. There was traffic on the road, cars and trucks on their way to and from Miami, bypassing the tolls of Alligator Alley. Nick wondered how many of them had any idea what they were driving through, the unspoiled land and wildlife they were passing by.

My wife is out there, he thought.

He drove through the intersection with highway 29 and slowed down to a speed ten miles below the posted limit. He was looking for the landmarks he had been told about, and the dirt road that was supposed to take him from the highway down to the banks of a creek. The canoe he had tied to the roof of his car slid suddenly to the right as a large eighteen wheeler passed him in the other lane, speeding.

"Asshole," Nick swore, then forced himself to relax. This is not the time, he thought. Don't lose it now.

He drove past a group of one piece picnic tables on his right then slowed down even more. If he hadn't made a mistake and already missed it, on the other side of those trees up ahead should be a small break and the road he was seeking.

He saw the break and put on his turn signal but there was no sign of a road. He thought about what it would mean if he couldn't find it, if he missed his rendezvous and lost this chance to find Katy. Fuck it, he thought and turned toward the break anyway. As he brought the car around from the opposite side Nick could see the faint but unmistakable tracks that must have constituted what his mystery man had described as a road.

Slowly, with low branches scraping the sides of the fiberglass canoe, Nick rumbled across the uneven ground, giving silent thanks for the recent lack of wet weather. As things were, the car bottomed out repeatedly in the soft dirt/sand mixture as he slowly picked his way along the path.

The tracks did indeed stop at the shallow bank of a small creek, a current of slow brown water flowing past. The afternoon sun was oppressively bright and a butterfly danced around Nick's face as he stepped out of the car.

A natural gap in the vegetation along the creek bank somewhat explained the presence of the dirt road. It was a natural place to put a small boat into the water. Nick wondered how useful it could have been to legitimate hunters on protected land but in any case, the man on the phone had known about it and it had brought Nick here.

But where was the man?

Nick turned and looked back in the direction of the highway. He had driven maybe five or six hundred yards once he had found the tracks and now the only sounds he could hear were the buzzing of the flies around him and the soft gurgle of the moving water. No sight, sound, or sign of another living person, Nick thought. Total isolation.

He turned and walked down the soft slope at the bank of the creek, stopping just short of the edge of the water. To his right the creek continued southward until it bent sharply away and was hidden from sight.

To his left was a leafy mangrove tree and as Nick bent froward at his hips, trying to see upstream past it, a low voice with a pronounced southern drawl said, "Don't get too nosy."

Nick straightened and took a step back, away from the water, staring at the tree. A few seconds later, the faded green bow of a shallow water bass boat eased noiselessly around the overhanging branches. Inside the boat sat a man, red faced not from alcohol or poor health but from over exposure to the intense semi-tropical sun. He was wearing a pair of well worn blue jeans, a plaid collared shirt, and hiking boots. On his head was a filthy baseball cap with a patch sewn to its front that was too dirty to read.

"You Kingman?" the man asked.

Nick nodded.

"You got my money?"

"It's in the car."

The man reached down and started the boat's small motor. He turned it around against the current and gently grounded on the shore at Nick's feet. Nick reached ahead to pull it further in but the man said, "Don't worry about it. It's not going anywhere."

Nick stood back as the man stepped warily out of the boat into almost knee deep water and slogged his way onto the bank next to Nick.

"Let's see it," he said.

Nick went to his car and removed an envelope from the glove compartment. He also took a semi-automatic .45 caliber handgun and jammed it into the waistband under the front of his untucked shirt. He got out of the car and handed the envelope to the man.

"Aw, shit," the man swore. "You're giving me damn check?" He didn't open the envelope.

"That check is guaranteed. Write your name on it and you can deposit it in any bank you'd like and the money's yours, no questions asked."

"Shit," was all the man said. He was staring at the ground in front of his boots, feeling jacked around again.

"Look," Nick told him. The money was out of the country. This was the only way I could get it here in time. When this is over, after we get my wife, I'll help you convert it to cash, traveler's checks, gift certificates, whatever the hell you want. But for right now, please, take the damned check."

The man looked up, studying Nick. He didn't have much of a choice. "How do I know it's really good?"

"How do I know you're really going to take my to my wife? You could be working for the men who took her. Something could happen to me out here and nobody would ever know it." They both knew the kind of something he meant.

The man turned his head to his left and spit a brown stream of tobacco and saliva into the ground. "I ain't working for nobody, 'specially those two sons a bitches." He nodded his head upward at Nick. "That your gun?"

Nick looked down at his stomach. The slight bulge was shapeless and barely noticeable under his shirt but this man had known it for what it was. "Yes."

The man opened the envelope and looked inside without

removing its contents. "I guess we got to trust each other somewhat," he said and handed it back to Nick. "But when this is over I want this in cash. Don't want to deal with no banks." He looked at the canoe. "What's that for?"

"So we can get closer without them hearing us."

"Shit. What makes you think I want to get that close?" But he wasn't looking at Nick and he walked to the rear of the car and began to untie the canoe from the rack. Nick moved to the front and undid the rope ahere and together they lifted the canoe and carried it to the water, placing it next to the bass boat.

"What should I call you?" Nick asked.

The man spit again, this time into the water. "Call me Gene, I guess," he said. He didn't offer his hand.

He tied a line to from the canoe to the back of the boat while Nick removed two paddles from the trunk and handed them to Gene, who tossed them into the canoe. "You 'bout ready?" he said to Nick.

"Let's go. You drive."

"Yeah, I'll drive alright," Gene said and pushed the boat off the shore into the water. "Get in."

Nick walked into the water, thick soft mud sucking at his shoes, and carefully climbed into the bow of the boat. Gene pulled himself into the stern, not nearly so smoothly, forcing Nick to grab hold of the seat in order not to fall off. Gene started the motor and slowly turned the boat upstream.

There were no other people anywhere on the water. The swamps weren't like the oceans or the rivers in the cities where hordes of pleasure boaters, fishermen, and jet skiers clogged the surface exploring new ways to bend nature to their recreational pursuits. This land had so far been spared that. Instead, much of the fresh water itself was simply diverted for farmers and ranchers, slowly choking off the supply as the swamps and Everglades flowed gently south.

Toxic mercury levels were found in fish and the remaining wildlife was just a small fraction of what it was a hundred years ago. Man's finely honed ability to take what it wants, consequences be damned.

Nick knew that somewhere around them there were other people like Gene, people who spent a lot of time in the swamps, hunting and trapping, maintaining the style of life of their grandfathers or even their fathers. Nick had no particular wish to know who they were or what exactly they were doing out there.

All of which, he thought, made this a perfect place to hide someone.

A part of his brain was on autopilot, guiding his body but refusing to think of Katy, of how close they might be to finding her. The present would end when they got to the place where Hill and Fetterman were holding her and it would start up again depending on what happened after that.

Gene guided them onto a larger river with banks thirty or forty yards apart. There was a place where hundreds of birds, mostly white ibises and American egrets, stood along the sandy shore and inches into the water, ignoring each other as they searched and probed for their food. As the boat approached, the birds gracefully lifted off and flew away, disappearing somewhere over the acres and acres of sawgrass and palmetto.

Several times they saw alligators swimming in the water, like bony logs propelling themselves quietly against the current.

Eventually Gene brought the boat into the shelter of a natural depression in the shore line and grabbed onto the branch of a small tree. He tied off the boat and killed the motor. From his tackle box he removed a plastic bottle of insect repellent and applied to generously to his body.

"Swamp angels are about to come out," he said to Nick, indicating the declining sun with a nod of his head. "Want some?"

"Thanks," Nick said and reached toward Gene to take the bottle. As he rubbed a palm full of the white lotion into his face he asked, "What do we do now?"

Gene looked at Nick impassively, deciding whether or not to enter into a conversation with his passenger. Then, "We wait until it's dark. If they're where I think they are, it's not far from here."

"And if they're not?"

Gene shrugged.

Nick tossed the lotion back to Gene and studied the man's face. He decided not to say anything as he slouched back against his chair and tried to get comfortable.

To the west, the sun looked like a big orange ball, sliced horizontally into sections and pasted onto pieces of gray felt. They were stacked one on top of the other and lowered slowly in minute increments into the horizon.

Gene untied the canoe and refastened it to the bass boat as Nick watched from the bow, then put his head back and closed his eyes. Nick didn't move, gradually becoming aware of a low humming sound, as if someone were blowing across the end of an empty tube, listening to it grow in the air around them.

"Song of the swamp angels," came Gene's voice, as if he were reading Nick's mind. "Enough mosquitoes to pick your ass up and carry it to Cuba." Nick didn't reply.

An hour crawled by, Gene apparently napping in the bow and Nick not able to really relax or concentrate on what would happen next. It was hard being so close to Katy and not knowing if she was alright, not knowing what had happened to her during the past two days. What could be happening to her now...

Nick turned his head to where the sun was just visible above the western edge of the swamp. *Drop, you motherfucker,* he swore silently, suppressing a rage that threatened to erupt out of the calm of the evening. He felt the grip of the pistol through his shirt. He thought of the feel of it in his hand and the expression on the two policemen's faces seen past the sight on the end of the barrel.

The boat rocked gently as Gene sat up, his eyes on Nick's. "There'll be time enough for that gun later," he said. Nick left the gun where it was and stared back into the western sky. Gene did not lay down again.

Something plopped in the water about fifteen feet behind them, something big sounding, and both men started, though Gene only in his eyes. Nick turned his head around, straining to see the ripple pattern as it pulsed in all directions through the now black water. He turned back to Gene, who said simply, "It's the swamp."

They sat that way for another half hour, each man with his private thoughts and reasons for being there. Clouds of mosquitoes buzzed constantly around their bodies despite the repellent, and Gene finally pulled the canoe alongside the bass boat and said, "It's dark enough. We might as well get going."

Nick stretched his tired legs in front of him and held the canoe in place as Gene gracefully moved from one craft to the other. Nick waited until Gene said, "Come on," then crossed over to the front of the canoe and sat down, reaching for one of the paddles they had placed on the bottom.

"Keep that gun of yours handy," Gene said as he released his hold on the bass boat and bent to pick up the other paddle. "They weren't too shy with theirs."

Both men put their paddles in the water and began to work their way against the current toward the middle of the river. "Too many submerged tree trunks next to the shore," Gene said in a low voice. "We need to stay out here a bit."

There was enough light from the half moon to be able to see the individual trees pass by as they stroked past the shore. The persistent humming of the mass of mosquitoes gave way to the steady trickling and light splashing noises made by their paddles. Other sounds, louder and intermittent, punctuated the darkness as they passed, reptilian croaks tearing the quiet fabric of the night. Under the best of circumstances, the scene would have been unsettling, spooky and eerie in a place not belonging to man.

After ten minutes that seemed like ten hours to Nick, Gene whispered, "To the right. We go in there."

They paddled toward an opening in the shore line, a wide crack through trees that even in the dim light Nick could see would have been hard to spot had they been coming from upriver. As they passed through the mouth of this branch, Nick stared ahead, looking for any odd or irregular shape that could turn out to be an airplane. He skipped his paddle off the water and simultaneously felt and heard the whump of his paddle as it glanced off the water and smacked the side of the boat. He sensed Gene stop paddling and turned his head around to look.

"Be careful, God damn it!" Gene hissed. Nick nodded, feeling stupid, though he wasn't sure the other man could see it. Concentrate, you dumb son of a bitch. You'll get your own wife killed.

They drifted with the current for a few minutes, back the way they had come, slowly rotating in the water until Nick felt Gene begin to paddle again. Nick followed suit and they resumed their slow but steady progress up the river.

Perhaps fifteen minutes later, Nick felt a sprinkle of warm water drops fall across the back of his head. He turned to look at Gene who held his arm out, pointing to a spot ahead of them on the left bank. Nick tried hard but he couldn't make out anything other than the miscellaneous shapes of the trees and bushes.

Gene began paddling again and guided them gently to that same shore, planting the blade of his paddle into the river muck to keep them from losing ground to the current. Nick turned to face him and Gene motioned him closer with his free hand.

Nick turned around in the canoe and moved into the middle of the craft. He kept his hands on either side of the boat, not allowing it to tip too far one way or the other. "I don't see anything," he whispered as he settled into a crouch in the place where a middle seat would have been.

Gene put both hands on his paddle and leaned into it with his upper body, slowly forcing the canoe sideways. When they had stopped turning, he pointed again to a spot ahead.

"Look at that big tree there," Gene whispered. Nick followed the man's outstretched arm to a tree that was taller than the others around it. "Follow it down." Gene slowly lowered his arm.

Nick finally saw it. There was a slightly irregular block shaped object beneath the tree's canopy that appeared to be manmade. Once he had spotted it, he felt his pulse quicken. Katy was there.

"Got it," he whispered back.

Gene began to paddle ahead slowly, and Nick turned and quietly took his paddle from the bottom of the canoe. He sat on his knees and paddled from that position, carefully matching Gene's strokes. A few cautious minutes later they were in front of the shack at a makeshift landing. There was no sign of any airplane.

Still whispering, Gene said, "Looks like this is the only place to land." There were no breaks in the trees and bushes that were close enough to allow direct access to the cabin other than the one leading to the front door.

Nick was about to ask Gene what he planned to do when a sudden noise and a broad shaft of light erupted from the cabin's front door. Both men instinctively ducked their heads below ground level as the door banged shut and the figure of a man moved toward the side of the cabin. When they regained their focus, the man was gone.

Nick grabbed Gene behind his neck and pulled his head to within inches of his mouth. "You coming or staying?" he demanded.

Gene pulled away, shaking his head. Nick turned and presented his ear. "Staying," he heard. "I told you I'd take you here. If you're going to do something, go do it. I'll be right here."

Fair enough, thought Nick. This wasn't his fight. He put his paddle down and moved as fast as he dared to the front of the canoe. With some paddling by Gene, he was able to step from the canoe onto a warped section of plywood. He crouched low, hoping his silhouette would be swallowed by the mangroves and pulled the gun out of his waistband, quietly flicking off the safety.

The cabin was about sixty feet in front of him and the man who had come out had moved off to Nick's right. From the brief glance that he had gotten from the open door, he thought that it may have been Fetterman.

Nick took long, quiet strides toward the cabin, listening and watching for any signs of movement. Gene made no noise behind him.

At the door, Nick placed his ear as close to it as he could without making contact. There was no sound from inside.

Wanting to move quickly, Nick pushed the door open just wide enough for his body to fit through and slid in sideways, dropping to a crouch on the other side while using his hand to keep the door from slamming closed. He squinted fiercely against the new brightness, holding the gun in front of him.

Katy was on a chair in the corner, handcuffed with a length of light chain looped around the thicker one that connected the bracelets on her wrists. The chain was attached to an iron ring jutting from the ceiling and her head was slumped to her chest as if she were sleeping.

As Nick stood and began to move to her, his wife lifted her head and looked at him. For a moment her face carried a blank stare, indifferent and unfocused, but then her eyes opened wide and she took in a breath as if she were about to yell.

Nick fairly leapt across the room and clamped his hand over her mouth before she could make a sound. The chains made light chinking noises as he crushed her body against his, lifting her from the chair and almost tipping it over.

"Oh, Katy!" he breathed into her ear. The familiar smell and feel of his wife were overpowering. Nick knew they didn't have time for this but still he held on for twenty seconds before he lowered her to her feet. When he pulled away from her a look of panicked fear snapped onto his wife's face. Tears were streaming down her cheeks as she asked in a hushed voice, "Where is he?"

"I don't know, love. We saw him leave but I don't know where he went."

"There's an outhouse somewhere, I think," she said. "Somewhere close."

"Who is it? Did he hurt you?" Nick ran his fingertips across her swollen lower lip, the flecks of dried blood.

"Not too much, no. They're not interested in me for that." She swallowed hard. "Hill's not here, it's the other one."

"We've got to get you out of here."

"The keys!" Katy hissed. "They're over there!"

Nick turned to the table in the center of the room. It was a good five feet out of Katy's reach and on it were a small set of keys, a cellular phone, and what looked like the average contents of a man's pockets: Billfold, change, a few scraps of paper. The only other thing on it was the kerosene lantern that filled the filthy cabin with light.

He jammed the gun back into his waistband and used the keys to unlock the cuffs from Katy's wrists. "Hurry, Nick," she pleaded.

Ugly purple and red grooves were inscribed in wicked circles around her wrists. "I'll be alright," she said to Nick as he saw the marks. "Let's get out of here."

Nick kissed her forehead and pulled the gun free as he moved to the table and the cellular phone. He flipped it upside down and smoothly ejected the battery, sliding it into his back pocket. "Come on, sweets."

Katy reached forward and took his hand while Nick extinguished the lantern. They didn't move for several seconds, adjusting to the darkness, before Nick gently pulled his wife to the door. He had been inside almost three and a half minutes.

Slowly, he eased the door open, tensing at every rusty-hinged creak, until it was wide enough for them to fit through. He squeezed Katy's hand once as a signal then stepped outside, carefully placing a foot onto one of the mud covered planks leading to the river.

The sensation of cold steel appeared at Nick's temple while an arm reached across his body toward his gun. A pale hand clamped over Nick's with a firm, cold grip while a familiar voice said, "Hold it."

CHAPTER TWENTY FIVE

Nick didn't have a choice; he knew without looking what was pressed to the side of his skull, and he knew the voice of the killer that held it.

Fetterman took the gun out of Nick's hand and stepped around in front of him. "Back inside, Nick," he said. There was not a trace of emotion in his voice. Another day at the office.

Nick backed slowly into the darkened shack, feeling Katy yield and fold into his side as he moved. Fetterman threw Nick's gun over his shoulder into the swamp and followed them inside, pulling a disposable cigarette lighter out of his pocket..

"Into the corner," he prodded, motioning with the gun though Nick cold barely see it.

Nick guided Katy to the chair he had found her in, then stood beside her as Fetterman activated the lighter and relit the kerosene lantern. As the lamp flared and filled the room with light, Fetterman stepped in front of it, reducing the glare in his own eyes and extended his gun toward Nick.

"Don't get any ideas," he said. "I can see you better than you can see me."

Nick looked at Katy and felt a surge of anger but choked it back. His wife's eyes were squeezed shut and her shoulders were tense; withdrawing inside herself.

"Pick up the handcuffs, Nick. Put them through the big chain and clamp one on your wife and the other on you."

Nick stooped and picked the handcuffs off the floor and did as he was told.

"Now sit down and throw me the keys."

Fetterman caught them with one hand and dropped them

onto the table behind him. Nobody moved or said anything for several minutes. Nick covered his wife's hand with his own and tried to will her to relax. Except for the nocturnal background music of the insects he couldn't hear anything from outside of the cabin. Gene was probably halfway back to the other boat by now.

A dry grin cracked across Fetterman's face. "This is an unexpected pleasure, Nick. What brings you to visit?"

"Shove it, Fetterman. The snappy patter works better for your partner. You don't carry the weight."

The wry smile on the policeman's face disappeared instantly. He clenched his eyes shut then allowed them to open slowly. A different voice, much quieter, said, "Do you wish he was here, Nick? Did you hope to see him?"

Kingman didn't reply. He didn't know what to say.

"Did you wish to see him?" Fetterman roared and stepped forward, sending a vicious kick at Nick's head.

Kingman ducked but not fast enough and not low enough. The light flared and his vision went black as the force of the blow spun him ninety degrees and left his back against the side of Katy's chair.

"Nick!" Katy screamed and tried to take his head in her hands.

Fetterman stepped back and leaned on the edge of the table, tucking in the front of his shirt. "He likes you, you know. He told me once."

He placed the gun on the tabletop and reached behind him to get at the rest of his shirt. "He said you were a good cop. He said it back when you were one of us, then he said it again when we brought you in on this." Fetterman seemed calmer now. "Did you know that? Do you even care?"

Nick was holding the top of his head waiting for the pain to subside. He didn't say anything.

"He's never said that to me. Not ever. Not even once." Fetterman reached into his pocket and came out with his knife. "I can't kill you, he wouldn't like that." He wrapped his long pale fingers around the knife and caressed it like a baby. "But I can play. He lets me do that sometimes."

Lifting his head from his palms, Nick opened his eyes and turned to look at Fetterman as he extended a miniature corkscrew from the body of the knife. Nick thought of the marks and wounds he had seen on the breast of MamaLu Bates.

"If you fight me, Nick, I'll practice on her first."

Twinges of animal panic flickered around the edges of his nerves as Nick watched Fetterman stand and walk toward him. Katy clenched his hand fiercely in hers. "Don't worry, love," he told her. "They need me to get their money."

Fetterman took a determined step forward, eyes locked on Nick's. Katy let out a shrill "No!" screaming as loud as she could. Fetterman didn't blink. He took another step.

"He's going to be so proud of me."

The door of the cabin crashed inward, slamming into the interior wall. Fetterman whirled, instinctively looking for the gun he had left on the table while the narrow edge of a canoe paddle cut through the air and collided with his temple.

Fetterman went down in a pile, knife skidding across the floor, with Gene McFarlane standing over him, breathing hard like a prizefighter. Fetterman tried to sit up but Gene brought the butt end of the paddle down on the dazed policeman's forehead, bouncing his skull off the hard wooden floor.

Gene raised the blade of the paddle into the air above the unconscious man's throat, poised for a killing blow. "No!" Katy shouted.

"Don't do it, Gene!"

Gene looked at the man lying at his feet, then at the paddle he held in his hands. Slowly, his features relaxed and he took a step back. "That's the son of a bitch that was going to shoot me," he said.

"He's done now," said Nick. "You stopped him. Thanks for coming back."

Gene turned to look at Nick, still pumped on adrenaline. "Didn't go far. After you went in, I saw this one come back from around the side of this place, then creep down to the water. I just pushed off and moved behind some trees. I waited for a while after he was gone but when I got back up here, I couldn't see neither one of you."

"You could have left."

"You still got my money."

That was true. The check was still folded in the envelope in Nick's back pocket. In fact, Nick thought, Gene could take the check from him now and simply leave them chained together next to Fetterman's unconscious body. "So what do we do next?" he asked him, holding his eyes.

"You got a way to get unhitched from there?"

"Keys are on the table behind you."

Gene looked down at Fetterman. "Let's get out of here. We had a deal and I don't need to do these motherfuckers no favors." He sent a light kick into Fetterman's side then swept the keys off the table and tossed them to Nick, who caught them with his free hand.

As Nick moved to unlock the handcuffs, Katy said to Gene, "Thank you for doing this." He looked at her once, then turned away, mumbling something she couldn't quite make out.

Nick freed them both, then leaned on Katy for a moment as he got to his feet. A lightning bolt pulsed through his head where he had been kicked.

"You okay?" Gene asked him.

"Yeah," Nick said. "Let's go."

"What about him?"

"Let him stay until his boyfriend comes. He's not going anywhere."

Gene shrugged. "Guess not." He turned and held the door for Nick and Katy as they held onto each other and left the cabin.

The night sounds seemed louder now, yet somehow more peaceful. Nick was aware of the sound of the black, unseen water as it flowed past the banks a few yards in front of them. Katy tripped once on the loose boards and Nick kept her from falling by squeezing her more tightly around her shoulders. "I feel like I could sleep for a week," she said.

They climbed aboard the canoe with Gene taking the back

and Nick crawling up to the front as before. Katy sat in the middle, reluctantly letting go of her husband and folding her arms around her knees. Gene pushed off from the bank with a gentle shove of his paddle and they were moving, gliding slowly away from the edge of the river.

"How far do we have to go?" Katy asked. Her voice was quiet with the weight of the swamp, a little more than a whisper.

"Not too far," said Nick. "This river flows into another one up ahead, and we have another boat tied up there."

"How did you manage to get out of there that time when you made it into my boat?" Gene asked. "What with the handcuffs and all."

Katy lifted her head from her arms and tried to see him over her shoulder.

Neither man was putting much effort into the paddling. An occasional stroke kept them in the middle of the river as they were content to let the soft current move them along.

"They left me alone after they first brought me here." She closed her eyes and concentrated for a minute. "We came in a small boat like this. When they left, they chained my handcuffs to that ring in the ceiling and said they'd be back. I stood up and turned around and around until the slack went out of the chain. Then I kept turning, using the handcuff chain to take the strain. One of the links opened up and I was free." She tried to stop a yawn with her fist but failed. "I'm lucky it was the kind of chain it was."

"You were lucky, period."

They moved on in silence for a few minutes, the silhouette of the overhanging point that marked the confluence of the rivers becoming visible up ahead.

"Thanks for coming," Katy said to Gene. "Thanks for helping me."

Gene didn't know what to say. He drew his paddle through the water while Katy laid her head back down.

"I'm getting paid," he said finally. His words were quickly swallowed by the night.

CHAPTER TWENTY SIX

Fetterman wasn't out long. The blows to the head had stunned him but the contact with the wooden floor had been what had knocked him unconscious. The realization of what had happened poured over him like a sudden rain and without looking, he knew that they'd gone.

He rolled over to his knees and felt a new pain in his side, a burning feeling in his ribs. He didn't know what that was but he pulled then pushed himself to his feet using the edge of the table. He'd worry about the damage later.

The cell phone was still on the table where he had left it. He snatched it up and began to punch in some numbers when he noticed something was wrong with the phone. There were no sounds accompanying the numbers and the keypad didn't light up. He turned it over and saw the empty battery compartment.

Damn it, he swore to himself and flung the phone away from him across the room. All their plans, all that money . . .

Hill was going to kill him. Maybe literally. Fetterman didn't care so much about the money, he was doing this for his partner as much as for anything else. But he knew Hill's motivations were a bit different from his own and he would not be so accepting.

There may be a chance to fix this, he thought. He didn't know a lot about the swamp, only what he had picked up from Hill, but he did know that the shortest way out of where they were was downriver to the south. They were probably headed downstream to the juncture of the two rivers.

There was a path behind the cabin that could take him there.

Hill had told him it had been made by Indians years before. Fetterman had no idea if it was even passable but it was his only shot.

He straightened, grimacing with the pain, then saw his gun on the floor where he had been lying. He picked it up, checked the clip, shot it back home. This'll work, he thought as he dropped it into the holster on his belt. If I can get there.

* * *

He was scratched and bleeding from two dozen superficial wounds caused by the wild branches and serrated edges of the sawgrass that lined the path. He had tripped twice while he ran, going down hard each time, and during the second fall he cut his forehead on a rock or a piece of shell.

The path disappeared behind the mangroves that formed the point of land that obscured the opening of the smaller river. He had to pull up before he got to the end so that he could see around the trees.

The light dripping sound of water on water that marked the unhurried paddling of the man in the back of the canoe drew his eyes to a spot on the river. Against the darkness he could make them out, moving slowly away from him and almost to the opening into the larger river.

He was too late. He couldn't reach them.

He thought about Hill and what he would say, what he would do, when he found out that he had let them escape. Bad things would happen and Fetterman didn't want that. He didn't want to be the cause of something coming between them. No, Fetterman thought. He didn't want that at all.

These people could not be allowed to simply float away down the river.

He felt for the gun in his holster, never taking his eyes from the pale, irregular shape of what was now his prey. He preferred to be up close, guns and bullets were too impersonal, but this was all he had. It would have to do.

Fetterman brought the gun up and held it with two hands, one supporting the other, and sighted along the pristine line of the barrel. There.

Slowly, precisely, he began to squeeze the trigger.

* * *

Katy had almost fallen asleep sitting upright in the canoe. Her arms were still holding her knees and she was resting her head on top of her forearms, fighting back her fatigue. She still wondered what this whole thing had been about and how it fit in with Tim's death, but she would find out later. Nick would hold her, touch her, and tell her everything he knew. In the end it would all come out okay.

A sharp crack sounded behind her, ending the comfortable mental drifting. Before she could focus her thoughts a second and third one ripped through the air. The canoe lurched sideways and she felt a sticky wetness spray across the back of her neck. At the same time there was an awful expulsion of air, of breath, and she twisted around to see the body of Gene McFarlane slumping slowly to the side. An ugly black hole had appeared in his throat.

"Katy, get down!" Nick yelled from the front but all she could do was scream. She knew that Gene was dead.

There was another crack and Nick suddenly threw his weight to the side, overbalancing the canoe and dumping all of them into the warm black water.

"Nick! Oh my God! Nick!" Katy flailed as she slipped under the surface of the water once, trying to touch the bottom and turn toward her husband at the same time.

"It's okay, honey, I'm here," Nick said as he slid an arm around her waist. "Are you okay?"

"Yes," she managed after a gulp of air. "He—he's dead."

Gene's body was floating face down on the surface of the water, the air trapped in his clothing yielding grudgingly to the pull of the water. The capsized canoe floated eerily next to him, a temporary marker for the man who had saved their lives.

"We have to swim, honey," Nick said, trying to pull her away as the two of them tread water.

There was another crack and Nick could see the flash of the gun from shore that marked Fetterman's position.

"Come on." He began to pull his wife down river, angling toward the shore.

"The canoe!" Katy said, starting to follow.

"The other boat's not far. Let's go!"

Behind them, at the place where Fetterman had been, they heard a shrill scream, a piercing yell carried across the heavy swamp air. Three more gun shots followed and then the sounds of a large weight entering the water hard, splashing and moving toward them.

Nick half pulled, half pushed his wife closer to shore where their feet could touch the muddy bottom. It was too soft to stand on, pulling at their shoes. "Keep swimming," Nick said. "Follow the shore." The mangroves lining the bank were far too dense to try to crawl through.

Nick looked back just once as he began to follow his wife into the larger river. He could hear something moving through the water but it was too dark to be able to see their pursuer. Silently he prayed the canoe had sunk by now.

* * *

Spiked on his own adrenaline, Fetterman howled like a half crazed animal, jammed the gun into its holster, then threw himself recklessly into the river. He wasn't sure if he had hit anybody but he knew something good had happened when the canoe went over. Their getaway wouldn't be so easy now.

He swam with his head out of the water as fast as he could to the spot his prey had been. The canoe was there, floating upside down with half a foot of its bottom breaking the otherwise smooth plane of the water. In his youth Fetterman had been a Boy Scout and he knew that a capsized canoe didn't sink; it trapped too much air as it turned over.

He held onto it for a moment as he caught his breath, staring at the river ahead for signs of his quarry, when he kicked something under the surface with his shin.

Something soft and heavy.

Warily, he probed beneath the surface with his free hand until he took hold of it. A piece of fabric connected the thing to a point somewhere under the canoe.

As he worked to free it, he felt the object roll over, part of it rising up and breaking the surface of the water. Fetterman found himself looking down into the dead eyes of the man who had hit him with the paddle. The man who was responsible for the others' escape.

The fabric of the man's shirt came free and Fetterman gently shoved the carcass away from him, looking briefly at the two holes, front and back, that marked the pale neck below the beard. You should have known better, you fool, he thought. He watched the body begin its slow glide beneath the surface. Gator food.

There was no sign of the other two. Kingman and his wife must have swam down river. Fetterman was familiar enough with this area to know that there was no way they could get through these mangroves onto any shore. There wasn't any solid land through here and the islands themselves were no more than tight stands of mangrove trees rising out of the water.

Holding his breath, he dipped below the surface and came up under the middle of the canoe. Gripping the sides, he pushed himself down until his feet sunk into the river bottom then straightened, extending his legs and arms, lifting the canoe as far as he could out of the water and dropping it to one side. The canoe rocked onto its bottom, mostly empty, and Fetterman grabbed for it as it began to float away from him.

One of his shoes stayed behind, buried in the mud but he couldn't worry about it. He was in a hurry and he needed to find a paddle. At least the damn things float, he thought.

The river bank in front of him formed a slight cup shape, one lip of it marking the end of one river and the continuation of the bank of the larger river it joined. If the paddles made it beyond that strip of land he would never find them but the direction of the current should have carried them into the natural depression.

Fetterman pulled the canoe around until he could grip the point of one of the ends of the fiberglass craft. Trailing down into the water was a length of tie down rope. Perfect, he thought, and let go of the canoe in order to lop the end of the rope around his ankle. He began to swim in a modified breast stroke toward shore.

* * *

Katy was struggling. The physical and mental ordeals she had been through had taken their toll. Her leaden arms were screaming for a rest and her mind was alternating between nightmare visions of what she had seen and imagined twelve foot alligators cruising the river looking for food.

She swam closer to the shore and folded her legs underneath her, settling her weight onto her knees. Nick came up behind her and took hold of her shoulders.

"What is it, honey?"

Katy couldn't answer. She was trying to both cry and gulp air at the same time. Nick wrapped his arms around her and pulled her close, kissing her forehead. When she looked up at him, even in the minimal light he could see the tears on her face. Her voice was shrill and her words were difficult for him to understand.

"I can't do this, Nick, I can't do it. I don't even know what's going on. They kidnapped me, they hit me, and they were going to hurt you with that knife. I don't want to die, I don't want to see you . . . " She trailed off, swallowing a mouthful of air. Nick gently pushed a strand of her hair off of her face.

"And that man, he helped us, didn't he? He was behind me, then he was dead. I saw his throat and I knew it. Why, Nick? Why is this happening?"

Nick squeezed his wife tightly to his chest. How was he supposed to answer her? She had been kidnapped, beaten, and shot at because of him, because of the thing inside him that drove him to find out who had killed his best friend. But what about Gene? What about Lu Bates and James Rooker? What about their best friends?

He thought about Fetterman somewhere behind them, maybe catching up, maybe not. Now was not the time for this. Whatever had come of the choices he'd made had happened and there was no going back. They had to keep moving.

"Katy, honey," he said, stroking her tangled hair. "We can't sit here, we have to keep going. It's not much further."

"How far is it?"

Good, Nick thought. A question: Her mind is functioning.

"Not far, honey. We're almost there."

In truth, he wasn't sure. Time, distance, and circumstance didn't translate their position well and Nick was at least as afraid they'd swim past the boat as he was that they wouldn't make it that far.

"Come on. Let's go."

Katy let herself be pulled gently forward to her knees. She began to swim away from the shore into the river. Nick stood for a moment, listening for sounds of man, but couldn't hear anything above the soft splashes of his wife's simple strokes and the more complicated sounds of the nighttime insects. Not wanting to be too far away, he slipped into the current and followed his wife.

* * *

Fetterman paddled hard, leaning into his strokes as he pulled himself through the water. He used long, straight strokes that directed the canoe off line with almost every motion, forcing him to shift the paddle from side to side as he zigzagged down the river.

His back ached and his bruised head throbbed with the beat of his pulse as he concentrated on both banks of the river. Hill would never forgive him if he let the girl get away. He wasn't sure exactly how he would react but he knew things wouldn't be the same between them. That was the worst part of all of this.

He thought that he should of caught up to them by now. He was sure there was no solid land around here so they couldn't have been able to leave the river. It was more likely that he passed by them in the dark. Maybe he should go a little further, turn around and wait for them to come to him. There really wasn't any other place they could go. They were frightened; they were running.

He imagined himself as a dark-winged bird of prey, circling high above his hunting ground, searching out his next kill. Swivelling his head from side to side he swoops down along the surface of the water, intent on finding movement, anticipating his prey.

There was something ahead of him, in the water.

Fetterman pulled the paddle out of the water and into his lap. Whatever was floating in front of him definitely should not be there. He stilled his breath as he stared at the shape, drawing nearer with the current.

It was a boat.

He withdrew his pistol from the holster on his hip, carefully forming his fingers around the grip. The damned thing should be dry enough to fire, he thought. If not, there were other things he could do. He moved his hand over the right front pocket of his trousers and froze. His knife was gone.

It had been in his hand when that hayseed with the paddle hit him in the cabin, he knew. When he came to he hadn't thought about looking for it.

The knife, like the gun, was simply a tool, and Fetterman considered himself a skilled craftsman. What mattered to the artisan was not the wielding of his implements, pleasurable as that may be, but the results that they produced. He weighed the gun in his hand and knew he would do fine.

He laid the pistol in his lap and held it there while he used the paddle to steer closer to the boat. From fifteen yards away he switched the paddle with the gun and waited for the current to carry him the rest of the way.

The bow of the canoe nudged the side of the boat and Fetterman grabbed hold of the craft with his free hand, pulling the canoe alongside it. Even in the dark it was clear the boat was empty.

There was no sign of Kingman or the girl. A life vest lay on the floor next to a gym bag and a windbreaker was tucked under a seat but that was all.

This wasn't right. He whipped his head from side to side, staring at the banks of the river. Where were they? This boat wouldn't just happen to be floating here, stationary, in the middle of the flaming river waiting for him to drift into it. They had to be here.

Something large erupted from the river behind him. He was half turned, leading with the gun, when a heavy object crashed into the back of his skull, turning the night into something blacker than it had been.

Nick gasped for breath as he pushed Fetterman's unconscious body the rest of the way to the bottom of the canoe. He swam around it than tossed the large adjustable wrench he was holding into the bass boat and pulled himself in over the side.

"Katy!" he called. "Come on out!"

His wife released the mangrove branch she had been hiding beneath and swam out to meet him. "Is it over?" she asked him as he reached over the side to pull her up. She was still whispering, afraid to relax enough to overcome her fear.

"Almost," Nick said. He grabbed onto the canoe before it floated out of reach and brought it in closer. He reached inside and took the paddle, handing it over his shoulder to Katy. "Take this."

As she did, she asked, "Is he dead?"

"No, he's not." Fetterman's gun was wedged between his body and the side of the canoe. Nick worked it free and sat up in the boat, releasing his grip on the canoe. "And he won't be needing this again." He flicked on the safety and jammed the gun into his waistband. The canoe began to float past them down the river.

"We're not taking him with us, are we?"

Nick turned to his wife and leaned towards her, taking her

face in his hands. "No, we'll leave him to drift." He kissed her forehead. "If he makes it far enough, somebody will probably find him. We'll notify the authorities when we get back."

Katy closed her eyes and Nick let her go. He moved to the rear of the boat and began to pull in the rope he had attached to Gene McFarlane's heavy tackle box before throwing it over as an anchor. When it cleared the surface, he rested it on the side as he cracked the lid and poured the rest of the water out. Then he stowed it under the seat and started the boat's small motor.

Katy folded herself into the other chair, never letting her eyes leave the canoe as the distance grew between them. She watched as it faded from sight. "God help me," she whispered. "But I hope you never come back, you bastard."

CHAPTER TWENTY SEVEN

Hill circled the plane once over the wide, straight section of river he used as a strip before he gently touched down on its surface. There was no sign of anything unusual, no sign of any other people, as he guided the plane downriver along the water's path.

In a bag under his seat were the items he had spent the past few days pursuing: New passports, new driver's licenses, virgin credit cards. All the trimmings of two new, manufactured identities. There was one more piece of business to conclude and after that, there'd be no more worries for the rest of his life. He'd simply be too rich to take notice of any.

The mid-morning sun sparked off the brown water into piercing shafts of light and into Hill's eyes. He squeezed them into a tight squint behind his sunglasses, already looking forward to the hour when he could kiss this snake infested bog of a state goodbye. In the future, it would be fine hotels and luxury resorts far away from the heat and high humidity of the horrid swamps of Florida. When the weather became disagreeable, it would be like nothing to climb aboard his new jet and fly off to a finer, more hospitable place. One that welcomed important self-made men of means like himself. A light tremor shook his body. He couldn't wait.

He had to look into the sun to find the point of land that covered the entrance to the other river when he approached from this direction. This was the only challenging part of the journey, successfully navigating the plane around the outcropping and up into the narrower channel that ran past the cabin. Hill accomplished this easily, however: He was too close to his goal to be put off by logistical details.

The cabin itself looked as it always did, shit brown, weather beaten, and looking like it could fall into itself at any minute. Ugly piece of crap, Hill thought as he brought the plane close to shore. But it did have its advantages and they'd used it well in the past. He thought about the body that was buried behind it, a foot and a half into the sandy muck, that had belonged to the two bit pusher that had tipped them off to the existence of all this glorious money. He thought of the things they had made him do both before and after he had told them.

Smiling, he thought about what Fetterman could get out of people with that little knife of his.

He killed the engine and pushed open his door as the propeller abruptly stopped spinning. Hill's ears adjusted to the new quiet and he looked to the cabin, expecting to see his partner but no one was there. In fact, there seemed to be a curious lack of activity.

Hill quickly tied the plane to a stump and drew his gun, clicking the safety off with his thumb. Damn it, he thought. Nothing was out of place and everything looked right, but where was Fetterman?

He kept his eyes on the cabin as he ran up to the door. The noise of the plane had certainly announced his arrival so there was no need for subtlety. There wasn't much for cover along the narrow dock anyway.

The lock was loose and hanging in the hasp, the way they always left it when they were there. He nudged open the door with his foot and entered in a crouch, leading with his gun. As soon as he was in, he could feel it. The place was empty.

What the hell is going on here, he thought as he stood and holstered his weapon, mind reeling with disbelief. Where was the girl?

The length of chain lay in a pile behind her chair, the handcuffs with the key still in the lock on the floor next to it. Did Fetterman take her somewhere? Why would he uncuff her?

He saw the cellular phone on the floor and picked it up. It felt light and when he turned it over he saw the empty compartment where the battery should have been. He recognized his partner's wallet on the table, as well as the other things Fetterman had dumped on the table to dry after the girl had kicked him into the river.

What had made him leave and take the girl?

The one idea that kept running through Hill's mind that made any sense was a double cross. Problem is, he didn't think Fetterman had the balls for that kind of move. But what else could it be?

He slammed his fist into the top of the table, spawning a new crack and upsetting the kerosene lamp. Hill swept it to the floor as it began to leak across the wood.

Did that slimy prick make a deal of his own with Kingman? When did he have the chance?

The mobile phone.

Damn it, it made sense. Otherwise he wouldn't have left his wallet behind, or the phone, all the things he carried with him everywhere he went. He just didn't need them any more.

He must have talked to Kingman and told him where to find them. He wouldn't have had any other way to leave.

A murderous rage washed over Hill and he gripped the underside of the table and heaved it to the floor. He moved to the corner where he had last seen the woman, helpless and chained to the ceiling, and kicked the chair into the wall. He picked it up and beat it into the wood planking until it came apart in his hands.

"You son of a bitch!" he yelled as loud as he could. *We were fucking partners, you bastard! I trusted you with everything. Everything! And you did this!*

Hill moved about the cabin, pulling the shelves off the wall, breaking out the painted windows, smashing and breaking until the anger caved in on itself, subsiding. It was when he got to the corner near the generator when he found the thing that made him stop fully.

His chest was heaving and he was dripping with sweat, his hands and forearms bleeding. He picked up the object and held it in front of him. He stared at it and tried to decide what it meant.

The anger slowly seeped away into the background of his mind, pushed out by this new and sudden revelation: Wherever Fetterman had gone, he hadn't gone willingly.

He folded the extended implement into the handle of the knife and dropped it into his front pocket. He took long, deep breaths while he tried to decide what to do. He didn't know what happened but the only thing that mattered, he thought, was if there was still a chance to get the money.

There was one place to go to find out.

* * *

Nick shook Katy's shoulder lightly. "Wake up, honey," he told her. "Today's the day."

Katy rolled over in the kingsized bed, uncurling her body into a feline stretch. She opened her eyes, a half dreaming smile gracing her lips, then she sat bolt upright. All of the fear and tension of the previous night dropped over her face like a leaden veil.

"Nick!" she yelled. She grabbed for him as she looked around the motel room, her sleep having made her forget where they were.

"Easy, sweets, easy," he said as he sat down on the bed and held her. "Everything's alright now." He held her until he felt her body begin to relax and she listened to his voice, slowly allowing herself to believe what he was telling her. Her hair smelled like plants as he stroked it, a pleasant shampoo bottle smell left over from the steaming shower they had taken when they had arrived here sometime after midnight. The stink and dirt of their time in the swamp had long since vanished down a sterile drain and he could remember few things as wonderful as the feeling of sliding his clean naked body between these soft cotton sheets.

"It felt so nice to sleep like that with you." She pushed away from him gently and laid her head against his chest. "Do we have to get up now?"

"You don't, honey, but I do." Nick kissed his wife's forehead and took himself off the bed. He went to a pile on the floor and began to pull on the clothes he had discarded the night before.

"Where are you going?"

"Well, first," he answered, fastening his belt. "I'm going to find some new clothes somewhere. Then I have to get to an appointment in Miami." He picked up his shoes and brought them to the bed.

"You don't have to go. I'm safe now."

"This thing isn't quite over, honey. And I have to pick up a friend."

"What about your friend Hill?"

"If he does what I think he will, he'll be there, too."

Katy put her hand on her husband's shoulder as he worked with the stiff laces on his shoes. "I don't want you to go."

Nick was sitting with his feet on the floor and his back to his wife. He stopped moving, holding the remaining shoe in his hand. "I know you don't, honey. But you're safe now and I have a friend who has been helping me do this. I need to pick him up, dear. There are a lot of things still going on that you don't know about."

"So tell me."

"I will, but not right now. I promise. I've slept too long as it is. I have to get moving." Getting to Miami from their Naples hotel was going to be close to a three hour drive.

"What about me? What do I do?"

"Stay here and rest. You'll be safe until I get back."

"The hell I will." Katy tossed the sheets aside and got out of the bed, stepping to her own pile of clothes.

"Katy—"

"Damn it, Nick. I've had enough of all of this. I didn't think I could deal with you going off and being Dick Tracy again. I've seen too well what it does to you, how it changes you. How I always get pushed to the side." She was dressing as she talked, looking alternately between her husband and what she was doing. "I just wanted to be included in your life, Nick, you know that. I wanted to share it with you, to be 'Katy and Nick,' not just 'Katherine Collins from Plantation, Florida.' But that can't work when there's this huge part of you I can't touch."

"Honey—"

"Let me finish." Katy moved to the small bathroom area, teasing her hair with her fingers as she spoke. "I know I made you choose before, and I shouldn't have done that."

"It was okay."

She ignored him. "But I left you before and I was miserable. Then when this thing happened with Tim, I knew what would come over you. I could see it coming a million miles away. And I left because I wanted to punish you. I left because I didn't want to be forgotten again."

"I'm sorry."

"And look what happened." She stepped toward him and held out her hands, which he took. "This just makes me think of one thing." She looked into his eyes. "I'm not going to be apart from you again."

Nick pulled his wife into his body, wrapping his arms around her and feeling the intensity of his emotions.

"My God, honey, if I had lost you . . . "

Katy said into his shoulder, "But you didn't. You came and you rescued me and now we have to go find your friend so we can leave all this behind us." She pushed her way backwards out of his embrace. "But after we find a clothing store, I think. We smell bad."

Nick laughed out loud. "I love you, Katherine."

"I love you, too, Nicholas. Let's get moving. You know you have a lot of talking to do between here and Miami."

CHAPTER TWENTY EIGHT

Fetterman woke up slowly, the skin on his face burning in the morning sun. He rocked the canoe as he pulled himself up into a sitting position then made the mistake of pressing his fingers into his head. There were several places that were very soft and very tender.

His mind was shouting questions but he didn't rush to come up with any answers. Instead, he lowered a hand into the river and brought up splashes of brackish water into his face.

The river.

The canoe.

The details of the night before filtered their way through the thick mental haze as slowly he began to remember what had happened.

He had lost the girl. Kingman, too, who wasn't even supposed to be there.

Weights were attached to his eyelids and he knew if he allowed them to close he would be sleep again almost instantly. He forced himself to sit hunched over forward so he couldn't lay back.

A tiny smile cracked his dry lips as he recalled one pleasant thought from the night before. Fetterman's eyelids touched and he visualized the black holes in both sides of the dead man's neck.

Open your eyes.

He dried his hands on the front of his shirt and checked out the canoe. There was no paddle in the bottom of the craft, no paddle floating in the water anywhere that he could see. They had stranded him.

Fetterman studied the land along the banks of both sides of the river. He looked upriver and downriver, trying to recognize the shape of its path, but if he could trust his mind it told him there was nothing familiar about any of it. There were some breaks between the mangroves, some treeless patches of dirt or grass where he might be able to climb to shore, but there was nothing but sawgrass and palmetto beyond them. He knew that he must have drifted a good distance to the south.

He slumped back into the point of the canoe, not caring about the uncomfortable pressure from the fiberglass sides pressing into his back. Unconsciously, he fingered the largest lump on his forehead, wincing when he pressed too hard. What was supposed to happen now?

At some point, Fetterman had no idea exactly when, Hill would show up at the cabin looking for the girl. When he found no one there what would he do? Would he figure out what happened and take off, try to save himself? Would he go on to Miami without them?

Would he come look for me?

A moment's hope but Fetterman let it die. He knew better than to think that he or anybody else would come between Hill and getting that money. Hadn't they proved that with all the bodies they'd left behind? Still, though, it was a pleasant thought if not a realistic one. The bitter scent of dreams that would never be.

He knew that the river eventually connected to the Gulf of Mexico and that there would be boats there, someone who would come to help him if he waved them down. If he were more himself, he could take their boat from them, he knew that. But then what? With Kingman and the girl loose he couldn't go back. And he had no money, no credit cards, nothing but the filthy clothes on his back. He'd have a hard time going anywhere.

He had cast his lot in with his partner's schemes and they had come up short. They had lost everything and it was just a matter of time before somebody named the price they'd have to pay.

His eyelids were so, so heavy.

Ahead of him the river bent sharply to the right and the current carried him toward the river bank that was now looming in front of him. He didn't notice until it was too late to try to do anything about it. He let the canoe carry him straight into the overhanging branches of a mangrove tree.

Leaves and branches scraped at his face as he threw his hands up, wresting his momentum from the current. He slowed to a stop, buried in the leafy canopy, then grabbed a branch and pushed hard backwards against the resistance. He moved and something heavy fell into the canoe.

He heard it more than he felt it and as the canoe pulled away from beneath the tree he saw what it was. A large, dark snake twisted its body into a tight compressed S, its head, wider than its neck, facing Fetterman from six inches in front of his feet. The thing opened its mouth, exposing a milky white interior and Fetterman knew what it was.

It seemed that he only thought about moving after the cottonmouth struck him the first time. A pair of needle pricks pierced the inside of his thigh, leaving a tremendous burning feeling, and Fetterman panicked. He kicked at the snake in desperation while he tried to sit up, to leverage himself so he could get out of the damned canoe. The snake bit him again, lightning fast and this time burying its fangs deep into the calf muscle of his other leg.

Fetterman went over the side, rolling the canoe and inhaling water directly into his lungs. He came up coughing, facing the shore as he fiercely began to push himself backwards through the water. His heart felt like it was beating two hundred times a minute as he saw the snake swimming alongside the overturned craft. Its head was well out of the water and it seemed to be looking at him, as if in some way it was admiring the damage it had done.

Fetterman couldn't stop coughing. He had inhaled so much water he couldn't breathe without gagging. Powerful fits shook his body as he continued to move awkwardly downriver, still panicking over the thought of the snake in the water with him. The wounds on his legs felt as if small puddles of molten lava had been poured onto his skin.

There was so much adrenaline in his system, Fetterman couldn't have stopped swimming if he had wanted to. He was into the middle of the river, still coughing and gagging when the feeling began to leave his legs.

His brain was telling his legs to kick, to keep him afloat, but no matter how hard he tried each movement became smaller than the last, each kick carried less and less force. Waves of nausea began to ride through him and it was terribly hard for him to swim with only his arms. His face bobbed beneath the surface and again he inhaled part of the river.

Oh my God, Fetterman thought. Oh my God. Never before in his life had he felt so weak, so vulnerable and not in control.

He had to get out of the water. He knew that but he didn't know how. His arms were tired, exhausted, and his strength was ebbing from the nausea. His useless, swollen legs hung like burning anchors, dragging him down beneath the surface. With each wracking cough he grew weaker and weaker. If he could just clear his lungs, breathe normally . . .

Fetterman tried to roll onto his back but it made the coughing worse and again his face went under. For a moment his mind seemed to detach itself from his body. I've failed myself, he thought. My badge, my partner, now me. He realized he was looking up at the burning Florida sun wondering why he felt so cold.

Overhead the roar of an airplane engine tickled his consciousness, disturbing the peace of the blue sky and the emerging thunderheads. Hill? he thought. Are you there?

It didn't matter. A larger part of him simply didn't care. Go away, Fetterman wanted to shout. I don't need you anymore. A coughing spasm shook him and he inhaled some more water as he struggled to hold his head above the surface. I don't need you.

Still he could hear the sound and it was disturbing him.

Fly on, he thought. I don't want you.

A thin current of warm brown water slipped past his sunburnt lips and Fetterman thought about the creatures that lived there in the swamp, that surrounded him at that moment. The snakes, the alligators, the bugs, the birds. I am the alligator man, now, he thought. I belong to the swamp. I was wet when I was born.

I am wet when I die.

* * *

Hill flew his plane to the small airport in Homestead and called a taxi to take him the rest of the way to Miami International. This way he didn't need special permission to land and if things worked out right it would be easier to abandon the Cessna without drawing much attention.

Once inside the airport, he saw the usual crowds of travelers and Spanish speaking employees that trafficked through the terminal building. Hill checked his watch. There were still three hours before he was supposed to meet with Kingman.

He walked into one of the numerous food shops that lined one wall of the terminal building and stood in a short line for a hot dog. It took five minutes before a Cuban woman finished servicing the two customers ahead of him and finally asked him what he wanted. Damned refugees. Couldn't work fast enough in this stupid little job no wonder their own country had gone to hell.

Someone had told him a joke once about how you could drop an atomic bomb on Miami and kill maybe six Americans. Based on his experiences in this town he couldn't argue.

He finally got his lunch and looked about for a place to sit. The little restaurant itself was full so he wandered back into the terminal and found a group of chairs that had their faces bolted to an otherwise bare wall.

He was impressing himself with how cool and calm he was. He let it go back at the cabin but he got himself under control once he got back into the airplane. Once he had a handle on what must have happened and what he was going to do.

Whoever had taken the girl had done something to Fetterman, probably killed him. That was too bad; he had been good for a certain number of things. He wouldn't miss him, exactly, but it would make things different.

The big question was who had taken the girl. Unless Fetterman had tipped him off, Kingman wouldn't have had a prayer of figuring out where they were keeping her. That was impossible. But if there was some way it could have been Nick, about a thousand other cops wold be out hunting for Hill right now, most of them right here. And that just wasn't so. He had called his office from Homestead and everything had been normal. He hadn't been missed.

So who took the girl?

He popped the rest of his lunch into his mouth and wiped his fingers on the fabric of his pants. Probably some renegade band of swamp mutants, out avoiding civilization and poaching for some gator tail. Didn't matter who it was, really. So long as Kingman didn't have her he had a chance to buffalo him into paying off the money. Failing that, of course, he would have to kill him. Hill stood up, excusing himself for an abrupt belch. Maybe he'd go get himself another one of those hot dogs. That Cuban woman was good for burning some time.

* * *

Reed Larson stepped out of the jetway and into one of the concourses that belonged to Miami International Airport. He followed the clear plexiglass enclosed ramp down and into the customs area along with the rest of the passengers that had disembarked with him. None of them, he thought, had checks worth nearly sixty million dollars burning holes in their jacket pockets. None of them had come to Miami to meet a murdering Tampa policeman who was holding his friend's wife as a hostage.

Clearing customs was a formality of course and Reed immediately exited the concourse and walked out into the main terminal building.

Miami International was an old airport, originally built in the late fifties and added on to in order to keep pace with the explosive growth of the city. The terminal building itself was a long, crooked structure with a multitude of concourses branching out and away from it. As Reed walked along looking for concourse G, he saw a sign advertising rooms at the hotel that was built onto the terminal: "It's all here . . . At concourse E, 2nd Level. Miami International Airport Hotel. 260 Completely Soundproof Rooms."

He came to concourse G, which branched off to his left before heading past a row of metal detectors and x-ray machines before disappearing behind a set of thick glass doors. Across from the security checkpoint, to his right, were the lockers Nick had described. There was the wall with the elevator set next to a pair of automatic doors that led outside.

Reed dug a handful of quarters out of his pocket and carefully placed the cashier's check for twenty six million dollars into one of the lockers. Ten feet away, the elevator opened unexpectedly and the he started as he twisted and removed the small plastic headed key. A group of chattering teenagers speaking French pushed behind him into the terminal. He hadn't heard the chime announcing the elevator's arrival and it made him nervous to be standing there.

He picked his one bag up by its shoulder strap and slung it over his shoulder, pocketing the locker key. He walked quickly away from the money and the elevator, feeling as though a hundred sets of eyes were watching him. He didn't stop until he was almost out of the terminal, past the first concourse and in an alcove of fast food restaurants.

Despite the heavy air conditioning, Reed was perspiring. He wiped at his forehead with his sleeve and set his bag down on the floor. Staring into the terminal, back the way he had come, he looked to see if anyone was showing any interest in him. He let out his breath when he couldn't see anybody even looking in his direction.

Two things I don't need, Reed thought as he checked his watch, are gangsters and bad cops. This day can't end too soon.

There were almost three hours to go before he was to meet with Nick, and Reed made a decision. Pulling more quarters out of his pocket, Reed moved to another set of lockers and gently slid his bag into one of them, dropping the change into the slot. Before he removed the key, he pulled the remaining series of checks out of his pocket and held them out of sight inside the locker.

Thirteen checks of roughly two million dollars apiece. Again the weight of the money nearly staggered him, with flashback visions of Lu Bates's body, sprawled out on her kitchen floor, dead eyes staring into Heaven and assaulting his imagination. He wiped his forehead again and left three of the checks in the locker with his bag.

Before he could give himself time to reconsider, Reed shut the door and twisted the key, pushing away from the lockers and walking back into the heart of the terminal. Three more hours.

* * *

Hill had spent most of his time walking end to end through the airport, and the last hour examining every square foot of concourse G. He wanted to know the exact layout, all the nooks, the crannies, every inch of Kingman's chosen meeting place.

It really was an inspired choice, thought Hill as he finished counting the actual number of jetway gates. An airport concourse with its security would keep out their weapons, and since the concourses themselves connected directly to the terminal, there were no overhead trams or underground trains that could be used as a bottleneck to trap either party. That would have been the weakness with the Tampa Airport. Kingman was good, Hill thought, but he would be better.

He felt the weight of Fetterman's pocket knife bouncing heavily against his thigh as he walked. They had let him take it through security. Apparently they didn't classify the small tool as a weapon. He smiled wryly as he thought of some of the things he had seen Fetterman do with it.

He checked his watch again. It was almost time. He began to work his way back down the concourse, to the deli booth Kingman had specified. Hill's eyes worked every face, saw every motion, led him around each food kiosk and newsstand. There was nothing suspicious going on around him. He stepped over and around waiting passengers and greeters as if they were pieces of furniture placed in a jumbled arrangement on some massive living room floor.

Hill was halfway to the deli when his eyes locked on something familiar. The face of someone he knew was walking through a small knot of people in the middle of the concourse.

Without turning his head to give himself away, Hill kept moving at the same speed, angling himself toward a stainless steel drinking fountain that was set into the wall on his left. He ben over, briefly touching his lips to the arcing water, then stood and turned casually toward the person he had seen.

Thirty feet away from him, moving with the crowd in the direction of the deli, was the face of a young man that he knew. It was Kingman's little helper.

Oh, this is too good, he thought as he jammed his hand into his pocket and pulled out Fetterman's knife. He shrugged off his light jacket and draped it over his arm. With the knife out of sight, he extracted one of the blades and moved into the slowly moving stream of people.

* * *

"It's Reed, isn't it?" Hill said softly as he moved in behind the man, extending his arm underneath Reed Larson's jacket and pressed the knife into his side.

Reed whipped his head around and tried to stop but Hill turned his shoulder and bumped him forward. "Keep walking, kid," Hill said as he pressed the razor edge of the blade into the soft flesh just above Reed's hip. "I mean it."

The two men caused a ripple of annoyance as their stutter step disrupted the rhythm of the people walking around them.

"This is the edge of a very sharp knife you're feeling in your side. Maybe Kingman told you what we could do with it."

Reed swallowed and nodded once. Hill was pressed against the left side of his body, keeping himself just behind the man. Sweat broke out along his forehead.

Dead bodies on kitchen floors.

"Where's Kingman?"

Reed tried to speak but his throat had gone dry. Hill pulled the knife along his side and Reed could feel the cold steel slice through his shirt and into the surface of his skin. "I haven't seen him yet. I was on my way to the deli up ahead."

"Does he have the girl?"

"What girl?"

"Don't fuck with me, boy!" Hill hissed, again sliding the knife. Reed could imagine himself opened up at the side, spilling blood and entrails as an anonymous figure stepped away from his body, losing himself in the crowd. He cast his eyes about frantically but there was no one looking back at him. Everyone was busy with their own little activities.

"Settle down, God damn it!" said Hill. "Where's Kingman's wife?"

"You're supposed to have her." Reed's stomach was in knots and he was feeling sick. What was happening here?

Hill could tell from long experience that the kid was terrified and probably not lying. So someone else had found the shack and had taken the woman. She was probably scrubbing pots and trimming the fat off gator tails for inbred first cousins like he thought. Hell only knew what would have happened to Fetterman. Life's a bitch.

The deli consisted of a long counter surrounded on each end by stainless steel coolers that held fruits, vegetables and sterile premade sandwiches and salads. Twenty or thirty small round tables filled an area bounded by a decorative rope. Hill led Reed to one of the ones toward the rear corner that was furthest from the counter and mostly free of customers.

With his foot he slid one of the green wooden chairs over to another one and prompted Reed to sit down by altering the pressure and angle of the knife.

"Okay, listen to me, kid," Hill said, sitting next to him. "There is only one thing in this world that is going to make everybody happy and that is me getting out of here with that money. Got it?"

Reed nodded. Their backs were to the wall and they were falling the steady stream of people walking past.

"Good. Put your hands up on the table where I can see them."

Slowly, Reed took his hands out of his lap and folded his arms on the table in front of him.

"The only thing standing between Kingman and me, Larson, is now you. We had his wife but that arrangement sort of fell through. Do you want to live, kid?"

Again Reed nodded.

"Say it."

Without looking at Hill, Reed said in a quiet voice, "I want to live." There was no doubt in his mind that Hill would bury that knife halfway to his spine if things didn't go his way. He could feel the sweat dripping on his forehead while at the same time a numbing chill was spreading throughout his arms and legs.

"That's good, boy. Now I want you to tell me everything you know about Kingman's plans. Start by telling me what it is you're supposed to be doing here." Hill gave the knife a small twitch to get him going.

Reed jumped but didn't say anything. If Hill didn't have Katy, did that mean Nick had been successful? And if he had been, would he still show up here? He opened his mouth to speak but then shut it.

"I'm not playing, boy. Start talking." Hill pressed the blade deeper into Reed's side. For the first time Reed could feel a warm stickiness at his hip.

"He's here," Reed said.

"What do you mean? Where?"

Reed nodded with his head and Hill followed the motion. Across the concourse, standing next to a square support column, was Kingman. He was staring at their table, a hard look on his face, oblivious to the stream of people moving between them.

Hill smiled.

"You say one word about the girl, boy, and I'll make you pay."

Nick took a step away from the column and as he moved a figure moved with him. Katy Kingman was holding her husband's hand as they walked slowly toward the deli.

The smile disappeared from Hill's face and he pressed himself closer to Reed's side. What the fuck was this? How the hell did he get her?

Nick and Katy moved to the table directly in front of Hill and Reed. Two of the tables between them and the counter were occupied but they were both at least ten feet away and the people there involved in their own conversations.

"Sit down," said Hill. "Looks like we both have us a surprise."

Nick sat without taking his eyes off Hill. Katy moved a chair closer to her husband and sat down slightly behind him.

"We meet again," Hill said to her, nodding.

"Don't talk to me, you pig," she breathed. Katy grabbed Nick's arm and looked at the table.

"Whatever you say."

"Are you okay?" Nick asked Reed.

Hill answered for him. "Do you mean does he have a razor sharp knife pressed into his side at this very moment?" Hill smiled again. "He does."

"I'm bleeding," said Reed.

"Back off him, Hill. You'll get your money."

Hill chuckled. "I know that. First tell me, Nick. Where's Fetterman?"

"You mean what happened to him after I slugged him with a wrench and left him in a boat floating down the river? I have no idea."

The smile never left Hill's face. "Did you kill him?"

"One can only hope."

A chuckle. "Oh, well. More money for me, then." Still looking at Nick, Hill used the knife to make Reed jump again. "Where is it?"

Nick didn't answer him. Instead, he looked at Reed.

"It's where I put it," Reed whispered.

"What did you say?"

"Tell him," said Nick.

Reed opened his right fist, spilling a red capped airport locker key onto the table. It bounced and clattered, stopping at a spot near the center of the table.

"Let him go, Hill."

Hill reached out with his free hand and picked up the key. "Where's this at?"

Nick told him in a quiet voice. "Walk out of the concourse, cross the terminal, and you'll see a bank of silver lockers near an elevator."

"Just like that, huh?"

"Just like that."

"Well," said Hill as he pocketed the key. "I think someone needs to show me the way. How about you, honey?" he said to Katy. "You know your wife, Nick, she cleans up nice."

"You're not taking anybody, Hill. Not if you want all the money."

A noisy group of a dozen or so men wearing yellow tee shirts emblazoned with the words "Ft. Lauderdale" across the front piled into the deli, forming an unruly line.

"Oh, Nick," said Hill, all humor gone from his expression. "You don't want to be fucking with me now."

A new wave of sweat broke out on Reed's brow. Some of the yellow shirted tourists began to sit at the empty tables to his right as others moved to the coolers.

"Listen to me, you son of a bitch. There is nothing I want more than to see you walk out of this concourse and get that money. All of it and without taking anybody with you." Nick leaned forward, keeping his voice low so he wouldn't be overheard. "But when you took my wife I had to come up with some way to get her away from you before you got what you wanted."

The smile was back on Hill's face. "Did you do it?"

"I think so. In that locker is a cashier's check for one half of the money I cleared out of Lankford's."

"I hope you're not trying to be cute. The other half is . . ." Hill twisted the knife and Reed squirmed in his chair.

"The other half is in a series of smaller checks." Nick looked at his friend. "Reed?"

The younger man reached into his jacket pocket and grabbed the remaining checks. In one motion he pulled them out and flung them into the air high above the deli. The men in the tee shirts looked up to see what was happening.

"Son of a bitch," growled Hill as he pushed Reed off his chair and jumped to his feet.

Reed rolled away from him as Nick and Katy helped him to his feet.

"I'm okay," he told them as they pulled him toward the boundary rope and away from the commotion.

"Let's go." Nick lifted the part of the rope that was closest to them and held it while Reed and Katy ducked under to the other side. Hill was snatching checks off the tables and out of the hands of the men from Ft. Lauderdale.

"What do we do now?" asked Katy.

"We disappear." Nick ushered the two of them into the crowd moving down the concourse and away from the terminal. A few seconds later, Hill and the deli were out of sight behind them, obscured by the weekend travelers and their people.

When they got to the end of the concourse, the trio leaned their backs against a railing and the windows overlooking the runways and watched the thinning tide of people flow toward them.

Katy leaned into her husband's side and asked, "Are we safe?"

Nick kissed her on the forehead. "I think so, honey. Hill's got no reason to come after us, he's busy grabbing the money he's been after for so long, and there are too many people here for him to try anything against the three of us."

"He didn't have much trouble with me alone," said Reed. He was examining the narrow slice in his shirt and the thin layer of sticky blood inside it. "I'm okay," he told Katy as she moved to help. "He just cut me a little."

Nick asked him about the other check. "Please tell me you put it in the right bank of lockers."

"I put it in exactly the place you described to Hill."

"Good."

Katy was incredulous. "You mean he's going to find the money and get away, just like he wants?"

"He'll find the money, sweets," said Nick. "But I don't think he'll get away."

* * *

Hill had to pull out his badge before he could get all those yellow shirted faggots away from his money. It was a good thing he had brought it with him. He had planned on dumping it along with the rest of his old identity.

One asshole wanted to fight but Hill had all the checks he had seen the kid throw and he had already drawn too much of an audience. Damn that Kingman, he thought. The man knew what he was doing.

Hill stormed out of the deli and out of the concourse, looking for the lockers Kingman had described. He crossed the wide hallway of the terminal and there they were, just as Nick had said.

He stopped in front of them, looking back the way he had come. No sign of Kingman or any pursuit whatsoever. He didn't think there would be. The man would have been figuring a way to get his wife back, not a way of capturing Hill or keeping the money. It would have been much too high of a risk for him to do anything else.

Hill had won.

There were two Hispanic men standing next to the lockers and another one in a dark suit next to the nearby elevator but after a glance Hill ignored them. He took the key from his pocket and located the corresponding locker. Subconsciously he held his breath as he fitted the key to the lock and turned it to one side, listening for the sharp metallic click.

He pulled back the locker door and it was there. A negotiable cashier's check in the amount of twenty six million dollars.

Strong hands gripped both of his arms and a heavy metal object was jammed into the small of his back. Hill tried to turn but another hand gripped the top of his head. A line of dark suited Hispanic men screened what has happening from the rest of the terminal.

"There is a gun with a silencer pointed at your spine," a voice spit into his ear. Before Hill could react, he was forced into the elevator next to the lockers. The men spun his back to the wall and a man in a suit, the one that Hill noticed earlier, pressed the barrel of a gun into his forehead.

They had taken him in seconds and nobody had seen a thing.

As the doors of the elevator slid shut, the man with the gun said, "Please do not even blink your eyes."

A pair of hands worked at the sleeve of Hill's right arm. A moment later he felt a sharp prick, then a smooth numbness began to work its way up his arm and into the rest of his body. My money, he thought. My money . . .

Ten seconds later he was out.

* * *

"There's something I need to show you."

Reed used the second locker key to open the locker where he had stored his bag. He withdrew the three cashier's checks and handed them to Nick.

"I don't know why I did it. Some kind of impulse, I guess."

Nick looked at the amounts printed in the boxes on each of the checks. Almost two million dollars each. Jesus fucking Christ. He didn't want to deal with six million dollars of blood money.

"The question is," Nick asked Reed slowly. "If they decide they miss it, do you want them coming after you looking for it?"

"Will somebody please tell me what's going on?" Katy asked. "Hill's gone but now you two are frightening me. Who are you talking about?"

Nick reached into the locker and pulled out Reed's bag and handed it to him. "Come on," he told them. "Let's get out of this damned airport."

Together they walked out of the building and into the humid afternoon sunshine. Massive cumulus clouds threatened showers as they crossed through the busy traffic and up a small ramp toward the short term parking lot where Nick had left the car.

"After these past few weeks, I feel like somebody just drove a truck off my back," said Reed.

"We all feel that way."

They climbed into Nick's car, left the airport, and began the long drive north out of Miami towards home. Nick didn't tell Katy what had happened until she insisted, about twenty miles later north on I-95.

"Please, honey," he told her. "I'd rather not talk about it." *I'll be thinking about it long enough.*

"You have to, Nick. No more secrets, remember?"

Maybe she was right. Perhaps Katy could one day help him look past what had happened, help him forgive himself for the lives he had seen lost since the day he had been approached by Hill.

"Okay," he said. "After Hill had taken you, I went to see one of the men who had given that money to Lankford's company."

"Wasn't he in jail?" Katy asked.

Nick nodded. "Up in Starke at the state prison. I told him three things." He took a long breath and blew it out from his cheeks. "I told him that Hill and Fetterman had stolen his money, I told him where they would be, and I told him when they would be there."

"Oh my God, Nick," Katy said. She closed her eyes and leaned her head into his shoulder. "Those people were here?"

Nick shrugged. *I hope so*, he was thinking.

"What do you think they'll do to him?"

Nick didn't answer. He was thinking about each of the people that had been hurt or killed since he had agreed to work with Hill. Katy could figure that one out herself.

Nick had been after justice, but was it justice that Lu Bates was killed? Or James Rooker? Or Gene, a man who had made such a difference to them but who hadn't even mentioned his last name?

Would it have brought Tim Clayton back or made any real difference to Marie if Hill and Fetterman had simply gotten the money and quietly slipped out of the country?

So what if in the end Hill pays the ultimate price for what he has done. Is that finally justice, and does it make up for the rest of it? Does it excuse Nick for what had happened because he wanted to be the one solving his friend's murder?

He drove on in silence. He was finished talking. Tell it to me later, he thought. I'm through coming up with answers.

CHAPTER TWENTY NINE

Isabella Santorro made a mark on her clipboard then hung it from a hook on her cart. With her key she opened the door to room 512 and kept it ajar by moving the cart halfway into the entrance. I hate Monday mornings, she thought. All the guests party then fly home, leaving what were by far the biggest messes of the week.

The metallic smell of drying blood hit her three feet into the room. Isabella recognized what it was immediately and looked around her curiously, but the bedroom was empty.

She turned down the short hallway to look into the bathroom.

The first time she had seen a dead body in Miami, for that matter the first time she had seen one in this hotel, she had become violently ill. She had thrown up repeatedly and had experienced trouble sleeping for weeks afterward. Eventually the nightmares stopped and she became used to such things. Life in Miami, after all, was the life she had chosen.

The body and most of the mess was in the bathroom. Thank God, she thought, at least they put him in the bathtub for a change. She recognized it as a man, coated with so much dried blood that it took her a moment to realize that he was naked.

His hands were bound in front of him and the body was slumped forward onto its knees. She took a step into the small room and saw that a large part of the front of his head was missing. She couldn't tell for sure but he didn't look like anyone she should have known. Disturbing possible evidence didn't bother her. The police would never solve this one, she knew.

Isabella turned to leave. This room wouldn't be cleaned anytime soon. Shortly the police would be here and she would be answering their many questions. She already knew what she would answer. She understood why a hotel attached to an airport would advertise soundproof rooms but the management here needs to realize the kinds of people that such a feature can attract.

The only thing that would shock her, she would find out later, was how badly tortured the man had been before he was executed.

* * *

Too many sleepless nights had taken their toll on him. Deep purple grooves sagged underneath his eyes as he carelessly passed an electric razor back and forth over his face. Silver hair, once combed and gelled meticulously into place each morning before he left the house, was merely pushed back away from his forehead and allowed to lie where it fell.

Sheila, his wife for the past thirty two years, knew of course that something was wrong at work, had been wrong for days, but her husband refused to talk to her about it. She had laid an elegant blue Italian suit on the bed for him, along with a freshly pressed shirt, silk tie, and comfortable hand tooled leather shoes. She knew how good it made her husband feel when he was dressed to kill.

If he noticed the care with which she had selected his outfit he gave her no sign. He was so distracted and so uncoordinated from lack of sleep that Sheila actually had to help him knot his tie properly. When he tried it himself the ends kept coming out wrong.

"I have coffee downstairs, dear," she told him. "And I could make you an omelette."

"I'm not hungry," he answered. Then, noticing the concern on her face as she helped him shrug his way into his jacket, he said, "I'll get something at the office."

"Of course you will." But she knew better. She followed him into the living room and then into the kitchen where he had left his briefcase and his car keys late the night before. He gathered these up and turned to the door where Sheila stood, offering the morning paper.

He took it to be polite but he knew he wouldn't look at it. Sheila opened the door for him and said, "I love you, dear."

"I know," he said absently. "I love you, too."

She watched as he moved down the short sidewalk to the silver BMW parked in their driveway. She waved once as he got in but he didn't see her.

Out of habit, Walter A. Lankford checked his mirrors before slipping the car into reverse. Ten seconds later, after he had backed to the end of his driveway and into the street, he was gone.

The shock wave from the explosion blew out every front window on the block.

Before the end of that month, some very large checks arrived at the homes of three very different people.

One went to Marie Clayton in Sarasota.

Another was delivered to a divorcee named Elizabeth Rooker in Bradenton, Florida.

In Minneapolis, a man named Carl Pantucket cried out loud when he realized that his dream of a chain of 24-hour sidewalk doughnut stands could finally come true.